Hare House

Sally Hinchcliffe

MANTLE

First published 2022 by Mantle
an imprint of Pan Macmillan
The Smithson, 6 Briset Street, London EC1M 5NR
EU representative: Macmillan Publishers Ireland Ltd, 1st Floor,
The Liffey Trust Centre, 117–126 Sheriff Street Upper,
Dublin 1, D01 YC43
Associated companies throughout the world
www.panmacmillan.com

ISBN 978-1-5290-6163-5

3 5 7 9 8 6 4 2

A CIP catalogue record for this book is available from the British Library.

Typeset by Palimpsest Book Production Ltd, Falkirk, Stirlingshire
Printed and bound by CPI Group (UK) Ltd, Croydon, CR0 4YY

Visit **www.panmacmillan.com** to read more about all our books
and to buy them. You will also find features, author interviews and
news of any author events, and you can sign up for e-newsletters
so that you're always first to hear about our new releases.

To my parents

Hare House

Hare House is not its real name, of course. I have, if you will forgive me, kept names to a minimum here, for reasons which will be understandable. There are many houses which might answer to its description, at least in general, and many places which might have formed the backdrop to the events I am about to relate. Dumfries and Galloway is a big place, and sparsely populated. The whole county is a patchwork of hills and moorland and forest, of tiny roads and dykes and scattered houses; the same pattern, endlessly repeated. Those who actually live there might recognize the place, and the people – and even the story, but if they do, I expect that they will keep it to themselves.

part one
enchantment

I T WAS MELISSA who succumbed first. She fought it; I could see the rising panic in her eyes. Her hands flailed as she reached for the chair behind her, but even as she grasped at it she knocked it down. She swayed for a moment and then she was falling and the chair only served to take her down harder. She fell between the desks, sprawling awkwardly. Before I could react, the girl next to her had fallen too, and a third was already swaying, her eyes wide and unseeing. Three, then four, and then it was all of them, passing through the classroom like a wave.

In my memory, as each girl fell, she fell in silence. They made a kind of sigh, nothing more, the sound of the breath being expelled from the body by the impact of landing. They crumpled as they fell, forwards, sideways, one after the other without a word said, not even by those initially unaffected. Those left upright just seemed to stare at their fallen classmates, blinking a little, until they too succumbed. And then the last one had gone and there was nobody left standing but me, silent among them.

Memory is a tricky thing, a construct. It isn't some unchanging reel of film that can be rewound and played exactly as it was. We recreate it afresh each time with all our human inaccuracies and bias. It couldn't have been like that, not the way I recall it. Not that strange, bewitched calm, the silence, the girls sliding to the floor without so much as a cry. They would have been panicking, those girls, as they struggled for breath. Everyone said, afterwards, that it was the commotion that brought them running – screaming, crying, the clattering of chairs – to find the girls fallen around me, as I stood rooted to the spot, unmoving and apparently unmoved.

Yet that is the memory I have, the one I cannot shake, the one that has haunted my sleep these past few years. It reaches to me in the small hours of the night, fresh and crisp, false though it might be. The classroom and the desks, the tumbled chairs, and the girls as they fall in silence – yes, silence – like petals from a rose.

CHAPTER 1

For me the story really begins on the day the bus hit the hare, the day Janet caught me cowering behind the barn. Despite everything else that happened before and after, I cannot shake the sense that that incident contained the seeds of everything else that then unfolded. As though, had I done something differently, it might have been in my power to stop the events of the days and months that followed, ridiculous though that might seem.

It was a couple of months after I had left London to start a new life in Scotland – almost a decade ago now, incredibly, for it is still as fresh in my memory as if it were last week. They had been happy, peaceful months of dreamless nights and busy days. I had quickly fallen into a routine of work and walks, exploring my new surroundings, filling my eyes with the views, as if I could literally absorb the beauty of the world around me. I felt myself changing physically as I shook off the confines of the city – growing stronger, fitter, standing taller. I felt it in the way my shoulders no longer tensed about my ears, the way I strode out now, walking to my own rhythm with no need to match my steps to the shuffle of the crowded streets.

That day I was on the bus, just gathering my shopping together, standing up to ring the bell. I was the only passenger, the driver and I hurtling together in silence between the confines of the dykes. He had already started to slow, in fact, knowing the place where I got off. Ringing the bell was redundant but I reached for it anyway, city habits dying hard. The button was under my thumb when he slammed the brakes on hard, hard enough to throw me forward, wrenching my shoulder. The bus stopped, stalled into silence, its engine ticking furiously as it cooled, the bags in my hand still swinging wildly against my legs.

A hare. Just that. Lying injured on the road, a mangled mess of fur where its hind legs had been. I got out and the bus driver, still silent, got out too. He looked at it and shook his head as if it was not what he had expected. The creature looked back at us, at him, at me, its ribcage heaving. I could not look away. There was no fear in its eyes, but something else, something watchful and knowing. It seemed to be waiting for us to act. I wanted to ask the driver to put it out of its misery, but I knew how my voice would sound: English, foolish. He said nothing, just climbed heavily back into his bus and drove off, safe in his empty lighted box with its half-fogged windows, leaving me with the hare. I could hear the bus engine for a long time after it had disappeared from view, and then there was just silence.

I expected the hare to die and yet it panted on, watching me. I looked around in the vain hope that someone might come, someone who would know what to do: something swift and merciful. There was nobody. The hare waited, still alive, asking me for something I could not give. I knew I ought to kill it. A rock, a twist of the neck, dispatching it before it suffered any more. I knew I did not have the courage.

It took too long to die and it watched me the whole while. It was only when it was dead that it became pitiful in a way it had not been when it was alive. I stood there for a moment longer and then I picked up my bags and set off on the two-mile walk for home.

You could say I had dreamt of this place. Not in the usual meaning of the phrase; I had had no waking thought of leaving London at the time. But I had gone to bed one night at a time when things had been at their lowest and I had woken the next morning with an image in my mind of a place clothed in silence, a place that seemed familiar long after the dream had fled. I could not tell you where it had come from, this image, only that I woke rested for the first time in ages, calm and serene as if freed from some imprisonment. A grey morning light was battling it out against the streetlights and the sirens were starting up in the distance – if, indeed, they had ever stopped – but if I closed my eyes, I could almost see the dream image still lying there: a house alone among the hills, the forest behind it stretching to the horizon. A place of peace, where I might find refuge.

It might have lain there till it faded had I not, some time later, taken it into my head to have a brief holiday among the hills of south-west Scotland. I was on my own for although various friends had reacted enthusiastically to the idea when it was first discussed, in the end none of them had been able to commit the time. And perhaps, looking back, I might not have made the most inviting of holiday companions. I have never had, nor needed, an extensive social life but I had valued my small circle of friends. They had been supportive when I had been forced to give up teaching – extravagant, even, in their offers of support. But when the immediate crisis had passed and I had refashioned a life for myself from the wreckage, it seemed they had found other priorities.

Pride made me go ahead on my own anyway, but even as I set off I was beginning to regret my decision, half minded to turn around and cancel the whole enterprise. I barely glanced out of the window as the train made its way north through hills that seemed to rise bleaker and wilder with every mile that passed. It was only after the taxi I had taken from the station had started to thread its way through narrow lanes, all flooded then with May blossom, that my mood had started to lift a little. The taxi climbed up a hill and the countryside widened out around us, fields giving way to moorland, open to the skies. As it crested the top of the hill, I caught my breath and leaned forward, only just preventing myself from asking the driver to stop.

There it was, just as I had seen it in the dream, laid out before me, as familiar as my own hand. Caught in a fold of land, the house and its buildings huddled together, quite alone. Behind them, only the hills, clothed in endless ranks of trees.

'That's the spot,' the driver said, as if he had read my mind. 'That's where you're going, isn't it? Hare House Cottages, you said.'

He spoke quickly, with a heavy accent, and it took me a moment or two to disentangle what he had said. He let the car slow and pointed through the windscreen.

'That's the main house just there, Hare House. Awa' i' the woods. And the cottages are next door.'

I must have made some noncommittal remark in reply, although I have no memory of it. All I can remember is the way the clouds moved swiftly across the landscape, the sunlight and shadows patterning it in shades of green and gold, and the feeling – ridiculous though it was – that the indifferent world had spoken to me, and to me alone.

As the taxi turned up the track that formed the driveway to the cottages and rounded the corner into a small cobbled yard, I saw a figure standing on the doorstep waiting, gilded fleetingly by the sun. It was Grant – Mr Henderson as I knew him then – the owner. On the phone he had been clipped and efficient, briskly authoritative, and I had not imagined he would be so young, not even thirty, as it turned out. He sprang to open my door with old-fashioned gallantry and shook my hand as I got out. His manner was touched with a seriousness that belied his years.

'Just you then?' he asked.

'Just me,' I replied, and I liked the way he didn't probe any further but took my bag in through the open front door while I paid off the taxi.

'No need for a grand tour,' he said. 'I'm afraid it's rather small.'

'It's perfect.'

The view from the kitchen window was a dance of spring leaves in the wind. He leaned against the counter, quiet for a moment, looking around the room as if seeing it for the first time. I was struck by his air of sadness, even as he recalled himself and smiled at me again, a rueful smile.

'Too small, really, for holiday lets. The world seems to want somewhere that sleeps six.'

Another time, another year, another life, and I might have let it slide. But the dream image and, more importantly, the sense of peace that it had brought me, spoke to me in that moment. What, after all, did I have to go back to in London? I had a job that I could do anywhere, a rented flat that required no more than a month's notice to leave, no ties – or no real ones, anyway. For too long these things had made me feel like a failure, my life stalled. Now, for the first time, I saw them as a freedom. Before I could stop and think further, I spoke.

'You wouldn't be looking to let the place out long term, then?'

For the first time he seemed to really register me, his eyes meeting mine, appraising.

'Would you be interested?'

I'm not stupid. I know that all that had really happened with my 'dream' was that my waking mind had pieced together a partial image out of scraps and I had mistaken déjà vu for recognition. I had freighted a random blip in the brain's sequencing mechanism with a significance it could not bear. Partial recall, confirmation bias – I know how much we are prey to the irrational when making up our minds. I was at a dangerous stage in my life: middle age is bad enough at the best of times but here I was, abandoned by the only career I'd ever wanted, and with nothing of substance to take its place. I know that now; part of me knew it even then, deep down. It didn't – doesn't – matter. The image still lay there in my mind, and with it the sense of calm and peace and healing that it seemed to bring. Whether it was the indifferent world that had spoken, or my subconscious, it made no difference. It had chosen its moment well. I saw no reason not to seize it.

'I'd love to, yes. Why not?'

He named a monthly rent that seemed ridiculously low. We shook on it, his face suddenly splitting into a smile that lit his eyes and swept away his air of restraint and melancholy. His hand enfolded mine and I had the sense that we were sealing a friendship as much as striking a deal. Just then, a bird started singing outside the window and I can still bring it to mind, that moment, complete and perfect in itself.

Normally I enjoyed the walk from the bus. It was the same route I'd taken the day I had arrived, the road rising steadily from the wooded river valley, out onto the open moor. It had been raining on and off all week and as I climbed, the sound of running water rose all around me. Streams had started to spring everywhere out of the hillsides, ignoring the roads and the walls and finding their ancient courses. I stopped at the top as I always did, and took in the view of the house and the cottages, waiting for the sense of rightness they always brought me, but this day it did not come. The hare, accusing, seemed to stare at me still, asking something of me I could not give.

The clouds were closing in on all sides, dark and ragged. Even as I watched, the forest started to disappear beneath the veils of coming rain. The sunlight briefly painted everything a spectral glowing green, unreal in its intensity, and then it vanished, the clouds sweeping in and obliterating everything. The rain started and I put my head down and hurried on.

By the time I had turned onto the track that led to the cottages, I was soaked through. As I approached, I saw with a sinking heart that my neighbour Janet's car was still parked in the yard outside. She should have been gone by now if she had stuck to her normal routine. She should have knocked on my door and found I was out and then left, allowing me to return unnoticed. Worse than that, as I rounded the corner of the old stone outbuilding that guarded the courtyard, I saw Janet herself standing at my door, her head covered with a plastic rain hood, the fabric of her anorak darkening with spots of rain. She seemed to be neither knocking nor ringing, just standing there waiting with her hands down by her side, patient as the grave.

Without thinking, I ducked around the side of the building before she could spot me. It just seemed the easier option, the coward's way out. While we had never exactly had a formal arrangement that she would give me a lift into town, it had become a regular enough thing that it would be hard to explain to her why I had preferred the vast inconvenience of the bus, with its attendant waiting and long walk to and from the stop. Easier just to hide and wait, and slip home unnoticed when she had gone.

If she ever would go. The rain intensified as I stood there, finding its way through every defence. There was no sound of the car starting, her driving off. I risked a peek around the corner and saw that Janet was still waiting on my doorstep, apparently there for the duration. I quickly withdrew before she sensed my gaze, crouching in what little shelter the building afforded. To be caught now, hiding like a naughty child, would only make things worse. I shifted my weight, my back pressed hard against the cold damp of the stone wall, looking out at the rain passing in skeins up the valley, thickening and thinning with the breeze. *She must surely give up soon*, I thought. I would hear her car start up, and then I could make my move. All I had to do was wait. I closed my eyes and willed myself to patience.

If there was a fly in the ointment of my new life, it was Janet. When I first moved in, I barely understood a word she said, for she spoke with a thick Scottish accent, an accelerating tumble of unfamiliar words. Otherwise, she had seemed unremarkable, with her sensible clothes and her rather doughy face, her wiry grey hair that retained no trace of any original colour. The outer walls of our two joined cottages were thick stone, but the inner ones were not and I was aware sometimes of her movements on the other side, as she, no doubt, was of mine. Apart from Grant, she was the only person I knew to speak to in the place. After the crammed anonymity of London, at first I had rather liked the fact of knowing my neighbour's name, and being on more than just nodding terms with her.

Certainly, the first time she had given me a lift I had been nothing but grateful. It had been on a morning when it had been raining steadily since I'd got up, with no sign that it might ever stop. I'd had to nerve myself up for the walk to the bus stop and it was only the fact that I was almost out of food and in danger of missing the only bus for hours that forced me to step out into the downpour. My shoes and my jacket, supposedly waterproof, quickly proved useless and I was barely at the end of the drive before I was wet through. I had resigned myself to a miserable walk and a miserable dripping trudge around the supermarket when Janet appeared in her car beside me like the answer to a wish. I had been so sunk in my misery I had not even heard the engine.

'I'm away off to town now if you'd like a lift,' she'd said.

It was only some time later that it occurred to me – one of those thoughts that strikes you in the early hours when everything seems equally probable and significant – that Janet might well have watched me set off in the rain that day and let me leave, in the full knowledge that she would herself be setting off just a few minutes later. She did take a sort of grim satisfaction in watching people do something she considered foolish and then suffering the consequences. And while the thought was absurd and I soon dismissed it when daylight came, I couldn't quite shake the suspicion off. Spending time with Janet had that effect on me, I found – suddenly the least charitable interpretation became the obvious one.

That first day had set the pattern for the rest. Janet took to appearing at my door twice a week, just at the point when I would otherwise have been setting off for the bus, as if it were a settled thing between us. She must, I suppose, have observed my movements in the weeks after I moved in and divined my habits. She drove impatiently, dashing at the puddles that stretched across the narrow roads, sending bow waves of water cascading over the drystone dykes on either side. The roads were for the most part single track but she did not give way to oncoming traffic, what there was of it, but barrelled on, forcing the other car onto the verge. She had the habit – terrifying to a non-driver – of taking her eyes off the road while she waited for me to answer her questions and it was always a relief when we reached the outskirts of the town. We split up to do our actual shopping – to my relief, for I wasn't sure that I could face doing it under her dour scrutiny – then once we had loaded our bags into the boot of her car, we headed off for what seemed to have become the real business of the day.

It had been my idea, the first time. It had seemed only right that I should thank her for the lift with the offer of a cup of tea or coffee somewhere before we both returned. I wasn't even sure if she would accept – why spend good money on something you could perfectly well make at home? – but she did, steering me firmly past the cheery-looking place on the main street whose door always opened with a burst of fragrant steam. Her favoured spot was down a side street, a grim and usually empty cafe where we were guaranteed a table by the window. There she sat, commenting on everyone who passed before her gaze, and I sat opposite her, quickly realizing how little we had in common.

On that first afternoon she soon filleted my life for the bare facts that I allowed her. I saw myself through her eyes: single and not getting any younger, childless and increasingly likely to remain so, friendless enough that I had been able to uproot myself from one life to another with barely a wrench. She pressed me for details of what I did, refusing to be put off by my attempts at generalities until finally I was backed into an admission of something concrete.

'Tutoring,' she said. 'That'll no pay well.'

'Well enough,' I said, trapped into snappishness, then regretting the implication that she had found a tender spot.

'But you were no always a tutor, were you? And what did you do before that? Teach?'

'I was a teacher for a while, yes,' I said.

'Why did you give it up? Couldnae hack it?'

Those who can, do; those who can't, teach – I had been hearing it all my adult life. And then later, unspoken, the question: what about those who can't teach? I could see it now, written in Janet's tight and satisfied smile, her narrowed gaze. She was a turner-over of rocks, I realized, not giving up until she had exposed something grown pale and hidden in the darkness, something that fled the light. She watched me until I looked away and then she smiled again and let my silence be her answer.

Looking back, I wonder now why I never asked her anything about herself, how she had ended up living in that little cottage next to mine. It was as if she had always been there, always been the same, sitting in judgement through the cafe window. She seemed to know the worst of everyone who passed under her gaze, transforming them into so many specimens: of broken marriages, spoiled children, drink problems, lingering and self-inflicted illnesses. I had no doubt that I too would be added to the catalogue of cautionary tales.

I have never been one for gossip, never. Even before I learned for myself the destructive power of the whispered rumour, I have never been comfortable with hearing someone else's shame dissected among the coffee cups, picked over, every last delicious crumb hoovered up. I grew to dread the moment when Janet's eye would pick out some hapless mortal in the street and bring her head closer to mine, lowering her voice, her cold eyes sliding towards the victim so that they must know, surely, that they were under discussion, must feel it like an itch beneath their collar. And I, weakly complicit, could do nothing but lean forward too, see the person take on a pinched disreputable look, forever tainted. It left a taste worse even than the thin and bitter coffee the cafe served. As we walked back to the car I knew that the whole evening would be soured by it, discontent spreading like spilled milk, getting into every corner. Each time on the drive home I told myself that I would call a halt, that next time I would refuse to hear it.

And yet I didn't. Each time I sat in silence and let her talk – until it was Grant who happened to pass us as we sat there. I saw him first, and his face shone out in that grey street as if some stray shaft of sunlight had caught it. Janet was distracted by something – berating the waitress, probably – and I found myself willing him to walk on, quick, before he too fell under her eye. But he stopped to greet an older woman and stayed courteously passing the time of day, gravely tilting his head to catch what she was saying, flashing that brief, transforming smile. He was dressed in an old waxed jacket, a pair of cords rather frayed and worn about the knee, but he moved with his usual easy grace and as he reached to touch the woman's shoulder in a gesture of farewell I saw her face light up with an answering smile that would linger even after he had gone.

Unconsciously, I was smiling too, I realized. As soon as I had moved in, Grant had encouraged me to go wherever I wanted in the grounds around the main house and we met occasionally when our early-morning walks intersected. He would fall in with me and we would walk together for a few hundred yards, sometimes longer, as ready to be silent as to talk, however our moods dictated. We said nothing much of any consequence – remarking on the turns of the weather, the passage of the seasons as summer turned to autumn. It didn't matter; those brief encounters, side by side, were enough to lift the day for me. All I knew of him – and this was from Janet, who else? – was that he had already suffered tragedy: first his parents had died, killed in a car crash, and then his brother, an officer in the army, had been killed too, leaving just him and his much younger sister, still away at school. Though he never said anything about it, I wondered if he might be lonely, rattling around in the large house on his own.

A stillness alerted me to the fact that Janet, too, was watching. Not Grant, but me, cold and knowing. My smile died on my face.

'Don't,' I said, before I could stop myself. 'I don't want to hear it.' I hadn't meant to say it out loud but it was true, I didn't want to hear it, whatever shabby episode she had in mind, real or imagined. I thought she might laugh, but she just sniffed and went back to checking the bill, carefully counting out the money for her allotted share. It was only after we had paid and left and were walking back to the car that she spoke, apparently apropos of nothing.

'Oh, there's things I could tell you would make your hair curl.'

That morning, the morning of the hare, I had woken and realized that it was one of Janet's days, and my heart sank. I couldn't face the prospect, especially after my outburst the previous time. The day had dawned with deceptive brightness and as I lay and watched the sunlight send its shafts around the edges of the curtains, it occurred to me that I didn't have to. After all, we had never had a formal arrangement that she would give me a lift. No, I would get the earlier bus, could even have lunch in town – somewhere nice, a fresh book from the library for company. By the time I was halfway over the hill the rain had started lightly, but I didn't care, the prospect of escape dangling in front of me like some successful prank. Childishly, I'd been full of glee and it was only seeing her just now, waiting, that it occurred to me how rude my behaviour would seem to anyone else.

I don't know how long I had been waiting behind the barn before the idea came to me to just abandon my shopping where it was and emerge empty-handed as if I had simply been for a walk, perhaps having forgotten the time, or even what day it was. Not long, perhaps, though long enough to have got chilled, the damp soaking through to my bones. I had not heard the car, but surely she must have given up by now and retreated to her own cottage. If I was quick, she might not even see me, assuming she was not keeping vigil at her kitchen window. I tucked the tops of my shopping bags over to try and shelter their contents as best I could, so I could retrieve them later, after dark. The rain and the wind rattled them, loud as chains.

I straightened, took a deep breath, rehearsed my surprise at seeing her waiting, if she was indeed waiting, suddenly realizing the time. She might not actually believe me, for she was no fool, but it might serve to paper over the cracks. I risked another look around the corner and was relieved to see my doorstep empty. Perhaps I might get away with it after all. I thrust my hands into my pockets, ready to make the move.

'You've forgotten your wee bags.'

She had the gift of silent movement, I'll give her that. She might have been there for ages for all I knew, standing four-square at the other end of the barn in the rain, knowing exactly what I was up to, watching me dig myself in deeper. In the silence that followed I could hear the stir of the wind setting the last of the leaves in motion, and the rain as it fell and pooled and dripped and flowed, the rush of it in the drainpipe by my head. Cattle bellowed somewhere and distantly a tractor passed and repassed, tirelessly. Then, above us both, high above the clouds, a skein of geese passed over unseen, calling as they went. Hundreds of them, thousands even, bird after bird, the sound of them the sound of exile and longing. Many as they were, they seemed to fill the sky with loneliness.

As the last mournful note faded off into the south, I picked up my bags. There was nothing to say, no explanation to make. I shrugged and walked away and left her where she was, the rain still pattering around us.

Chapter 2

It was the next morning that I first met Cass, although 'met' is perhaps too prosaic a word to describe our first encounter. I had woken at my usual hour and gone for my usual pre-breakfast walk through the grounds. They must have been grand, once; several acres of semi-parkland, shading into a fine beech wood. Beyond that lay the plantation forest, separated by a high drystone wall which had started to tumble in places. Like the wall, the grounds showed signs of gathering neglect. What must once have been a series of vistas and avenues and glades had been overtaken by undergrowth, and when I first arrived the air had been full of drifting seeds and thistledown. Now the dead seed heads stood cracked and dried in clumps beneath the trees and only the moss, which coated every available surface, retained its bright jewel green. Grant might swipe at the odd snaking bramble, and mutter something about sorting the place out, but he seemed to confine himself to mowing the grass, keeping a few lawns clear around the house and weaving a network of green pathways through the encroaching wilderness.

There was no sign of Grant that morning, and I had the privilege of enjoying the early-morning calm alone, broken only by the alarmed scatter of birds fleeing my approach. After a while, tiring a little of my own company, I decided to finish by visiting the hens, as I sometimes did. Behind the house but screened from it by a fringe of trees lay the remains of an old walled garden where half a dozen hens scratched within their wire-fenced enclosure. It was a pleasant, sheltered spot and the hens provided an undemanding background murmur of conversation. Sometimes Grant would be there, collecting the morning's eggs, but mostly I'd have the place to myself. I had taken to bringing them a few treats, clumps of chickweed or kitchen scraps, so when they saw me coming through the gap in the wall where the gate had once been they would hurry over with their dumpy wide-legged run, wing stubs flapping in their excitement. But that morning there was no crooning chatter as I approached, no scramble to greet me, nothing but a continued silence.

As so often happened after a day of rain, the morning was a bright one, washed clean and full of golden promise. The grass was frosted with dew and the slanting morning light gave it a subdued sheen. Each hen lay where it must have fallen, a heap of bright russet feathers against the green. Crouched among them was a girl, who straightened slowly at my approach. She held one bird cradled in her hands and the fall of her hair matched the colour of its feathers exactly.

I knew who she was, of course: Grant's sister, returned from school, perhaps for her half-term holidays. Cass, her name was – Cassandra. Young madam, Janet called her. The wee besom; the afterthought, with a twelve-year gap between her and her brother; the by-blow – 'for where's the red hair in that family, that's what I'd like to know'. Packed off to school even before her parents had been killed, seventeen now, spoiled, left to run wild; Janet's contempt for her had been clear.

What Janet had neglected to say – and perhaps in her book it counted as another flaw – was that Cass was beautiful, and not in the commonplace way that most seventeen-year-olds are, just by dint of being young. She had the most striking appearance, that unusual combination of red hair and brown eyes that made both appear to be the same dark red, like some exotic creature from a fable. Her brother was handsome enough in an ordinary understated way, but Cass seemed not quite real as she stood up before me with a single graceful motion, glowing against the subdued green and grey of her surround-ings, her eyes lit from within.

The silence stretched between us. And then she smiled, a smile full of warmth and welcome that I could not help but return in kind.

'I'm Cass, by the way, Grant's sister,' she said, as if meeting someone in an enclosure full of dead hens was an everyday occurrence, nothing that couldn't be carried off with a little charm. 'And I bet I know who you are too. You're the mystery lodger who nobody knows anything about.'

She was barefoot, I noticed irrelevantly, her feet long and pale, half buried in the grass. She must have been frozen, standing there with the dew soaking into her jeans. She walked towards me still carrying the dead bird and her feet seemed to find their own way through the tussocks and bare patches that the scratching hens had left in the grass.

'Fox?' I said at last, for it seemed I had to say something, although I would have expected more damage: feathers scat-tered, heads missing. The birds were all there, all apparently untouched. The one in Cass's arms was lifeless, its comb pale and its eyes glazed, but there was not a mark on it.

'It must be,' she said. 'I should tell Grant.'

She handed the body to me while she stepped over the fence of the enclosure, disdaining the gate. I saw from her footmarks in the dew that she had come the same way. Looking back, I could see my own marks, a parallel track of brighter green. There were no others.

'He'll be devastated,' she said.

'Was he fond of them?'

'They were Rory's hens,' she said simply. 'He was the one who got them. Said they made more sense than most people.'

Rory. It took me a moment to place the name. The brother, the other brother. The army officer, killed in action.

'Oh God, I'm sorry,' I said, and instantly regretted the emptiness of my words.

'He loved these hens. Loved them. It was all he could talk about. Like nobody had ever kept chickens in the entire history of the planet.' She looked down at the bird I was still holding and brushed her fingers against its feathers, but made no move to take it from me. 'He gave them all names, used to call them and they'd come charging over. This one was his favourite, the boss hen, the alpha female. He always said she made sure she got the best of everything.'

She glanced at me sideways, through her fringe, and I was struck once more by the match of her eyes and her hair, the contrast with the creamy smoothness of her skin.

'What did he call her?' I asked, even though I had the feeling I was feeding her her cue.

'Cass,' she said. 'He said she reminded him of me.'

24

Before I could react – and what reaction might have been appropriate to such a remark, I have no idea – her face changed in some indefinable way, her eyes blanking, all animation gone for a moment as she swayed and I was forced to take her arm to steady her.

'Are you all right?' I asked. 'Cass?'

There was no response and for a moment I feared she might collapse. I felt my heart quicken and my fingers tighten into the flesh of her arm before she blinked and returned to the present.

'Head rush,' she said at last. 'Stood up too quick. I'm famous for it, actually, at school. Total dizzyhead. You should have seen me in biology when we were supposed to dissect some rat or mouse or something. Bang, gone, on the floor. They hadn't even started, hadn't even got them out. It was just the thought of it. No wonder I got an E.' I let go and she looked at me, rubbing her arm. 'Are you all right? You've gone a bit pale.'

'Me? I'm fine. I was worried about you for a second, that's all.' I proffered the body of the dead hen, hoping she would take it from me, but she just hooked her arm back through mine, tilting her head a little so she could look at me. With one of the mercurial changes of mood with which I was to grow familiar, she was suddenly intense, serious, pleading.

'Come back to the house with me,' she said. 'Help me break the news to Grant. I can see you would be exactly the right sort of person to do it, where I'd just get it all wrong.'

I laughed, shifting a little in her grip. I'm not really a touchy-feely sort of person, especially with someone I've only just met, but there was something in the way she seemed to cling to me that made it hard for me to disentangle myself.

'He'll blame me,' she said, widening her eyes.

'Of course he won't,' I said. 'You just found them, that's all.'

'He will. He might. You don't know him. I'm always being found at the scene of some disaster and I totally get the blame, even when it's not my fault.' She broke her gaze and looked down at the hen, letting her fingers brush its feathers again. 'You could tell him it was you who found them first.' Her glance up at me was candid and open.

'I could, but that would be a lie.'

'Only a tiny little one.'

'All the same.'

She cocked her head, looking to see if I would relent, but then shrugged and seemed to forget it, urging me to come down anyway, chattering away beside me as we walked, full of the relentless egotism of youth. I learned more than I wanted to about how pointless her school was, how empty-headed her fellow pupils and how ignorant her teachers. She seemed once more completely unconcerned and yet I felt that there was an undercurrent of uneasiness beneath the flow. Her arm felt tense in mine, as if I was the only thing holding her up.

As we came to the yard at the back of the house, she stopped. 'Have you been in the house yet?' she asked. 'Have you seen it?'

'Not really,' I said. I had admired Hare House from afar, the way it seemed to be framed by the landscape, classically proportioned, a harmonious assemblage of grey stone, subdued against the vivid greens around it. It was not particularly large but it had a sort of reserved grandeur about it. It did not seem the sort of place one could simply drop in to.

'Oh, you have to see it. I can't believe my brother hasn't shown you round.'

She started towards the back door and I went to follow her, but she stopped me.

'No, no, no, you've totally got to come in the front to experience it properly. Go on round and ring the bell and I'll let you in. Oh, I can't wait to see your face.'

I hesitated, feeling ridiculous, but she waved me off impatiently and disappeared into the house. Annoyed at what seemed to me to be an unnecessary charade, I walked around to the front of the house. It was surrounded by a springy lawn, rather better kempt than the rest of the grounds, and at the front a sweep of gravel, somewhat taken over with weeds. There was a magnificent view from here, a version of my own but wider, the rolling hills golden in the October sunshine and the trees aglow with all the changing colours of the leaves. The house, though, was blinded, its shutters closed up, and when Cass opened up the front door with much sliding of bolts I could see nothing but the slant of light it admitted across the floor, and the darkness of the interior. Her cool hand went over my eyes even as she pulled me in, so that I half stumbled over the threshold.

'Come in, come in, don't look until I've turned the lights on properly, I want you to get the effect all at once.'

She closed the door behind me and scampered her way up the staircase. Her injunction not to look was entirely unnecessary for I could see almost nothing after the bright sunshine outside. Some light filtered down from upstairs, outlining the curve of the banisters and catching against some glass display cases that appeared to line the walls. Otherwise all was shadowy and dark, the air smelling a little musty and unused.

'Hello? Cass?' The space around me seemed to ring with

my voice. I could not shake off the feeling that I was being watched, judged, by hundreds of pairs of eyes and I wondered for a mad moment if this was some sort of a practical joke, a set-up of which I was about to be made the victim.

'Cass?' There was no answer, but the lights suddenly flooded on, leaving me blinking. The sensation of being watched had not been entirely in my imagination, for there they were, the eyes, the hundreds of eyes: the glass unblinking stare of dead animals ranked around me in the cases. Not the usual hunting trophies I might have expected, but something much more peculiar. I took them for dolls at first, or toys, animals dressed up in Victorian clothes. One case held a wedding with a bride and groom, bridesmaid, vicar, a whole congregation packed into the pews. Another was a school, a third a drawing room with lace-decked creatures taking tea while one sat at a miniature piano. A closer look showed that each character in every scene was in fact a hare, stuffed and awkwardly posed in its crudely made costume.

'Macabre, isn't it?'

Not Cass, but Grant. I spun around from the wedding tableau I had been looking at with horrified fascination and saw him standing in one of the doorways that led off the hall, his face unreadable.

'Cass about?' he said.

'She headed upstairs,' I said. 'She was just going to turn on the lights.'

'It was I who turned on the lights.' He had not moved from where he stood and I saw that his hand was on a bank of switches. 'I was wondering who it was in here.'

He moved at last, to the foot of the stairs, and bellowed up them. Cass replied faintly and inaudibly from some far reach of the house. 'I should apologize for my sister,' he said. 'She genuinely would forget her head if it were not screwed on.'

There was an awkward pause. I had got the impression that Grant was someone who valued his privacy, and yet here I was, standing in the middle of his home, as if I had just barged in.

'I'm sorry; Cass insisted I come in and see,' I said.

'That's all right,' he said shortly. 'Have a proper look. I forget they're there half the time.'

I could not imagine passing up those stairs each night without being acutely aware of the creatures, frozen though they were. Even dressed up in their costumes, raised up on their hind legs, the hares had nothing human about them. Their glass eyes gave them a look of watchful contempt. Turning back to the wedding scene again, I could not help but feel the bride and groom were glaring at me, resentful at being disturbed. I couldn't shake off the memory of the dying hare the day before, the quality of its gaze.

I became conscious that Grant was staring at the dead hen, still in my arms. I felt a flush of colour rise. 'Did Cass not tell you? About the hens?' I asked.

He put his hands out and I passed it to him. Distantly we heard the crash of pipes and the run of water, explaining Cass's absence.

'She came dashing through the kitchen just now saying you'd found them all dead this morning.'

It was ambiguous, in a sense. The English language has long since lost its plural 'you', an omission we should perhaps regret. I could not tell from Grant's words whether he thought that I alone had found them, or Cass and I together. A fine distinction, perhaps. I rubbed my hands to clear them of the sensation of the hen's feathers, which still lingered like a stain. Caught red-handed, caught holding the body. I could find no way of phrasing a clarification that would not have sounded like something else. I let the remark lie.

'I'm sorry,' I said again. 'You must be very upset.'

He shrugged. 'It's annoying. But hens are funny creatures. These things happen.'

'Yes, but these ones particularly. Rory's.'

He stiffened, jerking his chin upwards. 'Rory's hens? Who told you that?'

I caught a movement and looked up. Cass, silent on her bare feet, was standing at the turning of the stairs as if she had materialized there. She ran down the last flight and hooked her arm through his in an affected sort of way, demanding our admiration of the tableaux. Grant tolerated her for a second, then disengaged his arm and reached for the light switch.

'Easier to go out the back,' he said, as the hall once more went dark. 'We don't really use the front door much. Cass, if you could lock it up again?'

She moved off easily through the gloom. All I could see once more was the outline of the cases, although now that I was aware of them it seemed to me that the faint unblinking gleam of all those eyes could still be made out. Grant opened the door into a back corridor and he and I entered it together. He paused at an open door that led into the brightly lit kitchen, the light spilling into the dim corridor.

'The kettle is just boiling,' he said. 'You'd be welcome to join us for a cup of tea.'

'Oh yes, do, and toast – I'm ravenous and utterly parched.'
Cass had skidded up to join us and clutched my arm. Grant's
face had been polite and unexpectant when he had made the
invitation and I had been about to refuse, but Cass was unstoppable and dragged me in, grabbing three mismatched mugs,
then heaving the huge kettle off the Aga with both hands. The
kitchen was large and warm, much warmer than the rest of
the house, and cluttered with things that had no business there
but that seemed to me to be exactly right – even the dead hen,
which Grant had left casually on one of the counters. It was a
room for living in, with a fireplace in the corner surrounded
by a collection of shabby armchairs, as well as the large kitchen
table, which was almost entirely covered with paperwork.

'I can't stay,' I said. 'I really should be getting back. I've
work to do.'

'No, stay,' and it was Grant who said it, sweeping some
papers into a pile, making a space for me at the table. 'It's about
time we had you around.'

Cass brought over the tea and my fingers found the warmth
of the mug, welcome after the chill of my walk. We chatted,
the three of us, with the ease of a much longer acquaintance,
and when I did reluctantly finish the last dregs of my tea and
stood to go, it was Grant who rose to see me out.

Out in the dimness of the corridor, he led me down towards
the back door, his heels ringing against the stone flags. At the
door, he paused, and his face once more was blandly polite,
closed off, unreadable.

'You're very welcome to drop in any time,' he said, and then
after a pause added, 'You know, when it comes to our brother,
I'm afraid you really don't want to believe everything my sister

says. She's never been one to let the facts get in the way of a good story.'

I nodded, grateful for the dimness of the hallway, feeling a sting in my cheeks. I had no doubt that he was right about Cass and her imaginings. But all the same, as I walked through the cool morning air back to my cottage I had an image in my mind as vivid as if I had seen it with my own eyes: a young army officer leaning over the fence to absorb the murmur of the hens, finding peace in their company in a world of war.

CHAPTER 3

THE NEXT MORNING, Cass turned up at my cottage, announcing her presence with a brisk rattle of knuckles against the door. I found her dressed up like a Victorian orphan in black and grey, complete with a hooded coat and ankle boots. I had to repress a smile at the theatricality of her outfit, although I had also to concede that it suited her as well as her jeans and oversized jumper had the day before.

She didn't waste time with any greetings, but addressed me as if continuing a conversation. 'Come and keep me company – Grant won't.'

'Come where?' I asked.

'You'll see.'

She seemed to harbour no doubt that I would simply drop everything at her whim. And, in fact, although I had work to do, I found myself shrugging on my coat, reasoning that a walk would probably do me good. When I got outside I found her staring at the empty spot in the yard where a car would be, if I owned one.

'You don't have a car!'

'I don't drive.'

She widened her remarkable eyes. 'How do you get about?'

'Walk, bus, lifts occasionally.'

'Lifts from who? Grant?'

I smiled. 'I've not troubled your brother, no. My neighbour mostly. We go into town together.'

'You get a lift from Janet?'

'You make it sound surprising.'

'I wouldn't get into a car with her,' she said, giving a shudder that seemed only partly feigned. 'You should let me drive you.'

'Have you even a licence?'

'Oh well. Provisional. But I've been driving for yonks. Round the estate, everywhere. Nobody cares round here. Anyway, it doesn't matter today because we can walk there; in fact, it's better that way.'

'Walk where?' I asked, but I might as well not have spoken. She linked her arm through mine and once more I was struck by the way she seemed so familiar and easy with me, as if we had known each other for years.

'No wonder you're so fit and healthy, striding around everywhere like some sort of advert from the government about the joys of fresh air. Come on, we'll go up through the forest – it's quicker that way, and so much better than risking getting into Janet's car.'

'What's wrong with that?'

'Well, you know she's a witch, of course.'

I didn't challenge it at the time. I didn't even think that much about it, considering it one of those things that teenagers like to throw out in conversation to cause a stir. I was merely pleased to note that Cass wasn't the sort to keep repeating such remarks until she got a reaction. Instead, as we walked, she talked of other things and I began to see, beneath the adolescent posturing, glimpses of the young woman she might become. I have always cherished the way teenagers can do this, especially when they are on their own with an adult: suddenly surprise you with a flash of maturity. As she walked beside me, sometimes falling into an abstracted silence, chewing on a stray strand of hair, I wondered where her friends were. It seemed to me that a girl like Cass would have a wide circle of friends her own age. She should have had no need to seek me out, just for the company.

She led me up through the grounds, through the woods at the back and on through the gate into the forest. I had never ventured this way, repelled by the darkness under the trees. In the countryside all around, autumn had run through the hill-sides like a blown ember, bright rich reds and golds, changing from day to day, almost from moment to moment. But here, beyond the wall, the conifers stood unmoved and unchanged, the air beneath them silent of any birdsong. We soon fell silent too, and above and around us came the murmur of all the countless branches; a distant sort of a noise, ungraspable yet pervasive, like voices in another room.

The track we were following curved gently round until we could see nothing but trees ahead or behind us, each one no different from the other. Every so often a firebreak opened out with a startling slash of light, but then the trees closed in again as if they had never been interrupted. Only the tumbled remains of a wall beside us gave any sign that there had ever been anything but forest here. The ground was muffled by decades' worth of fallen needles, and nothing else could grow in the dim and shadowy light.

The ground rose, the gradient steepening, and it was an effort to keep pace with Cass. My heart set up a hammer in my ears and I was grateful for the respite when we reached a gap and she turned to follow another old track, one that ran along the contour of the hill. This was wider than the one we had been following, but it, too, had the remains of a wall running along either side of it, so covered by moss that it seemed to have grown there. The trees opened out a little, letting in a bright slash of green growth. Our feet crunched in unison on the finely gravelled surface.

'This used to be a road, once,' Cass said. 'You can still drive it, in fact, it's not bad. Grant lets me take the farm Land Rover up here sometimes, but he claims it's being fixed at the moment and he's a bit of an old woman about me driving the car off road. But anyway, I've decided walking is better; you're right – I'm going to walk everywhere from now on.'

I was not aware that I had said anything about the benefits of walking, but I was content to let her chatter away again, filling the silence of the forest, dispelling the mood of abstraction that seemed to have overtaken us both. The track followed what must have been the shoulder of a hill, hidden by the cloaking forest. We were joined by the sound of running water, and rounded a bend to find a little glade set in among the trees, half filled by the spreading branches of a vast ash tree that looked as old as time. The light seemed to pick it out, leaving the surrounding forest dark and untouched. A spring welled at its foot, the water deep and clear before it flowed across the surface of the track and down the hillside, opening a course of bright green vegetation between the ordered ranks of trees.

Cass skipped across and looked back at me. 'You can cross water, I suppose,' she said, a challenge in her face.

'Why wouldn't I?' I asked, although I was not shod for fording streams and ended up working my way around the head of the spring, my fingers clinging to the rough bark of the great ash for reassurance.

'Come on, we're almost there,' Cass urged, impatient now, setting off before I had regained the track.

'But where?' I asked and got no answer. I found myself reluctant to follow her down the track, where the canopy seemed to press closer than before, almost closing overhead. But I had to, or I would lose sight of her and find myself alone in the forest. I caught up with her as she turned up another side track, among older trees, taller now, their trunks rising uninterrupted, their lower branches bare and broken off. Darkness spread beneath them. It seemed we might walk forever through their ranks and never reach their end until I saw with surprise a gatepost, high and imposing, and a wall of mortared stone. Beyond was the square grey shape of a kirk, not ruined but intact, its door firmly locked and its windows protected by grilles. All around it stood gravestones, as grey as the church but tilting, crumbling; heading back into the earth.

As we stepped through the open gates we startled a pheasant that had crouched hidden at our feet. It erupted into the air with a great noise of clapping wing beats and frantic squawking, causing both of us to leap with fright and clutch each other, laughing when we realized what it was.

'Stupid idiot birds,' Cass said, but I saw that her face was puffy about the eyes and I realized that at some point on our walk she had been quietly crying, unobtrusively enough that I had not noticed. I was about to ask her what was wrong when I noticed among the older gravestones a newer monument, starkly shiny in polished granite and I understood suddenly what this whole expedition was about. She followed my gaze.

'Yep, the family mausoleum,' she said. 'They keep this whole place open just for us. I like to pop up and say hello when I can.'

She was suddenly all awkwardness, standing on the outside of her feet, her lip caught between her teeth. I guessed that she didn't know how to ask me if I could leave her for a moment alone.

'I think I'll take a look around,' I said. 'I like old graveyards.'

'Do you? How strange you are.' She smiled, though, and looked around her as if for the first time. 'It's Rory I come for really. I can't help but feel that, stuck up here with all these old people, he'd be going out of his mind.' Her smile was more practised this time, as if she'd brought this line out once or twice before. Then she pulled her cloak around her and stalked, straight-backed, towards the gravestones.

I went the other way so that the corner of the church was between us, giving her a little space. I had told Cass no more than the truth; old burial grounds have long interested me for their window into the lives of ordinary people, people the world has otherwise long since forgotten. The place was obviously still maintained and the grass had been kept more or less cut, but the trees leaned close against the perimeter wall as though they longed to creep in and close the gap. Moss grew everywhere, thick as fur. It had colonized even the inscriptions on the stones, lending them a vivid, borrowed life. The few that I could read were old, dating back to the seventeenth century. I stooped to try and decipher one. 'Know the hour of thy death,' it said in a roughly carved inscription beneath the naive depiction of a skeleton. Underneath, in a space cleared of moss, the words 'Exod 22:18' had been scratched.

I was puzzling over whether this was a recent addition when the sky was suddenly split with a noise – more than a noise: a violent assault of sound that came from all around, beyond description. I looked around, up, and caught a glimpse of a jet fighter hanging like a wicked toy in the clear sky above the trees, before it rolled and shot away. Another streaked across, black and bristling with weaponry. It seemed implausible that such a thing could even fly, as if it were an illusion conjured by the demon howl it raised around it. Two, three more came over, twisting, shrieking, then took their dogfight off across the forest, leaving only a shattered calm. Birds rose, calling – rooks, crows, I could not remember the difference – filling the air with their complaints, settling only slowly.

I should have been used to the planes by now, but their intrusion always took me by surprise. I shuddered, cold from standing still. The quiet contemplation of gravestones had lost its charm. I didn't like the place, didn't like the pressing trees that surrounded it, their restless endless murmur. The gravestones confronted me. So many short lives, all full of unknowable suffering and grief, and now that I had noticed it I saw scratched everywhere the same inscription, Exod 22:18.

Feeling the need to move, I continued slowly round the church. I was expecting more recent graves, Victorian perhaps, but here the graveyard was even older and long untended. The bracken and brambles were taking over and all the inscriptions had been worn away some time ago. The wall was breached in places and the trees were pressing through the gaps; not just the planted pines but also birch, hawthorn, a rowan still bearing its withered berries, poison red.

'It won't take long.' Cass's voice startled me. I turned and saw her standing watching me, her hood flung back, her hair flame bright against her pale face, the grey church behind. She might have been posed there by a cinema director with an eye for the melodramatic, and I could see that she was aware of the effect she had.

'What won't?' I asked.

'For the forest to creep back in and reclaim its own. Grant and I, we're the last of the Hendersons and when we're gone they'll shut this place up and lock the gate and fling the key in Maggie's Pool and then they'll leave it till the trees have smothered everything.'

'That seems unlikely,' I said. 'And besides, you're young, both of you. Hardly the end of the line.'

I walked over to where she stood and examined the headstones. The lettering on two of them was still sharp, newly cut. Cass's parents' names, and then beneath them, Rory's. I had not realized he had died less than a year before, in December. Next to it, an older stone marked what must have been the grave of her grandparents, also Hendersons. Her grandmother had died recently too, then, barely a month after her brother.

'He always said he wouldn't make old bones, and he was right. And he always said our family was cursed, and he was right about that too.'

'Don't talk nonsense, Cass. Nobody's family is cursed,' I said, perhaps more sharply than I had intended, and as I turned to look I saw the tremble of her chin, the way her mouth was working to stay still.

There are others who might have known how to offer the right words or the right gesture in the face of so much bereavement, but empty words of consolation do not come easily to me. In my awkwardness, I felt my impatience with her returning. What could I, a stranger, say to her anyway? Why wasn't Grant here, giving her the comfort that she needed? I waited, growing a little chilled, wondering if she would make a move to start back. In cold practical terms, I had work to be getting on with. I couldn't stand around in a graveyard forever. And perhaps sympathy – that cheap, easy emotion – wasn't what she needed. I saw her master herself in the space that I had left her, straighten her back, regain her composure.

To soften the silence, I put out a hand, a bare touch, just a brush against the wool of her coat. 'Shall we go?'

'You go, I'll follow.'

I hesitated, but she waved me on.

I was almost at the gate before she spoke again. 'He died a hero, you know.'

I walked until I reached the spring again and there I stopped to let her catch up if she chose to. The place was a relief after the close-packed ranks of the forest. The water welled, filled with a shimmering light from the sky. No ripples broke its surface but its reflections had a shifting quality, uneasy and unreadable, mesmerizing. In the water the tree branches crossed and recrossed, never still, my own face appearing and disappearing, illusions forming with the changing light. You might see anything in such a pool, if you looked hard enough. If you had that cast of mind.

I must have stood there, lost in thought, until Cass broke into my reverie. Her face appeared in the water, a pale drowned reflection, then when I spun round, real and alive, a hand snaked through my arm.

'I knew it,' she said, with unwarranted triumph. 'People are always drawn to Maggie's Pool. Especially those with a dark past and a history to hide.'

It took me a fraction of a second to realize that she was just teasing – long enough, perhaps, for her to register my reaction, as her eyes narrowed in a way that reminded me, incongruously, of Janet. Then she smiled.

'Aha!' she said. 'What is it, though? Were you wronged by your lover? Are you on the run from a *crime passionnel*? A spy, a murderess, an international jewel thief? Will they find you out and track you down? We'll be in all the papers – they always interview the neighbours. "Oh, she seemed such a quiet person, always kept herself to herself," we'll say. "We had no clue, not an inkling."'

There are ways of dealing with such nonsense: the pained smile, the quiet refusal to play along. Reacting makes it worse, and I knew that even as I shook my arm free.

But it was too late, for I had already spoken: 'Don't talk rubbish, Cass,' I said, and let the words come out as sharply as I felt them. Let her think what she liked; I didn't care.

I think she laughed, or said something, but I didn't wait to hear it. 'I've got to get back,' I said, pressing on down the path, regretful now at the time wasted. She was, after all, no more than a silly girl, and I was done with teenage girls, thank goodness. And yet, even as I walked away and left her standing there, I felt the regret rise at my hastiness, the feeling that I had failed her in some fundamental way.

My mood of regret did not lift as I came round the corner of the cottages and saw Janet emerging from her front door. Another person I'd offended. I knew I could not just walk past without some greeting, so I said good morning and she responded with a bare nod, her arms still folded. And yet she seemed in no hurry to either go back in or go and do whatever it was that had prompted her to come out.

'Turned into a nice day after all,' I said, filling the silence.

'Aye well, it won't last, mind,' she responded and the prospect seemed to cheer her.

'No,' I said, and then with an attempt at brightness, 'Well, I'd better get in then.'

She looked at me flatly. The memory of our last encounter lay between us: there, yet clearly not to be spoken of. I could not apologize and I could not explain and in the silence I heard my own words escaping before I could stop them, before I could claw them back.

'I'm just putting the kettle on now, if you'd fancy a cup of something?'

'You've no done much with it,' Janet said, as she stepped over the threshold and looked around her with little avid glances.

'You know the place, then,' I said.

'Oh aye, when it was young Rory's I was in here all the time.'

I looked at her curiously. She rarely mentioned Rory, a reticence unusual for her. She'd certainly never let on that they had been neighbours.

'I didn't know Rory had lived here.' I had assumed the cottage had always been a holiday let; it had that studied blandness about its decor. Just enough furniture and no more – even the kitchen, carefully supplied with its matching plates and bowls and cups, four of each. 'No wonder the place makes Grant so sad.'

She made a noise somewhere between a sniff and a snort. 'Huh. Well, I'm no one to gossip about other folk's troubles.'

The look she gave me was half a challenge, but I did not take it up. The coffee pot was sending up its rising note of hysteria and I busied myself with it, avoiding her eyes. Merely by sitting there, she seemed to cast a pall over the whole cottage, passing judgement. I had liked it for its simplicity, its suffi- ciency, but now it seemed merely bare, not a home at all and I regretted the impulse that had led me to invite her in.

I laid out the cups, milk jug, sugar bowl. The smell of the coffee rose up from the pot as I poured it, rich and dark and fragrant. I make good coffee; it's one of those small things I pride myself on. People remark upon the effort I put into it, but I see no point in not taking the trouble to make it properly. It's one of my treats to myself, a little moment of pleasure to punctuate the day. I handed Janet her cup but for the moment she was abstracted.

'He wouldnae stay at the main house, because of those creatures in the hall. You ken the ones I mean?'

'The hares?'

44

'Aye.'

'I'm not sure I blame him,' I said.

Her unexpected smile surprised me into smiling back. Her face took on a softer edge. Her eyes slid over mine and roved the room, perhaps recalling how it once had been. Army neat, perhaps, or bachelor slovenly? Had she come in here and drunk his coffee, shared gossip with him, what? My curiosity was piqued.

'I was up just now with Cass, visiting the churchyard,' I said. I remembered her parting words. 'She said he died a hero.'

I don't know what I expected. Some sour remark about every soldier dying a hero these days, perhaps. Or maybe something else, something that reflected that softening of her expression. But her face just closed, the remark bouncing off it as if it had never been uttered.

'Huh,' she said, all softness gone. 'Easy enough to visit when they're dead.'

'What do you mean?' I asked, but all I got was her usual challenging stare. She took her first sip of coffee and wrinkled her nose, ladling in extra sugar.

'Oh, you make that awfy strong.'

'I prefer it that way.'

'Your fancy pot and all. Plain old instant's good enough for me.' She seemed revived by this jab at my pretensions, straightening, looking around her with renewed criticism. 'Aye, you've no done much here with your few wee bits. Of course, you may no be planning on staying long. There's few folk come up here who last beyond their first winter. Whatever they may be running away frae.'

45

That evening, as I knew would happen, Janet's presence lingered, pervasive, casting a sour disappointment over everything. There was a moment I had come to look forward to, the point in the evening when the sun sank low enough to paint the hills beyond my window with its golden light, even as we fell into shadow below. This time, it didn't fill me with my usual delight as I watched, a cooling cup of coffee in my hand. The days were shortening, winter accelerating towards us. The fighter jets were up again, not overhead this time, but filling the skies with a distant disquiet. I watched but I did not really see them, my mind casting back instead towards the morning in the churchyard, Cass, the shimmering reflections in the pool.

That night I slept uneasily, and in my sleep the dream returned, the one I had not suffered since I'd left London. I don't remember it, I never do. I know it only as a wakening, my heart pounding as I fight my way to the surface, up through all the layers of sleep, gasping for clean air. Perhaps there is no dream, only a momentary sense of suffocation, some hiccup in my own body's rhythm, my breathing interrupted. It doesn't matter. Whatever causes it, it's then that the memory returns, the one I must play out in the quiet dark, must play out right through until the end, the images rising like reflections in the water – the classroom and the desks, the tumbled chairs, and the girls, falling in silence like petals from a rose.

part two
bewitchment

THEY WERE NOT dead, those girls. They had just fainted – although in real life there's nothing of the elegant swoon about a faint, nothing 'just' about it. The girls came round groaning and shaking, their breath returning in juddering gasps as if the very air was hurting them. It was no wonder that people thought it might be a poisoning, gas, chemicals, some sudden deadly virus. But girls faint. They just do, sometimes: if they haven't eaten, if they get worked up about something beyond the point of reason – which is common enough, God knows. And it can spread. One girl down and then another and another, as they see their fellows fall. Mass hysteria, they call it, and it has been recorded throughout history. Especially in close-knit groups of adolescent girls, so finely attuned as they are to each other's emotions.

The girls were coming round again by the time help arrived. I don't know how long it took. Later there were some who claimed I had delayed raising the alarm, but if I stood there stunned for a second or two, no longer, who could blame me? It wasn't as if it made any difference. The girls recovered completely, most of them. Even as they were being led away to the waiting ambulances you could hear their starling chatter rising in the corridor at the excitement of it all.

They wanted to take me too, to check me out, but I refused, for I was fine. Perhaps it would have been more politic had I allowed myself to be shepherded away with my charges, a blanket draped over my shoulders, to cool my heels in some accident and emergency department, but I have no patience for such charades. Later, it would be one of those things that would count against me, in some unspecified way. I suppose I should have long since stopped expecting stoicism and common sense to be regarded as virtues, rather than unnatural afflictions to be pitied and hence feared.

As it was, that day I found myself forgotten. Everybody else had gone, fled in fear of the nameless, invisible thing that had felled the girls. I watched the ambulances pull away, sirens sounding in pulses as if to blast their way through. The crowd at the gate knotted and struggled. Cars had been abandoned to the gridlocked traffic as parents rushed to retrieve their precious children, the news spreading as swiftly and mysteriously as gas.

I waited until everybody was gone and even then I did not leave the building, but walked down its deserted corridors, back to my own classroom. I could not explain that either, when they asked. The door was locked, but of course, I had a key. There was talk afterwards about a smell, some cloying scent, but that was just talk. The classroom smelled as it always did, of girls, of paper, of the markers we used on the whiteboard. The chairs were still scattered and fallen so I righted them, straightened the tables. There were two more days of the spring term to go. I did not want to come back to chaos in the morning. And then, in the absence of anything else to do, I gathered up my bag, the evening's marking, ready to go home.

Did I stand at the door before I closed it, looking in at the classroom that had been mine for so long? Probably not, because I had no inkling that it would be the last time I ever stood there, that that day marked the end of my teaching career. The girls were fine; they would bounce back unharmed, although a few would linger longer in the hospital, persuading themselves and the medics that there might be something seriously the matter. What I did not realize then, as I quietly moved around my classroom, restoring order, was that the real casualty here would turn out to be me.

CHAPTER 4

I WOKE AGAIN the next morning early, heavy with the weariness of a bad night's sleep. I lay awake for a while and watched the light seep through the curtains and let the concerns of the day pile up until I shook myself and sprang out of bed, resolving to make the most of the early start. A walk to set me up, and then a morning's hard work would resolve most of my problems, I decided. I found myself following the route that Cass and I had taken, up through the forest. I did not fancy the silence of the hens' enclosure, and I felt drawn to revisit Maggie's Pool. For all the gloom of the surrounding forest, there was something about the spot that promised peace.

It took me a little longer than I'd expected, so that I was wondering if I had lost my way before I rounded a bend and saw at last the ranks of trees give way to the glade I had remembered, the light of the water glowing with the sunshine filtering through the last of the leaves on the great ash. I had not noticed them before but I could now see that there were little scraps of cloth and ribbons tied here and there to its branches, fluttering like frayed pennants in the breeze.

As I reached up to touch the fissured bark of the bough above my head, I heard a voice say, 'Magnificent, isn't it?'

A woman had appeared on the track ahead of me, accompanied by two rough-coated long-legged dogs. She wore a coat the colour of spring leaves and she had grey hair, cut short, and skin as soft and downy as an old peach. Her eyes sparkled a clear and youthful blue.

'It is,' I agreed. 'It must be absolutely ancient. I'm surprised it has survived.'

'Oh well, no one would touch this tree.' She pointed down at the spring. 'South-running water, you see; and ash trees, of course, have a powerful magic of their own.'

I looked up at her, uncertain whether she was joking, but her voice had been as matter of fact as if she were discussing the weather.

'Magic in what way?'

'Well, once it would have been to cure the sick, but these days, people mostly ask the pool to bless them with a wean. Throw a stone in, make a wish. Offer up a gift if they're successful.'

'People still believe that here?'

Her eyes were level, kind. 'People who want a baby and can't have one manage to believe in anything,' she said.

'True,' I said.

One of the dogs leapt neatly over the stream, its companion following close behind. They circled, not quite touching me, their faces curious.

'They won't bite,' she said. 'Don't mind them.'

'I don't,' I said, pulling my hands up and out of the way of their questing noses all the same. I have never really been a dog person.

'They're lurchers. Sammy and George,' she said. Her voice

was softly Scottish, educated, sensible, matching her appearance. 'They're gentle souls, really, but with tinkers' manners. Just tell them to go away if they bother you.' She herself did not approach, nor did she introduce herself. 'I thought perhaps you might be here on the same mission, but clearly not.'

'It takes two to make a baby,' I said without thinking and was surprised at the bitterness in my voice.

'There are other things to wish for.'

'Well, if you believe in that sort of thing.' I caught myself looking down at the water, watching the shifting reflections scatter as a leaf fell and spun upon the surface. 'And besides, a wish can't change the past.' I looked up and caught the full force of her scrutiny. Her eyes seemed to see more than could possibly be there in my face.

'You stay up here, don't you,' she said, and it wasn't a question. 'One of the cottages, isn't it?'

'That's right.' No point asking how she knew.

'You're happy here then?'

'I love it,' I said. 'It's a beautiful place, and so peaceful.'

Her considering gaze seemed to imply that there was more to this exchange than mere politeness. 'Beauty is a rare thing. Peace is rarer.'

I did not quite know what to say to that. She tilted her head and waited, and I looked away, down, back at the spring at my feet. Between us the water welled and broke, the stream falling away down the hill, carving its clean line through the accumulation of pine needles. South-running, indeed. The stones at the bottom shimmered, the water clear enough to see each one. They were rounded, coloured, some with holes in them, the sort of stones you might pick up on the beach and keep in your pocket as a talisman, a comfort to the fingers. There were coins too, I saw, and even a seashell. Was each one then freighted with a mixture of hope and pain, a final act of desperation – but perhaps a release too? A wish can't change the past. And yet might it not be possible instead to package up all the futility of regret and longing and cast it into the water?

Something shifted in the forest light. I could no longer see the stream bed and the shimmering stones. Instead my own face was reflected back at me, cast with a pall of green. It was not flattering; the angle gave me a drawn and bitter look, as if I had aged twenty years. I could see myself, grown hard and disappointed, as narrow and disapproving as Janet. I shook myself and looked away from the seductive surface of the spring. A life spent dwelling on the past is no life. I had come up here to get away from such futile regrets.

The woman with the dogs was still watching me.

I smiled awkwardly. 'Well, better go – stuff to do. Work to finish. Deadlines to meet.'

'Deadlines? You're a journalist?'

'No, just the normal sort of deadlines. You know, work to be finished.' I could hear the evasion in my voice.

'What is it that you do then?'

Such a simple question. I found I could not bring out my usual lie about tutoring, not under that gaze. 'Oh, this and that. Freelancing.'

She did not probe further, only tilted her head a little as if waiting for my real answer. Once more I broke eye contact, disturbed by an inexplicable urge to tell her more, tell her everything. I was startled by the sheer irrationality of it and mentally shook myself, looking away and then back at her, really just a rather ordinary older woman with two poorly controlled dogs. I pulled my coat away from one closely pressing nose, and she too seemed to recall herself.

'I'm sorry, they are bothering you, aren't they? I should have realized.' She called them back and they came without a murmur, tails waving.

She gathered herself, preparing to leave, and then seemed to linger for a moment as if waiting one last time for me to find the right words, but I had nothing to say. Then she turned and headed off, her dogs slinking like shadows through the trees beside her.

I had told the truth about one thing: I did have a deadline to meet and I have never yet missed one; I can take pride in that, if nothing else. As soon as I got back from my walk, I settled down immediately to my computer. The job was a rush one – they almost always were – and it had arrived a couple of days before by email, the usual terse missive, no greeting, no sign-off except for the unadorned 'S. Robinson' at the bottom. In all the years of working for him – or her – there had never been anything else; no pleasantries, no superfluous communication. Just the details of the job, the deadline and the pay, which was not much, but now that I had moved out of London was more than sufficient for my needs.

I imagined this S. Robinson sometimes, a man with a glint

of gold in his smile, working in a bare-looking room in some warren of buildings in a shady part of London, the kind of place where the trains screech and rattle in the background, although the missives could just as well have come from Milton Keynes, or more likely Bangalore. We were scrupulous in our dealings with each other: I never let him down and he never let me down, paying me promptly and to the penny, and supplying me with a steady stream of work. I thought I detected in his manner – if emails so short can be said to have a manner – a certain respect, as one professional to another. And why not? For I was a professional, and I knew that I did a good job for him; far better, perhaps, than the work deserved.

This one was easy, something I could do in my sleep, although I would never skimp on my efforts in such a way. Each essay – it was laid out in the contract – had to be completely written from scratch, to evade plagiarism detection software. There was even a list of common spelling mistakes and grammatical errors to include, depending on the level of the student commissioning the work. Sometimes it was a ghost-writing job, taking the work the student had done themselves and shaping it into a coherent whole. This, though, was just a straight job: a title, a set text to refer to, and a deadline. I was paid extra for the rush jobs.

I never think too hard about the morality of what I do. It's advertised as a model answer service, showing students how it should be done so they can learn. Cheating is never mentioned, not outright. I write the essays and I write them well. I was always good at that at school and at university, and it wasn't as if people were queuing up to give me alternative employment. I enjoy it, if I'm honest, and I'm paid to do it. How many other people can say such a thing about their work?

It was five o'clock before I was finished. I had wasted too much time getting started to allow myself the indulgence of a lunchtime walk, although the clouds had never quite closed over and the sun had come and gone at the window all day, trying to tempt me out. As I stretched and unkinked my neck and gradually withdrew myself from the world of nineteenth-century corn laws to the present day, I saw that the light had taken on the slanting gold of the late afternoon. I was just considering getting out for a quick stretch of the legs when a knock came at the door.

I was not expecting it to be Cass. If anything, I thought it might be Janet, and perhaps that was the reason why when I saw Cass instead, I must have smiled more broadly than I would normally do, forgetting my earlier irritation. She answered me with a smile of her own, and all the slight cool-ness with which we had parted was forgotten.

'Have you been out cycling?' I asked.

She had a bike with her, but she did not seem to be dressed for riding, and certainly not on a bike like that, built for speed.

'Don't be daft, it's for you. I found it in the shed and decided I could just see you bombing about the roads on it, instead of having to walk everywhere. Look, it's practically good as new.'

She exaggerated somewhat, for the bike had a neglected,

dusty air to it, as if it had been more than just forgotten about, but deliberately shut away.

The idea was ridiculous. 'Cass, I haven't ridden a bike in years,' I said. And certainly not a man's bike like this, fast-looking, aggressive.

'You know what they say about riding a bike. And it's totally the ideal solution. You can go anywhere on it – into town, all round the roads, exactly as if you had a car. Never wait for a bus again. Never need a lift again.'

'Town is miles away,' I said, forgetting that when you start to criticize individual details of someone's plan you've already conceded the principle.

'Nonsense, it's hardly any distance at all. And think how far you have to walk just to get to the bus. Even if you leave the bike at the bus stop, you'll have saved hours and hours. Look, I even found a lock for it, and the pump. We'll get some air in the tyres and then it's all yours.'

She leaned the bike against the wall, fumbling with the pump until I was obliged to take it from her hands and do it myself. The fitting was different from the ones I remembered, but the action of pumping up the tyre was the same, so familiar that the sound of the air hissing through the valve instantly took me back – not to my student days when I had last ridden a bike, but beyond, to childhood. I remembered the satisfaction of a well-filled tyre, hard against my gauging fingers, the way the bike felt, rolling smooth as silk after its chain had been oiled, the satisfaction of making something work better. I remembered, too, the feeling of freedom, the ability to go anywhere at any time, without reference to anyone. I had forgotten that.

'Well, are you going to try it?'

It would not hurt just to try it out, I thought. It wasn't as if I was going to actually take it and use it, after all, but I could humour Cass in what was at root a kind idea. With some difficulty we lowered the saddle and I checked the brakes and then swung my leg over the back wheel, my feet finding their places on the pedals. It might be a man's bike, but whoever had owned it could not have been that tall for it fitted me perfectly, as if it had been built for my frame.

I circled the courtyard, a little wobbly at first, then tried it down the track, avoiding potholes. The bike felt fast, responsive. I reached the road in seconds, the tarmac stretching out invitingly, urging me forward. Even the slight rise of a hill didn't seem to slow it much. It would eat up the miles, a bike like this. I resisted the temptation to take it further and turned and pedalled back up the track to the yard where Cass waited.

'You see?' she said. 'You're grinning. I told you you'd like it.'

I had not been aware that I was smiling, and yet the bike had been – well, fun wasn't quite the word. Exhilarating, perhaps. I got off and stood holding it, reluctant to give it up.

'I can't accept it, though, Cass, even as a loan. What would happen if I damaged it, or it got stolen?'

'Oh that,' she said. 'It doesn't matter. It's not like anybody's using it. In fact, I'm sure Rory would have been pleased to see it getting used. He always hated the thought of bikes being locked away and forgotten in sheds. Used to claim that it was cruel.' As she spoke, her eyes widened and she flung her hands up against her face as though to catch the words. 'I didn't mean to mention that. That it was Rory's.'

'Why not?'

'Oh, I don't know. Dead man's shoes, I suppose. I thought it would put you off.'

The bike rested under my hand. Cass touched it too, her fingers running lightly over the black paint as if they might raise some meaning there. A blank mask of sadness passed briefly over her face.

'Why don't you ride it?' I asked.

'I can't. I'm going back to school on Sunday. Colditz. We're not even allowed bikes, in case we use them to make a bid for freedom. Or have some fun or something. Not ladylike. No, take it, I'm serious. I'll be able to think of you flying round the roads on it, the way Rory used to. It'll cheer me up.'

After all that, it would have been churlish not to invite her in briefly although, as with Janet, I wasn't sure that I welcomed the increase in intimacy that implied. As I made coffee, Cass roamed around, picking things up and putting them down in a way that made my skin itch. She wandered into my little sitting room, and even briefly into my bedroom, and there was no way to tell her not to without making it into an issue.

'When I leave school, I'm going to live exactly like you do,' she announced, once she had finished exclaiming at the braininess of all my books and other such nonsense and finally settled at the kitchen table with her coffee. 'I shall have an amazing coffee pot and make amazing coffee whenever I like and I shall live all by myself and go where I want and nobody will tell me what to do.'

'There are people who think it can get a little lonely,' I said.

'Nonsense – you're not lonely, are you? That's just the sort of rubbish people always say when other people want to live differently.'

I smiled at her. 'Did Rory not find it lonely living here?'

'Rory here? Who told you that?' She had the Henderson chin up again, suddenly imperious.

'Didn't he?' I didn't want to mention that it was Janet who had told me.

'Oh well. Only for the tiniest while. I mean, it was hardly at all.' She stood up and started roaming the kitchen again, moving so that she was behind my back.

'What made him move here, though?'

She didn't answer, although I could tell she had heard me by the way she paused and then moved on.

'What's this?' she asked. 'A lemon zester? Who even has one these days? I bet you use it too, for zesting lemons, whatever that is.' There was an edge to her chatter that hadn't been there before and then she broke off, silent for so long that I turned round to look at her.

'What is it, Cass?'

She was staring into the distance, her hand at her throat.

'Are you all right, Cass?' I thought it might be another bout of head rush, but she didn't have that absent look she'd had before.

'Don't you feel it?' she asked.

'Feel what?'

'The cold. It's creeping, creeping over me like fingers. Like freezing cold fingers.' Her eyes were on me but unseeing, and she was shuddering, shuddering all over like a horse plagued by flies. 'Don't you feel it too? Don't you feel it?' Her voice was urgent.

'Don't, Cass,' I said, alarmed. I stood up and went to touch her hand, but then drew back. It took a moment longer before the shuddering stopped, and she seemed to register me properly again.

'You didn't feel that?'

'No,' I said. 'It was probably just a draught.'

She laughed, but shakily. 'Not a draught. It was weirder than that, it felt like a sort of creeping dread.' Her hand rose up to her throat and for a moment I thought she might start up again but she didn't, shaking herself more naturally as if to clear her head. 'Look, I think I'd better go. Thanks for the coffee, anyway. And do please ride the bike, I mean it.'

Before I could stop her, she impulsively leaned forward and kissed me on the cheek, her own cheek damp and cool against mine. She laughed at my face, all her alarm forgotten, and then blew me another kiss and was gone.

I stood in the doorway and watched her go, my hand up against my face where Cass had kissed me. It had just been a causal gesture on her part, but it had been a long time since I had felt even the brush of someone's lips against my skin. Even those of us who make a conscious decision to live alone, we are still human. We do still sometimes miss the tender touch of another person, however lightly bestowed. The sensation still lingered on my cheek, cool, cold. And then without warning I felt the coldness deepen and start to spread.

A sense of creeping dread, Cass had said. A theatrical phrase, and yet the words held some truth. I could feel my skin contracting, as if crawling under the touch of something repugnant. It spread so that my whole body seemed to shrink away from it, a shudder I could not control passing over me. It was only for a moment and then it was gone, and I was left standing with my hand on the door, fighting a sudden reluctance to go in.

That evening, a chill seemed to creep in through the very walls of the cottage, settling on every surface. I had the heating on, but though the radiators felt warm to the touch they made no impact on the cold air. I had a restless feeling I knew too well. With the pressure of the deadline lifted, the evening stretched out endlessly before me, too silent and too still. I turned the radio on but got nothing but a rush of static. I sat at my computer, but there was nothing in my inbox but spam. The quiet outside was absolute. Even Janet, next door, was silent. Silence leaves too many spaces for memories to creep in, old regrets, useless remorse, things that should long have been forgotten.

Recognizing that I was having just such an unprofitable spell of introspection, I glanced around the sitting room, seeking some distraction. My eye settled on the fireplace. Of course. A fire would add warmth and movement to the room, and a companionable sort of presence, as if of another living creature. I had not sat at an open fire for years. There was wood stacked up beside it which had been there since I moved in – a nice gesture, a literal housewarming gift. This would be the perfect time to use it.

I knelt at the hearth and laid the fire. There were no fire-lighters, but there were some kindling sticks in a tidy bundle. I untied the string that bound them and they rang onto the hearthstone with a cheerful note. I built a careful pyramid over a scrunched pile of paper and then sat back on my heels to check my work. Just loose enough to let the air draw through and feed the flame, just tight enough that it would hold until the logs could catch. I had not built a fire since I was a child – it seemed to be the day for revisiting my childhood – and I was pleased that such a basic skill had not deserted me. I had an image of generations of people kneeling in this very spot, building just such a fire. The dreams we might all dream as we stared into the flames would differ, but the human impulse towards its light and warmth would be the same.

I leaned forward, first lighting a spill of paper to check the chimney wasn't blocked. The smoke unfurled as the flame brightened and lifted and I felt the tug of air against my hand. It was as I stared past the flame, its shape still dancing in a dark afterglow across my vision, that I saw the face peering out at me. For a moment I could do nothing but stare at it, transfixed, the spill burning almost to my fingers. It seemed so alive in that uncertain light, and not just alive but full of life, a sort of malevolent wicked glee.

The heat of the flame nearing my fingers brought me to myself and I shook it out. Without its dancing shadows, I saw that where the back plate of the grate met the chimney opening, crumbling mortar had opened out a little niche, the bricks themselves beginning to wear away. Wedged into this gap was a clay figure and it was this that I had seen in the flame. I pulled it out and held it in my hand. It was no more than a couple of inches high, the large head out of all proportion to its body. Now that I was looking at it properly, I could see that it was very crudely made, all illusion of life gone. The eyes were black holes, the nose pinched up out of the surface of the clay, the mouth a gash. It had not been fired and it had dried to a crumbling texture, grey beneath the caking soot. Its head was matted with something and as I turned to examine it more closely I saw that it was a clump of dark hair, pressed into the clay before it had dried, dull and brittle and dead.

I dropped it, rubbing my hands to rid them of the sensation of the hair and the powdery dust still clinging to my fingers. I was overwhelmed by the urge to destroy the thing, and the poker was in my hand before I had mastered myself. It was absurd. The thing was just a toy, something a child might make. Someone might want it back. I put the poker down again and set the figure aside, still startled at the strength of feeling it had engendered. I lit the fire and watched the shadows of the flames, and it was a long while before I could dismiss it from my mind.

CHAPTER 5

I WAS ON top of the world. I sat back on the bike at the crest of a hard-fought hill, regaining my breath, surveying the route ahead. The sun was bright, but it carried no warmth and the wind was cool against my face. I had climbed up far enough that I could see the whole spread of the land around me. The road unfurled ahead, the narrowest possible strip of tarmac, untouched by any white lines and roughly made, barely more than gravel at the edges. Seen close to, the green of the hills was a complex thing, grass thatched over with dead stalks and overtaken by bracken, spikes of sedges in damper hollows, patches of heather and gorse and broom. The walls that from a distance divided the landscape, here seemed in the process of returning to the stony earth, the scattered sheep stepping easily over them where they had fallen. Wandering lines of trees and shrubs marked the rivers, clinging to the steeper slopes. Directly ahead and below me, the forest flooded everything, a dark pool stretching unending out of sight, its grid of trees concealing even the contours of the land.

According to the map, my route should be downhill most of the way, a relief after the struggle of the climb. It had not seemed far laid out on paper, neatly squared off, so many inches to the mile. After the steady drudgery of walking, cycling was swift but it was not effortless. The muscles in my legs burned and my lungs felt as if they had been dredged right to the very bottom, clearing out the accumulated grime of the city. I felt alive in a way I had not felt for years.

The bike responded to the first turn of the pedal, sensing the gradient, quickening as the road fell away. It seemed sure-footed even on the loose gravel. I feathered the brakes, checking its speed, not sure that I could stop it if I needed to, but then I let it have its head, trusting it to stay upright. We spun down together, the bike and I, the wind singing in my ears and sharp against the burning of my face. Cass had been right: it was a fine thing to be out on the roads, speeding along under my own volition. All the vague malaise of the last few days was blown away and my heart lifted. I might almost have started singing, had I had the breath left.

The road banked and curved, dropping down into another river valley. I rattled over a cattle grid and came to a crossroads, stopping to check the map and reassure myself that I was where I thought I was. It was a cold spot, shadowed by the surrounding hills, a place the sun would not reach even in the height of summer. A single tree, ancient and blasted, stood just by the point where the roads met, and then the forest began, darker and more closely packed than ever. As at the house, it was enclosed by a boundary wall, drystone like the field walls, but much higher. Or rather, it had been enclosed, for here too this wall was breached, but not simply by the passage of time. It had been reduced to no more than a tumbled heap of rocks, as if it had been blown apart. At the crossroads, the stones were strewn into the forest, creating a gap several feet wide, and on either side the wall had toppled like a domino run. Vegetation had started to colonise it, but it was dying back now and among the stones I caught the glint of glass, a sight familiar from any urban street: brake-light red and indicator yellow, and the crumbled greenish white of a shattered windscreen.

I left the bike leaning against the tree and went to have a closer look. Among the dead plants at the foot of the wall a stone, ghost grey, lay streaked with a trace of bright colour. Paint, lipstick red, blood red. A car crash, no doubt about it, and a bad one from the looks of it. I felt the chill, more than just the sunless air. There was no sound, no birdsong, just the hushing murmur of the forest.

Into the silence came a whistling, the absent music of a man with his mind on other things. It neared, then stopped, and I turned to see the whistler emerging from the forest, staring at the bike where I had left it, and then at me. He had a dog by his side, some sort of sheepdog mix, its hackles raised. The man was tall, with the skin of someone who has spent his life outdoors, his age hard to guess. Not old and not young, his hair pulled back into a short ponytail, a gold ring in one ear. Dog and owner stared at me.

'Morning,' I said.

'All right,' he replied shortly. In the pause that followed I wondered if he was going to just stand there staring in silence forever. 'Nice bike,' he said finally.

'It's not mine, I was lent it,' I said.

'Aye, thought as much,' he said, and he seemed to dismiss me at that, turning to look at the breach in the wall. I saw that at one end, repairs had started, the stones not merely tumbled wreckage but laid out in a more ordered way, sorted by size.

'Fixing the wall?' I said inanely.

'Aye,' he said, and then a flash of private amusement briefly lightened his face. 'Well, I'm no taking it down.'

I smiled, but he did not smile back. 'Must be a lonely job.'

'You'd think,' he said, and the dry edge was unmistakeable. He picked up a stone and seemed to weigh it, the tendons of his forearm shifting a little as they accommodated to it. All this time, the dog's eyes on me had not wavered. I waited, but there was nothing more. He shrugged a little and the stone seemed to find a place in the wall and as I left him he was standing, rolling a cigarette and staring once more at the heap of stones at his feet. Only the dog watched me go.

It was a strange encounter, but I did not let it bother me as I cycled back, hurrying a little now for I had been out longer than I'd anticipated. I had an evening engagement to get ready for, a rare occurrence. An envelope had dropped through my door the day before, containing a thick cream card, Mr Grant and Miss Cassandra Henderson requesting the pleasure of my company for dinner. A nice gesture, I thought, though whether Cass's or Grant's I couldn't tell. I could have just rung in reply, but I decided to meet their old-fashioned formality with my own and had gone up to the house to drop off my RSVP. Cass had flung the door open wearing an apron, her hair pulled back behind an Alice band, rubber gloves on, a smudge of something decorating one cheek.

'We've got an old friend coming to stay, and Grant's been living practically in the kitchen all year, letting the rest of the house go to rack and ruin. Muggins here has had to turn herself into Mrs Mop. Honestly, it's an utter pigsty. And spider city.'

I had to laugh. I couldn't imagine her sticking at the drudgery of housework after the novelty had worn off, but she waved away my half-hearted offer of help with her duster.

'No, go, get out and enjoy yourself while I slave away. It's all right. Take the bike out cos I know you haven't yet. My spies tell me everything.'

Her joking reminder was still running in my head as I walked back, and my eye lit on the bike. It was a bright day, still and clear. I had risen to the first frost of the autumn, rime outlining each leaf and blade of grass. The cold had felled the last of the leaves still clinging on to the tree branches and as I stood there, I remember them spiralling around me, caught by the sun, flashes of russet and gold, setting up a constant soft patter all around.

The thought had come to me then – yes, why not take the bike out on a day as lovely as this? No matter that I might make myself a bit ridiculous, I'd have to either ride it or find some excuse why I hadn't and suddenly it seemed easier just to take it out that once; after all, she would be gone soon, and then I could decently put it away and forget about it.

I did not regret it now, bowling along the road, a river running by my side. The trees here were broadleaf, holding out against the plantation forest, oak and ash and birch, their shadows striping the road in a flicker of light and dark. Dried leaves whirled beneath my wheels and the small birds flicked away with chattering calls of alarm at my passage. The burn in my legs had gone, replaced with a feeling of strength and power. I was swift and silent, borne along, and everything felt effortless.

I was almost home and beginning to tire again when I encountered the hare. It was a place in the road where the walls on either side crowded in close, and as I rounded a bend, the hare rose up, huge-seeming on its long legs. It ran on in front of me, jinking sometimes from side to side, but seeming unpanicked, maintaining its steady, loping pace. And yet I could not catch it up, not even on the downhill stretches, no matter how I tried. I raced it, or rather the bike raced it, for I seemed to have no say in the matter, pedalling on blindly as fast as I could manage. It seemed we might run like that forever, the hare and I, until finally it rounded a bend and vanished through some gap I could not see and I could ease up at last, panting, before pedalling the last half-mile more gently home.

I might have guessed that Janet would be out there waiting for me when I got back. Or maybe not waiting; perhaps it was just coincidence that she happened to be stepping out of the door with an empty washing basket as I swept into the courtyard on the bike. I smiled hello, for I was feeling cheerful, the exhilaration of the ride behind me, the evening ahead to look forward to. In the look that she gave me I knew that I was at once dishevelled, sweaty, bright red, ridiculous. Then she smiled back.

'Is that no the Hendersons' bicycle?'

'Cass lent it to me, yes,' I said.

'We're awfy thick with the gentry,' she said.

'I don't know about that,' I said.

'But you're off to dine at the big house all the same,' she said. 'So I hear.'

I got off the bike and felt my legs quiver as the unaccustomed effort caught up with me. I was suddenly ravenous. The thought came to me unbidden of a bacon sandwich, thick doorstop bread, grease, salt, everything I might normally avoid. I had earned it, after all, and I could almost taste it, but Janet hadn't quite finished with me.

'Of course, he's a good-looking young man, is Grant Henderson, and there's money there and all, for all he walks about dressed like a tattie bogle.'

I opened my mouth to respond but found nothing to say. To deny anything would have been to acknowledge the accusation. I felt the deep hot spread of embarrassment rise, the kind that takes over the whole body, and was only thankful that I was flushed already from the ride. Was this what people thought of me? What Janet thought, what Cass thought, or even Grant?

She was watching me carefully to see if her bolt had shot home. I managed no more than a shrug, my face carefully bland. Was there disappointment there? Or calculation?

'Oh well, I'll just get the washing in before the day's done,' she said at last. 'Weather like this'll no last.'

'Indeed,' I managed, and even as I went in I saw that she was right; the clouds were gathering already behind the hill, the sunlight fading out, the bright afternoon vanishing as if she had rubbed it out herself.

Inside, empty but all appetite gone, I stood and watched the skies darken, evening coming early under the weight of the clouds. I thought back through every interaction I'd had with Grant, picking them over for anything on my part that anyone could hold up to any ridicule at all. Just our few walks together, accidental encounters, nothing I had even engineered. My conscience was clear. It was true I had been pleased to find someone even remotely on my wavelength, an evidently cultured man who had read enough and knew enough to converse beyond the generalities. And a kind man too, courteous in his way, reserved enough that friendship would not become a burden. But that was all. That was all.

There had been men in my past, of course, and one in particular: a married man, isn't that so often the tedious truth that lies behind a mysterious past? At the time, I squared it with my conscience in all sorts of ways, but really, it's just that the heart wants what the heart wants. Or wanted: by the time I realized that I had been in the end no more than proof to himself that he was still attractive, I had long since forgotten what it was that I had wanted for myself. And in the meantime, how many years had I wasted? Time passes whether you ask it to or not; it will not stand still while you're waiting for a promise to be made good. And after the first deadline has come and gone, the first milestone, the others come easier: the months and years of a life deferred until one morning you wake up and find your youth gone and your friends moved on and nothing to show for it except a certain tolerance for a life lived on your own.

He was a fellow teacher, of course; who else would I meet? He taught art, and he asked me to sit for him, and I should have known then that it was a well-worn technique of his, at once flattering and yet innocent enough on the surface of it, all above board. Or perhaps I did know, and that was the attraction: that he had thought me worthy of the effort of seduction. I am not someone people flirt with, as a rule. I never have been. It's not as if I welcome that kind of attention anyway. And yet, and yet.

I say sit for him, but that makes it sound more of an undertaking than it was. All I would agree to was a pastel sketch, dashed off in a single sitting. He had made it seem like an act of friendship, a pleasant way to spend an hour or two together. I had enjoyed the process well enough, unused to receiving such concentrated attention. I had soon relaxed as we chatted, and he had got me onto one of my hobby horses so that I forgot all about where I was and what we were doing. At the end he said it wasn't finished and he wanted to work on it a bit more, so I didn't press to see it, and in truth, I was a bit relieved not to have to admire something that might have turned out poorly; an awkward ending to what had been a pleasant Sunday afternoon.

And then I remember coming into the art room on the Monday morning – I had a message for him, nothing urgent – and seeing it, still on the easel. I had felt exposed to see it there: me, depicted with what seemed then to be a peculiar burning longing. He had caught me leaning forward, alight in some way that a photograph can never capture. The camera is not kind, not to me, mercilessly picking out the flaws. I stood and stared at the picture he had made and wanted both to hide it away and to place it on public display, flaunt it like a trophy.

I did not notice him coming in until I felt him at my back, the warmth of his breath on my neck, and he didn't have to say anything more. I knew. I knew what he wanted and despite knowing everything that was wrong with that – his wife, his family, the complications it would entail – faced with that image of myself, a different me, a passionate one, I wanted it too. I went into it with open eyes. I cannot blame anyone but myself.

The affair is long since over but I have the picture still, unlooked at now for many years. I daren't expose it to the light and find that it has become in some way ordinary, a trite collection of tricks, any resemblance to myself mere chance and wishful thinking. Or worse, that it might emit the same fierce charge of longing that I had put away many years ago, rolled tight against the light.

It doesn't matter. Not for this story, at least, except in the trivial sense that I was alone and unattached and able to uproot myself the way that I did. And perhaps in the wider sense that I had lived too long with my nose pressed up against the glass of other people's lives, waiting to be let in.

CHAPTER 6

I<small>N THE DARK</small> of the evening the house was lit up, the shutters at the front flung wide to flood the driveway with light. I stood in the shadow of the trees, my mind still not fully made up over whether to go in at all.

As I hesitated, a car pulled up on the drive, an old Range Rover. A couple got out, he springing round to open the passenger-side door for her. They might have been in their sixties or seventies, or even older, though both were very upright. I froze, not wanting to alert them to my presence, lurking there in the dark.

'Well, this should be interesting,' the woman said as he held out his arm for her to take. Her voice was clear, carrying, with all the self-confidence of the county.

'It will be fine, Helen,' he said.

They moved slowly to the door. I noticed that she walked with the aid of a stick and that the arm through hers was providing more than just gallantry.

'Lorna always liked to have the house ablaze with light like that,' she said. 'It takes me back. Terrible waste, of course.'

'Nice to see some life in the old place,' her companion said.

They were almost beside me, but oblivious to my presence.

I could hear the rasp of her breathing, the faint creak of his shoes.

'How did you think she was the other day?' the woman asked. 'The girl, I mean.'

'I thought she seemed on good form. Back to her old self, almost.'

'Hmph.' As they reached the door, I saw that she dropped his arm and straightened herself while he rang the bell, deploying her stick like a weapon. 'I thought she was brittle. As they used to say when I was a girl. Brittle. Just like her mother before her.'

The door opened in a flurry of greetings, Grant handsome in a dark suit, Cass behind him in a glittering emerald-coloured dress, everyone's faces caught in the warm yellow light. Grant leaned to give the older woman a formal kiss of greeting, shook the man's hand, and then they were all gone, swept inside, the door shut tight once more. I relinquished the prospect of my fireside tray with a sigh and went up to ring the bell myself. Cass would be gone tomorrow, after all, and why ruin her evening just for my own foolish pride? I waited, shoulders squared, resolved to face the evening exactly as I would have done had Janet said nothing. I knew my own mind, after all. I knew I had nothing to be ashamed of.

Any diffidence I might have had was swept away the minute I went inside. Cass greeted me like the arrival of the cavalry, confiding in my ear that the kitchen was in *chaos* and it would be a miracle if we managed to eat *anything* before midnight.

'Do you want a hand?' I asked.

'No, not at all, I shall cope. You're here as a guest. Have a drink, relax. Wait and see.'

I looked sideways at her but she just smiled and introduced me to the others gathered in the hall. Robert and Helen were the couple who had just arrived, old friends of Grant's parents. Dougie, round-faced and somewhat ill at ease in a jacket and tie, looked familiar to me as I shook his hand.

'I'm no usually dressed like this,' he said. 'Try a pair of overalls and a quad bike.'

'Ah, it's you,' I said, as he morphed back into the cheery presence I had seen buzzing about the roads or heaving bales of fodder across a field. 'Nice to put a name to a face.'

'Aye right, and likewise. This is my wife, Kirsty.'

She was thin where he was rounded, dark-haired and dark-eyed. 'I've seen you about,' she said, her voice barely rising above a whisper.

'Ah yes,' I said, although I had not ever noticed her. Her whole face seemed pushed forward, as if braced to meet some unknown challenge. She did not smile.

'Dougie runs the cattle side of the estate,' Grant said, handing me a drink. 'But more importantly, he and I went to the village school together, back when the village had a school.'

'Aye, that's gone now,' Dougie said. 'Closed down. Terrible shame.'

'Dreadful the way they shut down these local schools just because some dreary accountant deems they're not cost-effective,' Helen said, and Dougie turned to her, seemingly surprised to find that there was a subject they could both agree on.

The door to the back corridor opened and I was startled to see another face I recognized, the drystone waller. He had also dressed up for the occasion, his hair freshly smoothed back into its ponytail and his gold hoop earring swapped for a more discreet stud.

'And this is Davey,' Grant said. 'An old mate of Rory's who's come to stay and do some work for us on the estate. The insurance finally came through so we can make a start on that blasted wall.'

The remark attracted Robert's attention and he started waxing forth about some insurance claim of his own to Grant, leaving Davey and I standing together. So this was the family friend Cass had mentioned. I was surprised; somehow I had got the impression of someone older, their parents' generation.

'We meet again,' I said, a little wary after our previous encounter.

His hand was hard, slightly rough against mine, but his smile was genuine. 'I'm sorry if I was a wee bit offish with you this afternoon,' he said. 'I was thrown by seeing the bike. Thought for a minute it'd been nicked.'

'I'm hardly your stereotypical bike thief,' I said.

'Aye well. And there's been some ghoulish sightseers there up frae the town.'

I was surprised. 'Sightseers?'

'Wherever there's a death. More than one death. You'd be surprised what people will come up to see, leave flowers and that, even if they've never met the folk.'

I suddenly realized what he was talking about. 'Was that where—' My voice was suddenly too loud for comfort and I glanced involuntarily over towards Grant, who was standing talking to Helen. I had not realized the fatal car crash had been so close to home.

Davey glanced over too before he nodded.

'Memories must be long over here,' I said. 'I mean, that was over five years ago.'

There was a flicker in his eyes and for a moment I thought I'd got hold of the wrong end of the stick, but he just said, 'Five years is nothing around here. Try five hundred.'

I laughed, though it wasn't clear it was a joke, and then we paused for a bit.

'No dog?' I said at last.

'Jess is in the kitchen, cannae believe her luck. Lying belly up against the Aga. I'd have left her out in the yard but Cass wouldn't hear of it. She'll be spoiled rotten cause she's no an indoor dog at all.'

'Says he,' Cass said, laughing, as she paused in the doorway on her way to the kitchen. 'He takes that dog everywhere he goes. Not an indoor dog, my arse.'

'Well, I'm no really an indoor man.'

'Huh. Well, talk amongst yourselves. I may be gone some time.'

I saw Davey watch her as she went, his face thoughtful, as if he had just noticed she was no longer a little girl. She did look exceptionally beautiful that night, glowing and sophisticated, but underneath still filled with the excitement of it all, and when I think back to those days that is how she still comes to my mind, glancing back over the curve of her shoulder like an actress on a red carpet.

It seemed Davey was the last of the guests and once everyone had got their drinks and been introduced, we seemed to drift naturally towards the glass cases and their macabre contents. Helen's voice, clear and carrying, dominated the hall.

'They're relics of another age, aren't they?' she said, addressing nobody in particular. 'I've always thought these were the height of Victoriana. So hideous.'

I turned to see Grant's reaction, but he just smiled. 'I think Great-Great-Uncle Matthew was out on a limb with these.'

'Ah yes,' she said. 'The family murderer.'

I did not imagine the slight stiffening of Grant's shoulders, the short silence that fell, but when he spoke it was easily enough. 'I think you'll find he was acquitted of that,' he said.

'Is that who bought them?' I asked. 'Your great-great-uncle?'

'I may have missed off a couple of greats. And he didn't buy them, oh no. He shot every one of those hares himself, and stuffed them too. I don't know who made the clothes, probably some girl in the village.'

'But why?' I asked.

'I expect she was reasonably well paid for her time,' he said with a faint sardonic smile.

It was the school tableau we had gathered around. There must have been twenty hares in the case, the pupils all smaller – leverets, presumably. Only the teacher, severe in a black gown and cardboard mortarboard, was a fully grown hare. Stretched up, it was a good two feet tall. I remembered the animal I had encountered that morning, and before that, the one that had been hit by the bus, the look in its dying eye. This creature seemed grotesque by comparison, its head cocked, still seeming to watch us.

'He had the eyes made specially, at some glass manufacturer in Birmingham. The stock ones that taxidermists used were all wrong, apparently. These are very real. He had a notion that they would protect the house in some way.'

Someone laughed uneasily.

'From what?' I asked.

Grant did not answer and the silence after that lasted a beat too long before Dougie said, 'I mind the first time I saw them – gave me the screaming abdabs. Course, I was just a wean then. That school there, it's the spit of the school we was in, right down to the desks.'

I drifted away to another case and Kirsty drifted too, so that we found ourselves standing side by side staring intently through the glass at the drawing-room scene. I had not noticed before, but the hare at the piano was in an emerald coloured dress, similar to the one Cass was wearing. Kirsty, shorter than me, stood eye to eye with it.

'Witches,' she said in a whisper, a sharp hiss of breath. 'They're there to protect them against the witches.'

Chapter 7

I could see the minute we walked into the dining room that Cass had been over-ambitious. I didn't know what standard of entertaining she'd had in mind when she had planned this evening, but it seemed likely beyond the powers of a seventeen-year-old who'd never done this sort of thing before. Perhaps she was trying to bring some occasion from her childhood back to life, dinners her parents might have held. The table had been laid with silver and a dozen candles burned in elaborate candlesticks laid out along the polished surface of the table. She'd planned at least three courses, if the knives and forks were anything to go by, and the soup was already on the table. She came in through a side door that closed flush with the panelling, and handed me a basket of warmed rolls nestled in heavy white linen napkins to pass around.

'Have you someone helping you?' I asked.

'No no, it's just me.' She was pointing people to their places, each name written out in careful calligraphy on a card. 'I've got it all under control.'

I found myself seated between Davey and Robert, who asked me how I was liking the place. His conversation was bland and general, sticking to the weather, memories of winters past. Davey said nothing, but concentrated on his soup.

'And you're an historian, I hear,' Helen said to me, suddenly fixing me in her beam across the table.

'Well,' I said. 'In a way. That was my subject, anyway.'

'And do you teach?'

I kept my eyes on hers. 'I did,' I said.

'And now? I heard you did tutoring or something like that.'

'Something like that.'

If I had hoped she would be deflected, I was mistaken. 'And do you take pupils up here? There must surely not be that many around.'

'I do it online,' I said. 'Over the internet.'

'Over the internet?' She said it with a kind of blank astonishment, as if I had mentioned that I did it through alchemy, and turned her attention away from me and onto Davey instead.

I caught Grant's eye, and he seemed to share my amusement. We smiled, and I forgot my earlier resolution to maintain my distance. I leaned forward and said impulsively, 'Tell me about this murderous ancestor of yours, then. He sounds quite the eccentric.'

My words fell into one of those hushes that come across a room from time to time and I heard my own voice – pitched a little too loud, a little too arch. My wine glass was already empty and my pre-dinner gin and tonic had been poured with a generous hand. I felt the blood rise again in my face. Grant did not help, looking at me coldly.

'What do you want to know?'

They were all watching, even Cass, who had got up to see to the next course, her hand on the panelled doorway, her eyes darting between us. I glanced at Davey, who let his eyes slide away.

'I'm sorry,' I said. 'It just sounded as if it might be interesting.'

Grant took a small, controlled sip of his wine. 'In his day, of course, the insane were still considered to be fair game for the amusement of the masses. These days we consider ourselves more enlightened.'

My cheeks were really burning now. Everyone was looking down at their bowls – everyone except Kirsty, who was still watching us intently. I heard the door close as Cass left the room. Davey let his spoon clatter against the bottom of his empty soup bowl, as loud as a cannon shot.

'I wonder if Cass needs a little hand with the next course?' Helen said, and gratefully I fled.

As I had guessed, the panelled door opened into a short passageway that led down a brief flight of steps into the kitchen. The door itself was backed with baize, muffling any renewed conversation that I imagined must have sprung up in the silence after I'd left. Caught between the glitter and candlelight of the dining room and the warmth and clutter of the kitchen, it was a dark place, cold, stone-flagged, the one low-energy light bulb doing little to dispel the gloom. I felt a chill creep under my thin silk blouse – explicable, perhaps, in a damp cold place like this, but still a crawling sensation that my skin shrank from. I hurried through, pushing open the kitchen door, expecting to be greeted by Cass in full flow, but there was no sound at all, no movement.

Cass was standing, frozen, staring up at the window as if she could see something in the blackness outside. The dog stood beside her, ignoring the dropped dish of potatoes at her feet.

'Cass?' I said.

Only the dog reacted. It turned its eyes full on me, its hackles rising, a growl growing in its throat.

'Cass, what happened?' I spoke louder this time, but she still didn't move until I stepped forward and put my hands on her shoulders, startled at the icy coldness of her skin. The dog's low growl built, more menacing than any bark. Cass tore her eyes from the window and stared at me blankly as if she had no idea who I was.

'Do you see it?'

The way the house was constructed, the kitchen was half underground, the windows small and high, right at the top of the wall. It was pitch black outside, and in any case the windows were all steamed up. I could not imagine what she thought she had seen but when I looked up, I saw the writing.

'It just appeared there, right before my eyes.'

It's a simple enough trick, of course. Write invisibly with your finger on a mirror or glass and watch the words appear by magic as it steams up. Someone must have clambered up – for even a man would have needed a footstool to reach it – knowing the heat and steam of a busy kitchen would do the rest. The message was short enough, easy to fit on a single pane: the same cryptic phrase I'd seen scratched on the gravestones: Exod 22:18.

We got through the evening somehow. I rustled up some cous-
cous to cover the lack of potatoes, and a couple more bottles of
wine for the guests smoothed over the cracks. Cass rejoined us
in the dining room, a little pale, gallantly attempting to recover
the mood. She had, inevitably I suppose, drunk too much wine
herself, and it was not long before gallantry tipped over into
barely suppressed hysteria. After a look from Grant, I found
myself escorting her upstairs as the evening ended. The stairs
led up to an open gallery above the entrance hall, with two
dimly lit corridors running off it left and right to the bedrooms.
Cass's room was girlish, filled with the detritus of a younger life,
dolls and teddy bears adorning her dressing table. She sat on
her narrow single bed, her head in her hands, groaning.

'What was all that about, Cass?' I asked her.

She straightened and I was relieved to see that she looked
a bit less as if she was about to be sick, although there was a
sheen of sweat still on her face. Her hair was coming down in
loose hanks and she looked exactly like the child she was, a
child that had been allowed to stay up too late and get over-
excited.

'What?' she said.

'In the kitchen?'

Her eyes flicked away. 'I dropped the potatoes.' I saw the
effort she was making to recover herself and she looked me
full in the eyes again, all false brightness. 'You should have
seen Helen's face, by the way, when I came in with the main
course. Like she'd been sitting there waiting to see what the
screw-up was, so she could be all condescending about it. Ha!
I came in utterly as if nothing had happened and you could
see the disappointment. Total, total triumph!'

The edge was there in her voice, her eyes too wide, the words tumbling out too fast. Her hands flew wildly. Perhaps it would have been better just to take them, hold them still until she calmed herself.

'You know it's just a silly practical joke, writing things on the window so they appear like that.'

She looked away, all animation gone. 'There was nothing on the window.'

I could see she would brood over it, working herself up further, all the more toxic for being denied. 'I saw it, Cass. I saw the words. They were written all over the gravestones in the churchyard too. I know it startled you, and made you drop the dish. But it's just someone playing games.'

'I dropped the dish because you jogged my elbow, that's all,' she said stubbornly. 'You're always doing that – pawing me about, grabbing my arm. I mean, it's fine, I don't mind, it's not like I think there's anything creepy about it, but it's difficult when you're cooking, that's all.'

There was no point dignifying nonsense like that with a response. I stood up abruptly – too abruptly, because she giggled and the giggle became unstoppable, a paroxysm of laughter. 'I'm sorry,' she said, gasping. 'It wasn't really funny but you're so sensitive at times. Like you think I'm going to accuse you of something. Anyone would think you had a guilty conscience.'

'You're being ridiculous, Cass.'

She looked at me and it seemed, despite the laughter, that her eyes were shadowed, dark against the pallor of her face.

'I genuinely am truly sorry,' she said. 'You were a brilliant help this evening and I should be more grateful. I'm always being told I'm a complete ingrate.'

Only a seventeen-year-old can make even an apology entirely about them, but I accepted it anyway, and she laid herself down on the bed, still fully dressed, pulling the covers roughly over herself. I turned out the light and bade her goodnight and she was silent for a while and then spoke out of the darkness.

'I tell you one thing, you don't know your Bible, do you?'

'Excuse me?'

'You should look it up.'

'Look what up?'

'Exodus, 22:18.'

'Patient settled down then?'

I had thought that the guests might still be gathered, but when I reached the kitchen it was just Davey and Grant by the fire. The room had been somewhat restored to order, the dropped potatoes cleared up and the other dishes washed and mostly put away, and now the pair of them were relaxing in their shirtsleeves with a glass of whisky each, the dog flat out between them. Davey already looked completely at home in his armchair, his legs stretched out, one socked foot resting on the dog's shoulder.

'She'll live, but she'll have a sore head in the morning,' I said. 'I suppose it's a lesson we all have to learn the hard way.'

'She overdid herself, that's the problem. Insisted on doing everything properly, exhausted herself.'

'Seemed an awfy fuss for a bunch of tatties,' Davey said.

I thought Grant's eyes caught mine in warning, then looked

away. I could not help but notice that the window had been wiped clear.

'Sit down, have a drink – you've earned it.'

Part of me wanted nothing more than to join them and let the fire and the whisky warm me through. They looked so cosy there, and so at home. But I shook my head. 'I'd better go. It's late enough.'

I had not meant for Grant to offer to walk me home, but perhaps it was inevitable that he should. He helped me into my coat and we left Davey by the fire and stepped out under a surprise of stars, glittering across the sky.

'It was the night skies I missed most when I lived in London,' Grant said.

'You lived in London?' I almost added that I could not imagine him there, but stopped myself. It seemed too personal a remark to make, out here in the intimacy of the dark.

'For my sins,' he said and then lapsed into silence.

We walked on under the trees and I was conscious as I had never been before of his presence, his shoulders close to mine. He stopped me just before we reached the cottage, his hand on my arm, firm through the fabric of my jacket. I had left the outside light on and we stood just outside the circle it cast, his hand lingering just a moment longer than was necessary. The light seemed only to intensify the darkness. I wondered what Janet might have thought if she could have seen us, two figures in the dark, too close to be made out as separate people.

Whatever she might have expected, had she seen it, what I got was a warning. Politely done, of course – never anything less than polite.

'It's about Cass,' he said. 'As you may have noticed she's got a tendency to talk nonsense, especially if she's had a glass or two of wine. I know you're too sensible to give her any credence.'

I could see nothing of his face in the darkness but the faint gleam of his eyes.

'Nonsense?'

'Superstition. Fairy tales. Things that go bump in the night. You know how girls are at that age. Rory's death hit her pretty hard. Losing her parents, and then her brother. We try not to dwell upon it, but she gets these fancies sometimes.'

'Well, not tonight,' I said, perhaps more shortly than I had intended. 'The only thing that went bump in the night was those potatoes.'

'Oh,' he said. 'Well, that's good. Even so, if she does bring anything like that up, don't encourage her. And obviously it's not for wider circulation. I know what the village is like.'

I said nothing, for it was not an instruction that expected any answer. We stood for a moment face to face in the darkness and I thought he hesitated, unsure of how to say goodbye before he settled for an outstretched hand, at once a farewell and a sealing of a bargain, and then he was gone.

I stood for a while alone under the stars, then I turned and walked to the cottage, putting my key in the door. It was cold, the night chill sinking deep. The welcoming silence of the house awaited me, already filled with the familiar smell of home. I would kick off my shoes and have a nightcap; I would stand at the window in the darkened kitchen and wonder at the stars, listen to the strange night noises, fill myself with the peace I had discovered in this place. It was as I opened the door that I felt – imagined – something, a tugging or a plucking, then a jostling sort of a presence, as if something had pressed its way past me in the doorway. My keys fell with a clatter to the step. I froze, my heart beating hard despite myself. Just my sleeve caught on a nail, I reasoned, still standing there, staring down at the keys. Just that. And yet I was filled with a deep reluctance to go on, to scoop up my keys and step inside, back into my former refuge.

Chapter 8

'**D**AFT OF HIM to pay for that school if she's no going to go to it,' Janet said, stirring her coffee. 'He'd as well have Cass no go to the high school instead and save the money.'

How had this happened? Here we were at the cafe again, face to face at Janet's favourite table, for all the world like two best friends exchanging confidences. Janet stopped stirring and laid the spoon down, turning to watch the waitress threading herself through the tables towards us. She was a plump girl whose face was always a little moist with exertion and although the cafe was usually almost empty, the tables had been crammed in too close together, forcing her to turn herself sideways to make her way between them.

'Bet she eats all the leftover stock and then wonders why she cannae lose weight,' Janet remarked.

'You can't know that,' I protested, even though I thought she was probably right. The girl did have the air of someone who filled the holes in her life with sweet things. Once when I had stuck my head around the kitchen door to find her – desperate to pay and get away – I had seen her perched on a stool, her mouth crammed with something that left her speechless, her eyes like the eyes of an animal caught in a trap. 'People have different metabolisms,' I said lamely.

'Have they now?'

Janet started stirring her coffee again. I sat in silence, watching the small brown vortex she had made in her cup as though its depths might tell me something. I knew what she was doing, eking the information out, knowing she could make me wait. I was not going to ask her what she meant by her remark about the school and Cass. I had the sense that she would tell me soon enough.

She had turned up at my door that day at the usual time as if there had been no interruptions in our routine, and I had meekly gone with her. It was a wild wet day and I was half grateful not to have to face the walk down to the bus. As I got into the car the thought struck me that she would take the opportunity to pump me for the details of the supper party, but she didn't say much at all on the drive in apart from to ask me if I'd seen Grant at all that day. When I admitted I hadn't she had not responded, keeping her own counsel with a little half-smile.

'No so thick wi' them after all,' she said as we pulled into town, but it was almost to herself, as if at the conclusion of some long train of thought of her own. I said nothing and it was only as we arrived at the supermarket car park that she broached the subject.

'Have a nice time up at the big house, then?' she asked, accelerating forward to nip into a parking space that I felt certain someone else had been just about to take.

'I did as it happens,' I said, enjoying the chance to deny her any details.

'Enjoy your tatties?'

I glanced at her sharply but her eyes were fixed on her mirrors, seemingly fully absorbed in what she was doing.

'You'll miss that wee besom, I suppose.'

She got out quickly, not waiting for my reply. I was a little thrown by the remark. Would I miss Cass? She had certainly jolted me out of my routine, and perhaps I had been in danger of growing stale in my new life. She had mentioned something about coming to say goodbye and I had stayed in all of Sunday, catching up with some work, not wanting to miss her. It was not until the light had gone entirely and I had found myself sitting in the dark that I'd realized she must be long gone. Grant might even be back at the house again from having driven her back to school. I went around the cottage, drawing the curtains tight against the dark and I could imagine him doing the same, walking through the quiet of empty rooms, the silence of absence settling back into the walls. I imagined it so vividly that I might almost have been there with him, joined in a quiet kinship. I lit my fire as he must have been lighting his, watching the sticks kindle, the same dance of the flames. He would miss her, undoubtedly, and yes, I would do the same. It was unusually perceptive of Janet to have seen that, I thought.

The lights were on in the cafe now, losing the fight against the lowering grey of the afternoon outside. The rain washed the pavements. The few people who were out were bundled in coats, heads down, umbrellas useless in the wind. I realized Janet was watching me in the reflection in the window, waiting for a response. I sighed and gave in.

'What do you mean, if she's not going to go? Cass, do you mean? She went back to school on Sunday, didn't she?'

Dawning, malicious triumph. 'Oh, so you've no heard? I would have thought you'd be the first to know. Oh, she's no back there at all. First it was a migraine, the Sunday, so she couldnae stand to be in the car at all. So Grant was going to take her in the day instead, first thing, straight tae school. Only of course the next morning young madam woke up and what a stramash. She didnae want to go in the car, she didnae want to drive anywhere at all, she'd had a premonition.'

'A premonition?'

'She'd had a dream. She'd dreamt Rory had come back from the grave and he was going to drive her, drive her straight to hell. So that was it. She was hysterical, by all accounts.' Janet sat back, satisfied.

'Poor girl,' I said.

'Huh. I told that brother of hers to just give her a wee skelp and be done with it. She lost a whole three months last year wi' her wee nervous breakdown and I bet they've no repaid the fees for that an a'.'

I thought the loss of school fees might be the least of Grant's problems. 'Nervous breakdown?'

'Oh aye. Well, if you can call it that. Everyone heard about *that* one right enough, young madam made sure of that. No sweeping that under the carpet.'

I watched Janet drink her coffee with what seemed to me deliberate slowness. The wind was throwing handfuls of rain at the cafe window, the streets outside deserted now. Her eyes seemed to dare me to ask her more questions, to expose more layers of my ignorance. Instead I picked up my own cup and drained the last of my coffee, cold and bitter as it was.

If Cass was still around, I saw no sign of her that day. I got on with some work in fits and starts but found it hard to settle. The wind did not drop; it keened in the chimney, rattling the windows with every gust. At times the rain came in bursts so thick the view was obscured, the very air darkening. The cottage was full of the sound of water, running in the drainpipes, pouring from the gutters. I was restless, wanting to be out. In the end I pulled on my coat and boots and headed out anyway, into the storm.

I avoided anywhere near the main house. I did not want it to look as if I was prying. I took the path up into the forest where the close-packed trees offered some sort of shelter from the rain and the wind. Even there the air was filled with noise, each tree setting up its own murmur that together made a rushing roar, drowning out all other sounds. In places, sudden whirls and gusts broke through, tugging at my coat like a living presence, snatching at my hood. I battled on, upwards, reaching the track, passing along it until I came to the spring, Maggie's Pool. There was a lull here, the storm seeming to pass over the wide limbs of the ash tree, leaving it undisturbed.

There was a figure crouched at the pool, back turned, hooded and slim as a girl. Cass, I thought, and I hurried forward, pleased to see her, but as she turned I saw that it was not Cass but Kirsty, and that I had surprised her. She wiped her hand awkwardly against her trouser leg.

'Wild weather,' I said, raising my voice to be heard. She looked at me, and I felt the urge to explain myself. 'I just needed to be out, though, stretch my legs.'

'Me too,' she said and I realized how implausible it sounded. I was growing cold, the rain finding its way down my neck, soaking through my trousers. What was she doing out here in this weather? What was I doing?

I would have turned back, but I thought it might seem even odder, so I picked my way past the spring and continued a little way along the track, with Kirsty falling in unexpectedly beside me, pulling the zip up on her jacket against the renewed onslaught of the wind. It took me a moment to realize that she was speaking, her voice lost, the same expression on her face that I'd noticed before: a curious mixture of anxiety and urgency.

'Sorry, what?' I asked, slowing, turning so I could see her face. She did not raise her voice, preferring even in that gale a conspiratorial murmur.

'You were asking about the murder.'

I must have stared at her blankly. Then I remembered the conversation at dinner, with a flash of embarrassment. 'Oh, that.'

'He killed a woman, you know. Stove her head clean in two with a spade. Didnae even try and hide he'd done it.'

'So how did he get off?' Acquitted, Grant had said. I wondered if he had pleaded insanity. Would that count as an acquittal?

'People dinnae forget.' The trees around us were moving now, the whole forest stirring in the wind. 'Some said he was mad, but the village, they knew better.'

'What happened? Who did he kill?'

'Auld Isobel. That's who he killt, though she was no auld Isobel when he killt her. She came to him in the shape of a hare and it was a hare's head he put the spade through. No law then against killing sich a creature.'

'He claimed he thought she was a hare?'

Her face took on a look of slight contempt. 'Oh, he knew what she was then, right enough. She was a witch, that's how she changed her shape. She had the whole village in terror at her, she was a terrible woman. There wasnae a soul there would testify against him. They all of them said how they saw she was a hare when he brought the spade down. It was only when she died that she turned back into female form.'

I glanced at her, thinking I might be being teased, but she was in deadly earnest. 'That would never stand up in a court of law,' I said.

She shrugged. 'He walked out a free man.'

It was a wild tale, but that last part I could well believe. The local laird, his own tenants browbeaten into saying whatever he wanted, a sheriff perhaps chosen from among his own kind. No wonder Grant didn't want it discussed; it was hardly the most ringing of vindications.

'But why on earth would he want to kill her?'

Kirsty's voice got even lower; now she was barely audible. I sensed as much as heard what she said, caught it in snatches against the fretting of the wind.

'Because she had him bewitched. He was a fine young man

and she took a fancy to him, daft as it may seem, and when he laughed in her face, she cursed him. Cursed him far and wide. Tormented him until he could barely stand and every doctor baffled as to what was wrong with him.'

If this had been London, I would have been edging away from her, seeking my escape. Up here there could be none and I felt I had to play along. 'You've read about this?'

'I know it. People dinnae forget. They told us when we was kids, you behave or auld Isobel will get you.'

'Yes, but that's just . . .'

She looked at me narrowly, and then glanced over her shoulder as though we might possibly be overheard over the tossing gale. 'He thought that would be the end of it, but it wasnae. You can kill a witch, but you cannae get out of a curse that easy. He lived in mortal torment all his days. I can mind when I was a wean growing up, there was folk would still talk about him, a broken old man.'

The illogic of it infuriated me. 'Well, maybe it wasn't this Isobel woman who was the cause, then.'

The glance she gave me was pitying rather than anything else, but she said nothing.

'People don't still seriously believe in this, do they? Curses? Shape-shifting?'

Kirsty shrugged, her face closed off. 'Aye well, if you dinnae believe me, that's fair enough. It's no gone away, that's all. There's folk still have the gift. Cross them, and you'll be sorry.'

I might have laughed, I don't remember. I know I felt uneasy at the look she gave me. 'Well, I'll be sure to watch out for anyone slipping hemlock in my tea.'

'Oh, it'll no be anything in your tea. But watch out for someone who wants a lock of your hair or a piece of your clothes.'

'What for?'

'To make the wee clay figures with.'

She said it as if it were obvious, and perhaps to her it was, brought up in superstition.

'Clay figures? What are you talking about?'

She smiled a close-mouthed smile. 'You should look it up.'

If I hadn't laughed before, I might have then, except that we had reached the churchyard gates and were standing staring at them. The wind here was wild and gusting, the tops of the trees tossing violently, and for the first time it struck me that walking through forests in a gale wasn't that sensible an idea. But it wasn't that which had brought me to a halt, brought both of us to a halt. On the gateposts ahead of us, fresh paint stood stark red against the rain-blackened stone. It was crudely done, the letters crammed in towards the end, the paint running, but it was still clear. Exod 22:18.

By the time I reached the shelter of my cottage again the darkness was deepening, the sky a livid colour like a healing bruise. I fumbled for my keys, my fingers stiff and cold. I was in a hurry to get in, get the fire lit, feel the close protection of four solid walls. The wind snatched open the door and I almost had to force it shut behind me. Even then the wind seemed anxious to invade, probing the chimney, rattling the windows, prowling the perimeter as I went around, drawing the curtains as tight as I could. The storm filled the cottage with its discontent, its restlessness, the trees tossing outside. I was still in my boots, my raincoat, like an anxious visitor wishing to be gone. Something was unsettling me, tugging at my memory; something that made the cottage feel an unwelcome place – hostile, almost.

I sat down at my desk, still in my coat, as the computer sprang into life. I started to type the words from the gatepost into the search box but it was already completing them: Exod 22:18 *Thou shall not suffer a witch to live*. I stared at the words, replaying the conversation in the woods in my mind. Perhaps it had been Kirsty who had painted the gatepost? She had certainly shown no reaction to the words, as if she had always known they would be there – or as if they weren't present at all, except in my own head.

Now where had that thought come from? I shut down the computer and sat irresolute. I should get up, hang my coat up, remove my boots. Light a fire, and fill the cottage with warmth and light. I used to enjoy a good storm, knowing that I was safe and snug indoors. Yet something still left me uneasy. I stared at the fireplace and Kirsty's words came back to me: clay figures, locks of hair. The little figure I had found presented itself in a more sinister light. Vague memories of seventeenth-century witch trials floated back into my mind. People had once believed that you could harm someone that way, through a likeness. I couldn't imagine anyone making such a figure now except as a joke, but I wanted to have a closer look at it, or at least that's what I told myself. In fact, I wanted to find the figure so that I could get rid of it, banish it from my home.

I looked around for it, casually at first, then with increasing urgency. It was not in any of the obvious places – my desk, beside the fireplace, the kitchen, the windowsills. I tried the likely places and then the unlikely ones, and then all the places where I'd already looked. I stared into empty drawers as if that would make it magically appear, teased by the sense that something couldn't just vanish, that it had to have been hidden from me in some way. A feeling of frustrated helplessness rose up in me, a feeling something like rage. I searched the cottage – ransacked would be a better word – until the search had gone beyond all logic. I found myself kneeling before the fireplace where I had started, staring into the empty grate, as if that might make it reappear.

I shook myself, and the frenzy passed. I would light the fire, I would take off my coat. I felt no hunger for an evening meal but I would make myself some hot milk – how long since I had done that? I would enjoy the security of centuries-old thick stone walls. I would stop chewing over things that were long past and people who could no longer do me harm. I had let Kirsty's irrationality get under my skin, that was all. The cottage was still my sanctuary and my refuge. Someone else's supernatural fantasies could not change that.

I went to the kitchen and let the smell of the milk as it heated take me back to my childhood. It started to climb up the sides of the pan, always quicker than expected, and I burned the tips of my fingers a little as I snatched it off the heat and carried my scalding cup back into the sitting room, intending to settle down with a good book. I felt better with something inside me, able to enjoy the wild ride of the storm outside. The wind still howled and battered the house, stronger now if anything, but even the flickering of the lights as the wind shook the wires did not faze me. I had candles, if need be. I had everything I needed.

I don't know at what point that evening I became aware of something, a sense of being watched, the feeling unshakeable. The wind had just gusted down the chimney, sending the fire flaring, and the lights dimmed, stayed dim, the corners of the room giving in to creeping darkness. The pages of my book swam before me, the words becoming crawling black dots, unreadable. Looking up, I could see only the fire, and then, beyond the fire, eyes once more watching me from the niche in the chimney. Not just a single pair now, but two pairs, two faces, alive in the firelight.

I blinked, my vision occluded by the dance of the flames. There was definitely something there, two creatures watching, mocking, but I could not reach them. The heat of the fire drove my hand back. I tried the poker but it was a clumsy tool and I knew I must not dislodge them for if they fell, they would break, and I had the sudden unshakeable conviction that if they broke, something terrible would happen. In the end I managed to nudge them onto the flat of the little shovel that hung with the rest of the fire irons and draw them towards me so I could see them properly.

One was the original clay figure, although how it had found its way back to its earlier hiding place I did not know. The other was fresher, more finely modelled, the clay still soft in places, not quite dried. I turned her over – for somehow I knew that it was a she – feeling the heat of her in my fingers, knowing what I would find. On the back of the head was hair, human hair, matted into the surface of the clay. Even in the uncertain light I could see that it was fine and long, red, the exact shade of Cass's hair. I found myself pulling it free, my fingers burning, yanking it out to drop and shrivel in the fire as the two clay creatures howled at me, screaming in pain.

I woke, stiff-necked and cold on the sofa with the wind raging around me. I could hear every tree in motion outside and it felt as if the world itself had turned into a heaving sea, the cottage tossed upon it like a boat in a storm. A dream, just a dream, though it had seemed so real and concrete at the time. My fingertips were still tingling as if burned, but the chimney niche was empty and the grate strewn only with cinders and cold ash.

CHAPTER 9

W HEN I WOKE again it was the next morning, late, long past the time I would normally get up. A sickly yellow light shone through the window. Whatever else I had dreamt, the storm had been real, for I stepped out of the house into a landscape half uprooted. A tangle of leaves and fallen branches lay scattered and smashed over the cobbles. The main house, normally hidden by the intervening trees, appeared in jagged new gaps that had been left by the storm. As I picked my way along the path towards it, I saw that I was not alone: Grant was walking towards me, a mixture of relief and worry on his face.

'Thank goodness,' he said. 'I was coming to see if I could find you. Is everything all right your side?'

'I think so,' I said. I had not thought to check the back of the cottage, or Janet's half. 'And you? Did the storm do any damage?'

'No, no.' He seemed distracted, staring around him as if he had only just noticed the trees. 'At least, not in the house, though there's trees down everywhere and the drive looks impassable. Dougie's coming later with a tractor, as soon as he can clear his own track. No, I was looking for you for something else, in fact.'

'How can I help?' I asked.

He didn't answer immediately but pressed his toe into the sodden ground, staring intently down at it.

'I don't know who else I can ask. There's Helen – but she's my parents' generation. And it needs a woman.'

'What does?' I asked.

'Cass,' he said. 'You'd better come and see.'

All around me the world looked unfamiliar, as if more than trees had been wrenched out of place by the storm. The path to the house was blocked by a huge fallen copper beech and we had to walk around it. It had heaved the earth up as it fell, its roots clutching stones the size of boulders, gouging out a huge raw hole. I had blithely walked past it the night before, never imagining it could come crashing down with a force that had shattered its great branches into matchwood. It was madness to have been out in such weather and I could not imagine now what had possessed me.

We went in round the back of the house. I was expecting Grant to head for the kitchen but instead he led me straight into the dimness of the hall, up the stairs, past Cass's bedroom. Grant pushed open one door no different from the rest and revealed a bathroom, old-fashioned with its claw-footed tub and a huge porcelain sink suspended on two metal brackets with a mirror behind it. Cass was sitting there, staring into the mirror, wrapped in her dressing gown. Our gaze met in the glass and I did not see at first what she had done, noticing only that her eyes seemed huge and dark in her face. Then she turned and I saw the bare patches on her scalp, the fall of hair about her feet, vivid and red in the flat white light of day.

For a moment I could not speak. The dream returned to

me and as it did my burned fingers tingled. Her eyes on me seemed to be an accusation. I turned and looked at Grant and he too was watching me, as if assessing my guilt. I swallowed against a sudden rise of nausea.

'What happened?' I managed to ask.

'She was like this when I got up,' Grant said.

Cass said nothing.

'What happened, Cass?'

On one side of her head, her hair was untouched, as glossy as ever. On the other side, crazy tufts of shorter hair were mixed with patches of nothing at all, her scalp pimpling in the cold morning air. She tucked the ghost of her hair behind her ears and smiled.

'I thought if I cut it, it would make it look less obvious,' she said.

'I took the scissors,' Grant said, and something in his voice made me wonder if he'd had to take them from her before.

'Can I see?' I asked.

She tilted her head and I went to have a look.

'It was all on my pillow this morning,' she said.

I caught Grant's eyes in the mirror. The doubt in them was plain, but not directed at me. It was Cass herself he suspected, I realized. I felt a wave of relief, as irrational as my earlier worry had been.

'It can just happen,' I said to him. 'It's a reaction to stress.'

'Can it?' He sounded sceptical.

'It can,' I said, with more confidence than I felt.

'She can't go back to school like that,' Grant said. 'What can we do?'

'I don't think anyone's going anywhere at the moment, if

110

there are trees down everywhere,' I said. 'Who normally cuts your hair?'

It was Cass I was speaking to but it was Grant who answered. 'Can't you do something yourself? Cut it short properly?'

What did I know of cutting hair? I had used to cut my own when I was younger, but that had been a matter of practicality, and I hadn't done it with any great skill.

'I can't promise miracles,' I said.

Grant got a pair of clippers and went to ring the school, leaving us to it. I managed to fashion a neat if rather brutal crop and when I had finished I noticed with detachment that my hands were steady, the tingling in my fingers gone.

Cass turned her head this way and that, gauging the effect.

'It's still pretty patchy, but if it grows back it should blend in fairly quickly,' I said.

'If?'

'Well, when then.'

Cass pulled her dressing gown closer, shivering. We both regarded her reflection in the mirror and she smiled up at me. I rested my hands on her shoulders, just for a moment. It seemed the natural gesture to make. She seemed all fine bone beneath the silky cloth.

'I'll do,' she said.

'You'll do just fine.'

I thought I might find Grant in the kitchen, but the room was dark and empty. Davey must have gone out too, for there was no sign of him, or the dog either. I heard a sound, a rhythmic chop and thunk, and followed it out to the back door to find Grant chopping wood, a pile of it already at his feet.

'Is that one of the trees that was down?' I asked.

He laughed. 'Good Lord, no. This one must have come down two years ago. It's been seasoning. Thought I'd better get it chopped and stacked, make room for the fallen timber. Prepare for winter.'

He propped a fresh log upright on the block and the axe swung in an arc towards it. A flash of blade and the cleaved halves flew free, ringing against the stone flags. He stooped to pick them up and flung them on the growing heap, then took the next log and the next, each blow sure and easy.

'Satisfying,' I said.

'Got to be done,' he said. 'Got to be done.' He spoke without altering the rhythm of his work. 'You're never finished, getting the wood in. Always got to think ahead. Two hundred years growing, two years seasoning, two months burning. I planted two more trees to replace this one. Whatever else happens, we'll never want for wood.'

'Thinking long term.'

'It's the only way.'

The next piece was larger, awkwardly shaped and knotted, and he brought the axe down harder. The head jammed in the wood and he swung the axe back, log and all, thumping it down against the block until it shivered apart.

'How does she look?' he asked finally.

'Cass? Fine. A bit war orphan-ish. She's lucky she's got the bone structure to carry it off.'

He smiled faintly. 'What made her do it?'

'What makes you think she did it herself?'

In the pause that followed I could hear the rise and fall of a chainsaw, closer now, the outside world making its way through. My fingers tingled again, no more than a raw prickle of memory. Then the next log went onto the block and the axe resumed its rhythm.

'She was supposed to go back to school today, wasn't she?'

'You think it's about school?'

'In my experience, it almost always is about school,' I said. 'Does she seem to enjoy it there? It's all girls, isn't it?'

This time when he had struck the log, he did not stoop to pick up the pieces immediately. 'Yes, school. I hadn't thought of that. Perhaps it's that.'

'Have you talked to them about it?'

'Maybe I should.' He resumed his rhythm, the wood cued up ready.

'Was this what happened before?' I asked.

The axe came down harder and I saw he had to tug it slightly to free it from the chopping block. He had missed the centre of the log and the smaller piece flew off wildly. I retrieved it for him.

'Before?' I recognized the blank closing of the shutters in his face. Not a subject for conversation then.

'I'm sure she'll be fine,' I said, lamely.

'I should thank you for your help,' he said, all briskness.

'It was nothing.'

'All the same.' He resumed his chopping, evenly now, the axe swinging like a dismissal of the subject. I turned and left him still standing as if he had taken root there, wielding the axe as if he might never stop.

A few days later there was a gift waiting for me when I returned from one of my bike rides. The cottage had a woodshed, no more than a little lean-to, which had stood empty except for spiders since I had arrived. I had meant to find out where to buy more logs, for I had all but exhausted the stock that had been left in the cottage and I had grown used to the comfort of the fire. Now as I wheeled the bike into its shelter, I saw it had been filled up, packed to the roof with neatly split logs that smelled of dust and sawdust and underneath that the faint tang of long-vanished sap, the ghost of the growing tree. It was a generous gift, no doubt about that, and a thoughtful one, with the winter approaching. But I could not help but feel that it was more than that: a price, perhaps, for my silence, or a careful reckoning of the balance to ensure that my hosts were not in anybody's debt.

I saw nothing of Grant and Cass for the rest of that week, except once in the distance, walking close together, too preoccupied to return any greeting. I left them to themselves; I assumed that if they wanted my company or needed my help, then they would ask for it. There was no need for me to intrude. With October drawing in, I was seized by the need to be out and moving, away from the closeness of the cottage's four walls. After the storm, a calm had fallen like a truce and though the nights were cold now, during the day the sun still held the last ghost of warmth on my skin. I took the bike out every day, through a world still mangled by the storm, the road mulched with its debris of mashed twigs. The last of the autumn leaves lay scattered along the verges, bright russet against the spectral green of the moss and the grass. The complaining note of chainsaws clearing away the felled timber could be heard everywhere, but I saw almost no one.

I followed the same route I'd taken the first time, gauging the improvement in my fitness. The hill seemed easier every time I climbed it, and I gloried in the effort, feeling my legs stretch and work, the bike responding almost as if it was alive. At the top of the climb, I liked to pause, no longer heaving air into my lungs, but welcoming the chance to catch my breath all the same. The view opened out around me, the forest sometimes half shrouded in the mist that clung to it like smoke.

I grew more confident, too, on the plunging descent. I did not hold back or brake, pedalling even as the bike gathered speed on the downhill, taking chances on the curves. The wind rushed over me and around me, silky smooth, a solid force of air. The bike seemed to actively balance itself beneath me as we met each curve, turning almost without my volition. I felt that we could never fall, the bike and I, that we were two halves, one thing, perfectly fitted to each other. I felt more alive than I had ever done and it made me feel like laughing aloud; certainly there was nobody about to hear me if I did.

Well, nobody except Davey. All that week he had been repairing the drystone wall at the crossroads, a slow but steady process. I took to stopping to watch him working, fascinated.

I had not thought of these walls as being anything more than piles of stones, but watching Davey I could see that there was an order in the way he put the structure together. It was, in fact, two walls leaning in towards each other, holding each other up. Unlike the rougher field boundaries, which were loosely built, he had taken care to build this one neat and tight, each stone seeming to find the one place where it would go.

Absorbed, he did not always acknowledge my approach; only the dog would warily mark my arrival, its eyes never off my face, its body never quite relaxed. I watched, and Davey worked, and eventually – when some tricky passage of construction had been completed, perhaps – he'd pause, unbend from the work, roll a cigarette, ready to talk once more. All his earlier standoffishness was gone and he answered my questions, even let me have a go at choosing a stone from the pile at his feet and trying to fit it perfectly in the wall.

'Ah, see, you've got the knack already,' he said kindly at my efforts, although I saw him shift it slightly afterwards. He told me about the way the field walls here were built looser because the chinks between the stones made the sheep less likely to run at them if they could see through to the other side. He told me that the cattle could easily knock the walls over simply by leaning on them, yet they rarely did, preferring the comfort of remaining enclosed. And he told me, just as matter-of-factly, that in the time it takes a man to build a wall – especially up alone in the high moorland, where the walls stretch for miles – he builds a piece of his soul into it that never quite leaves.

'Oh aye, the old boys that built the walls, you know they're there, all right,' he said. 'You feel them watching you, making sure you get it right.' He gave me a look that was half challenge.

'What about this wall?' I asked.

'Oh well, this is no a happy wall. I told Grant he'd be better off no rebuilding it at all. It's not like these wee trees will go anywhere after all. But it's the estate boundary and he wants to see it made whole.'

'He thinks long term,' I said. 'I suppose he wants to make sure he passes the estate on in good condition.'

'Aye well. So it seems. I never knew Grant that well, before. Rory was the one I knew.'

I looked at him curiously. 'You were friends.'

'Aye.' A silence fell, and the dog shifted, her eyes on him. His cigarette had gone out and he flicked the twisted end of paper into the darkness of the trees.

I waited, hoping for more. Living in Rory's house, riding his bike, he had begun to take up a presence in my mind, made up as much of silences as of anything else. There was always a pause when his name came up; his death too recent, perhaps, for anyone to feel comfortable talking about him. And Davey was no more forthcoming than the rest.

'It's nice to see his bike out, anyway,' he said, nodding towards it. 'Someone getting some fun out of it.'

'I really love it,' I said. I had taken a slightly different route than usual, longer, glorying in my increasing fitness. I mentioned this, pleased with myself.

'Oh aye,' he said. 'That was one of Rory's favourite routes. I mind he used to ride it all the time.'

I said something about it being a nice road but my mind was elsewhere, back on the bike, racing between the dykes on a rolling ribbon of tarmac. Although I had never taken the road before it had seemed to unfold in a way that seemed inevitable, every climb and drop and curve just right. It was like the memory of the dream that had brought me here, that sense of everything falling into place. A feeling of rightness. I looked down at my handlebars, my hands gripping them, and I had that momentary sense of alienation you sometimes get, as if they weren't my hands but someone else's, seen from a very long way away.

Davey was still talking, rolling a fresh cigarette. 'Aye, it was when he stopped even riding his bike, that was when I knew something was seriously wrong.'

'With Rory?' I was brought up sharp, but he had already caught himself, all openness gone. 'Why, what was wrong him?'

He seemed to take an age to roll that cigarette, his fingers working the loose tobacco evenly along the length of the paper, the deft moment of transformation as he rolled it into a tube, then the final tamping and smoothing. I could see that he had one already rolled, tucked behind his ear. My words were left to hang emptily in the air. It took me a while – too long – to realize he simply wasn't going to answer. The cigarette rolled, he took his time lighting it, all his attention on the flame. He breathed out the first drift of smoke, his eyes sliding past mine, off and away. Only the dog watched me as I mumbled some sort of farewell and pedalled away, all the exhilaration of the day suddenly gone.

The next morning, I decided against taking my normal route. Perhaps, if I'm honest, I was a little annoyed with Davey and his abrupt closing down – or perhaps with myself, at being insensitive, pressing him with my curiosity. After all, whatever the truth of it, Rory's death must still have been quite raw. Either way, I had no desire to meet him again so soon, so I took the village road instead and started to navigate my way towards the town. I had not imagined that I might actually manage the whole distance, but coming across a familiar landmark and stopping to consult the map, I realized that I had got much further than I had dared hope, and more easily than I had expected. Within minutes I had reached the outskirts of the town and then was sailing down the half-deserted Sunday high street as if discovering it for the first time.

In Janet's company the town had come to seem a dour place, struggling to survive. On this bright brisk autumn day, however, I found it to be just another ordinary small town, no more depressed than any other. I stopped off at the supermarket, glad that I had thought to bring a small backpack with me, and bought a few things, including the rare treat of a Sunday paper and then, wheeling the bicycle, came across the other cafe, the one Janet usually spurned, which was open and doing a brisk trade. I went in and was hit by a wave of warm air and savoury smells and ordered coffee and a slice of cake. The staff were dressed up for Halloween, their faces round and smiling under their witches' hats.

'Is that your bike outside?' asked the girl who brought my coffee over. 'Did you want to put it safe in the yard behind?'

There was a chorus of admiration when they learned how far I'd ridden, and I felt myself the unaccustomed hero of the hour. As a result I probably lingered too long over my coffee and the weekend supplements, the chat of the cafe washing around me. My head was full of how I could make this a regular thing: a bike ride, a guilt-free slice of cake, my shopping done, no need to wait around or get a lift. I might not be able to carry a whole week's shopping on the bike but two or three times a week would be manageable, enjoyable even. I left feeling more buoyant than I had been for a while, a weight lifted that I had not even been aware that I was carrying.

I had forgotten, of course, about the clocks going back. I had dutifully adjusted my watch that morning when my computer reminded me about the time change, but I had thought no more about the impact it would have upon the light. It was only when I was halfway home, pedalling hard up a climb that had not seemed anything like so long or steep on the way down, that I realized how quickly the light was fading.

I was on an avenue of beeches, sunk down between two high banks. The road surface was already shadowed and becoming tricky to read. The sun was setting, bright on the hills, the darkness creeping up behind it. I plugged on, head down, hurrying against the wind. How long before it was quite dark? Half an hour? Twenty minutes? I had no lights; I had not even thought about needing them. I would just have to press on as quickly as I could.

By the time I reached the road end where the bus stopped, the sun was long gone from the sky. Climbing up gave me a little more light, for the day did not fade out on the open moorland so fast as it did in the valley, but as I reached the top I saw how the white-painted cottages were no more than a gleam in the dusk. Hare House, dark and stone and shuttered, was barely visible at all. As I dropped down into the valley and reached the fringes of the forest my eyes were straining to read the road in the last of the light. The bike wheel found a pothole and jolted me sideways, almost causing me to lose my seating. I slowed down, uncertain now. Nothing looked familiar. The trees seemed to have moved, closed in, leaning over the road and spreading their dark shadows. The walls and gates were not as I remembered them. I could have been on another road, another place, another time. The verges were filled with small night noises, sudden rustles and scuffles followed by outbreaks of frozen silence. I was barely pedalling, unsure about everything. Had I missed the turn? Could I possibly have got lost?

A car came up behind me, a four-by-four, filling the width of the narrow road. I pulled right over as it swept past, a blare of light and noise, its headlights throwing everything into sharp contrast. When it had gone, the darkness washed back and by now it felt absolute. The clear day had ushered in another frost and the air was turning bitter, my hands numb except for an ache in my fingers, the sharp throb of the cold.

I got off the bike and started to walk instead, wheeling it along beside me. I wasn't sure it was any safer along that narrow road, but at least I would not be jolted off by a pothole. My eyes slowly adjusted but everything now looked shadowy and strange, unfamiliar. My bike had become an awkward companion, its pedals constantly catching at my legs. I was seized by the unshakeable sense that I was lost, that I had gone wrong somehow, taken a wrong turn or passed the gateway to the drive. My steps faltered, fighting the compulsion to turn back and retrace my steps, even as I told myself that the idea was insane.

It was then that I saw the woman walking slowly and steadily down the road, just a few paces ahead. Silent and upright, her silver hair gleaming in the darkness, flanked by two dogs that wove through the shadows around her feet. The woman I had seen at the spring. I pressed forward, thinking at least she would provide some human company on this lonely road, but she must have sped up too because I did not overtake her, or even approach her, and I did not like to call out, not knowing her name. She walked on, oblivious, even the dogs not turning their heads, always just ahead of me.

I followed in her wake until I rounded the bend and recognized the pale pillar of the gateway looming out of the darkness. The uncanny feeling I had had of nothing being quite where it should be fell away abruptly and I now knew exactly where I was; I was almost home. And I was alone. The woman had gone, the dogs with her. I paused for a moment, straining my eyes. There was no sign of any life.

Even off the road, I dared not risk the bike on the potholes of the drive in what was now the dark. The light outside Janet's door was on, a welcome beacon, lighting me home. It was not until I reached the courtyard that I saw that Janet herself was standing in her doorway, caught in the light.

'You'll get yourself killt on that thing, one o' these days,' she said with a certain satisfaction.

'I'll need to get some lights,' I said. 'I forgot about the clocks changing.' I thought she might enjoy my discomfort, but she barely seemed to register it.

'Been up giving haircuts, so I hear,' she said. 'No exactly Vidal Sassoon.' This time she smirked and something about that smirk just got me, right in a tender spot I didn't know I had, like a finger dug sharply beneath the ribs.

'It's not a laughing matter,' I said.

'Is it no?'

'Well, I don't think so. And it's certainly not something for common gossip.'

'Ooh, we're very grand. Comes wi' mixing wi' the gentry. You should probably tell that to young madam hersel' then. She seemed to think it a high old joke, and her brother too.'

'That's up to Cass,' I said, and perhaps if I hadn't been a bit hurt, I might have left it there. But I couldn't believe that any joke Cass might have made of it with Janet would have been genuine. 'But seriously, I don't think it's a laughing matter. She might look like she's brushing it off but she's fragile underneath and she was genuinely upset. She's had to deal with a lot in her life, and that's got to have had an impact on her.'

Janet drew herself up, eyes hardening. I had never really stood up to her before, I realized. Now, in the uncertain light, she seemed to gather a strength to herself, all cold contempt. Weary myself, and chilled, at a low ebb, I felt then that this was more than a little sparring between neighbours.

'I wouldnae meddle in things I didnae understand,' she said.

'I think I understand adolescent girls well enough,' I retorted.

'Aye.' She looked at me for a long time and it seemed to me that she saw everything. I felt my breath catch in my throat as I struggled to hold her gaze. She couldn't know. 'Aye,' she said again, as if she had come to some conclusion. She started to turn away, dismissing me, but then she stopped, her hand on the door.

'I'll tell you this,' she said. 'She talks the talk all right, that girl. But one of these days something's going to come along

123

that will wipe the smile off her face, and that will shut her up once and for all.' She smiled herself, her smile more chilling than anything else, and then she pushed open her door and was gone, the light going out with a sharp snap.

CHAPTER 10

DARKNESS CLOSED IN on us with the clocks going back. Too long spent living in London had made me forget how dark the night could be, how early it could fall, and how cold it could get. The next day, I cycled once more into town and bought myself a set of lights for the bike and a bigger backpack. I rode back once more in the fading light, my legs heavy with the effort after the day before, my hands frozen, for I had once more neglected to bring any gloves. By the time I reached the driveway it was properly dark, my front light casting no more than a square of brightness before me. The sky was sharp with stars and there was no moon. On either side, the verges formed pools of blackness and I could hear, just faint above the whirr of the bike's wheels, rustles of life and movement, which stilled and hushed themselves as I passed.

Janet's cottage was in darkness, no light outside the door, no mocking greeting. I was grateful for the light outside my own as I fumbled with cold-stiffened fingers with my keys, the lock somehow not turning right. It was only after I had turned the key and felt the mortice slide home that I realized it was because the door had been unlocked already, and I had just re-locked it. And the light, too. The outside light was on, but it was not me that had left it burning because it had not been dark when I left. I turned the key again, cautiously, and stood on the threshold, listening. All was darkness inside, and a sort of expectant, muffled silence. I felt an undercurrent of unease.

I shook myself, recalling myself to the present. 'Cass?' I said into the darkness, opening the door to the kitchen. She waited until I had switched on the light – it was a fluorescent tube and it took a few blinks and flashes to warm up – before she sprang out from behind the table where she had been crouching.

'Trick or treat! My God, I've been waiting ages. Where have you actually been? I thought I was going to literally freeze while I waited. If I hadn't actually totally died of boredom first.'

If she had dressed up as anything in particular, it wasn't obvious. She was wearing the emerald green dress from the night of the dinner party, with nothing over it but an old-fashioned fox-fur stole, the kind with the head and the feet still on, its tail caught in its jaws. Her cropped hair stood out in crazed tufts around her head.

'What are you doing here?' I asked.

'I came round to invite you up to ours. And you were ages and I was frozen so I just pushed the door open a tiny little crack and slipped inside. Just like Goldilocks, or something.'

'Invite me up for what?'

'It's Halloween. I thought we'd celebrate. Come on, it will be fun. You've been hiding from us all week. I thought you'd quite gone off us.'

'Of course I haven't gone off you, Cass,' I said.

I was weary, chilled, the sweat still drying on my skin from the ride. I should have just curled up as planned beside the fire. I should have told her off for her unwarranted intrusion and her assumption that I wouldn't mind. But the truth is, I was pleased to see her. Even in the midst of my irritation, I felt my spirits lightening at the sight of her. And an evening in company with Grant and Cass would make a pleasant change. I had not spoken to Grant since Cass's haircut and I was pleased to be thought of, even at the last minute.

'Give me a moment to change then,' I said.

'Nonsense, you look perfect as you are. As ever. Come on, come on, let's go now before my arms and legs actually fall off from the cold.'

'Haven't you a coat?' I asked.

'I didn't need one, I only came from the house. I'm fine,' but I could see now that she was freezing, the goosebumps standing out along her arms and her lips and hands waxy pale. There was an edge to her impatience that brooked no delay, as if she might do something reckless if left to herself. I abandoned the idea of changing, keen to get her back home as quickly as possible, and lent her my own jacket for the walk back up to the house. She clung to my arm and chattered, breathless against the solid chill of the air. What she said was largely nonsense, but it barely mattered as she left no space for me to respond.

It was clear from the moment we stepped into the kitchen that Grant had no idea that I was coming, nor even that Cass had been out. I watched dismay and politeness do battle in his face and wished myself anywhere but there.

'We should stay up till midnight and tell our fortunes,' Cass announced, oblivious to her brother's frozen smile. 'Tonight's the night the dead walk and spirits roam and all the mischief is abroad.' She flung out her arms, still wearing my jacket, the hem of her dress bedraggled where it had trailed on the ground. I caught Grant's eyes on me and looked away again. I was acutely conscious of how I must appear, dragged off the bike, still windblown from the ride.

'Cass, you can't just assume people will drop everything at a moment's notice on your whim,' Grant said.

'I don't mind,' I said.

'Well, I mind. Not that you wouldn't be entirely welcome this evening, of course. It's just that Cass should learn that people aren't at her beck and call the whole time.'

If Cass was listening, she gave no sign. 'Grannie Campbell was always telling us how they celebrated Halloween back when she was a girl. Guising with a neap lantern, bobbing for apples.'

'Where would you go guising here? Are you going to call on Janet and see if she'll give you a penny and some sweeties?'

'She won't be in. She'll be up on Black Mag's Hill with the rest of the coven, holding her Sabbath and summoning the Devil.'

'Cass.' Grant's voice was sharp.

'OK, I was joking.'

'Not even in jest, Cass.'

'All right, all right.'

'I should probably go,' I said.

Cass was suddenly serious. 'You can't go yet, though, there is one thing we have to do.'

Grant jumped in. 'Cass, I'm not messing around with Ouija boards. I've told you.'

'No. I know. I know that. I'm not talking about that. It's just that we have to light the candles, in the windows. Like Grannie Campbell used to do.'

'What for?' I asked.

'To guide the dead home.' Her eyes darted back and forth between me and Grant.

'Cass . . .' Grant chided, though his voice had softened.

'Even though you think it's a nonsense, we still should. Just to say that we're thinking of them. It's like a symbol, isn't it?' She turned and silently appealed to me and I got the sense that this was what I had really been summoned for, the whole charade, to support her in this request.

'Sometimes it's healthy to make a little ritual of remembrance.' My words sounded trite even to myself, but I saw Grant giving in before he'd opened his mouth to speak.

'Not all the windows, though, Cass – just the one in the hall. Oh, that girl.' For Cass had darted out of the door before Grant had even finished his sentence.

He shook his head. 'I suppose in a house as damp as this I shouldn't worry about the fire hazard.'

'It seems harmless enough, I suppose,' I said.

'Grannie Campbell filled her head with a lot of nonsense,' Grant said. 'Our mother's mother. Second sight and little people and all that fey Gaelic superstition. Seances too.'

'You don't believe in it, then.'

'I don't believe in messing with it, anyway.'

'I really should go,' I said. 'I'm sorry you've been troubled.'

'Well, let her do this and get it out of her system. I really don't know why you had to be dragged into it, but that's Cass for you.'

How long had Cass been gone, at that point? Long enough, at the speed she had been going, to have gone right through the house and back again. I worked out later that she had dashed through the hallway in the dark, familiar enough with the layout of the house not to need to turn the lights on, in too much of a hurry to notice anything at all. In the dining room she'd grabbed the candlesticks from the table and lit one of them in the window there. She'd then carried another to the study and left it in another window, reserving one last candlestick for the hallway. Once back in the hallway, spotting the bank of light switches, she claimed she'd thought to add a little drama to the atmosphere by switching off all the lights at the source, plunging the rest of the house into darkness, before she struck a match to light the final candle. All we knew of this was that the lights went out and then in the darkness there rose a thin and wavering scream.

Grant reacted first. Clearly long used to power cuts, he strode to the counter and took up the torch that lay there ready. I felt him brush past me in the dark and then the room reappeared in the beam of the torch, light catching and gleaming in odd places as it reflected around the room.

'Cass!' he cried out, shortly. The scream shattered into gasping sobs. He did not pause but went straight out of the door, leaving me once more in the dark.

As my eyes adjusted, I made my halting way to the door and the light of the torch before it vanished. Once out in the corridor I could see better, and I hurried after him, into the hall. There, the candle Cass was holding guttered and danced, barely lighting her face which was wide-eyed and frozen. She had stopped screaming. Grant held her shoulders and I wondered if he had slapped her. The silence seemed to have that quality, of something interrupted. They seemed locked together. I could not see his face, only the set of his shoulders, the grip of his hands. The torch was on the floor, its beam striking nothing but dust.

'What is it?' I said.

Slowly, Grant turned and he must have looked at me, though I could see no more than his shape in the darkness.

'It's nothing,' he said. 'It's all right.' He bent to pick up the torch and I saw vague shapes, furred, the gleam of sightless eyes. He swung the beam round and it flared in my face before pointing towards the wall beside me. 'There's a switch over there which controls all the lights in the house. If you could just shed some light here?'

The electric light seemed suddenly very bright and glaring as I flipped it on. Cass was still frozen in the middle of the room, still clutching her lit candle. All around her, scattered at her feet, up the stairs, in every corner of the room, the hares lay, like victims of a massacre.

We put them away together, Grant and I, leaving Cass sitting silently beside the kitchen fire. I would have bundled them all up and locked them in a cupboard, but Grant wanted them back exactly as they had been. I gathered them up while he dusted each one off and set it in its place. My fingers recoiled from the soft brush of their fur, the smell of them, of mould and dust. Their straw-stuffed bodies were stiff in my hands and crackled slightly. I was relieved when the last one was settled in its place and the last case locked shut. Grant pocketed the key.

'Thanks,' he said, and his smile was weary. I looked at my watch, surprised that it was only seven. It felt as if it was almost midnight.

'Are they locked up all the time?' I asked.

'They're supposed to be,' he said. 'I've told Cass, but she's got this notion about drawing them. She takes them out and then forgets to lock up.'

Through the open doorways off the hall I saw the light of the candles burning forgotten in the windows. Grant went to the dining room, and I went into the other room where I was greeted by the smell of musty books, in what seemed to be some sort of a study. I had not noticed the door open before, and the room seemed half shut up, unheated, filled with the damp sort of chill that sinks into your bones. Even the candle flames burned small and dispirited. I switched the light on but it was an energy-saving bulb and barely seemed to cut through the gloom. Two sides of the room were lined with books, leather bound, packed tight from floor to ceiling. On another wall I made out a jumbled assortment of family portraits, photographs and paintings all muddled together. Nothing of any great merit or interest, except perhaps to the people who knew them, but one stood out among the formal shots of young men in uniform and stiffly posed family groups. A photograph, in black and white, but clearly modern. I thought for a minute it was Cass, for it had her cheekbones and dark eyes and her occasionally otherworldly air. But it was a young man, of course, with that cropped hair. He had been posed so that he was looking just past the photographer, as if he had glimpsed someone over his shoulder, his lips slightly parted as if in surprise.

I had to ask. 'Is that Rory?'

Grant was standing in the doorway as though reluctant to come in. 'Yes. Not a great likeness of him, I always thought.'

'He's very like Cass.'

'D'you think so? There's some in the village will tell you that Cass looks like nobody at all in our family. At least not on the Henderson side.'

'Oh no, there's definitely a family resemblance,' I said.

'Glad you think so.' His voice was dry, but amused, and with none of the warding-off that suggested I'd got too close to things he considered private. We stood in silence together, both staring at the young man in the photo, the dark intensity of his eyes, permanently caught in that moment of interruption.

'I was just going to blow these candles out,' I said at last, not wanting Grant to think that I had been simply nosing around. He said nothing, for so long, that I turned to look at him. His face gave me no clue as to what he was thinking.

Finally he said, 'Cass told me she saw the eyes gleaming in the candlelight and imagined somehow that they'd escaped and were still alive.'

'The hares?' I said. 'Well, no wonder she screamed.'

'You think?'

'I'd have screamed.'

'Really?' He looked at me. 'I'd have thought it would take a lot to make you scream.'

'Well, in the dark like that,' I said at last.

'It all just seemed a bit overwrought,' he said. 'But maybe you're right. I never know with Cass.'

'The real worry is who actually did it, surely. I mean, someone must have broken in.'

But he waved that away. 'Oh well. The back door's always open. Anyone could have done it for a laugh.'

Some laugh, I thought, and I started for the window and the candles.

'You know,' said Grant, 'I think we could leave them burning a little longer.'

I turned and looked at him, but his face was unreadable.

'OK,' I said.

'It's just a gesture, after all. No harm in that.'

'No harm at all,' I said.

The cottage seemed very cold and dark when I got home. The curtains were all open, the windows black and stark in the glare of the kitchen light. I went straight to the kettle before taking off my jacket, feeling the need for something warm to wrap my hands around. I wasn't thinking of anything in particular as I waited for the kettle to boil, just staring blankly at the uncurtained glass. The moon had risen while I was up at the house and had provided a faint light for me on the way home, but staring through the kitchen window I could see nothing but my own reflection. It was only as the kettle boiled and sent up a burst of vapour across the glass that the writing appeared, faint at first and then more clearly, as if even as I was watching it was being written over with a firmer hand. Exod 22:18. *Thou shalt not suffer a witch to live.*

I don't know quite what made me do it, but I took my cup

with the teabag still steeping in it around each window in the house in turn. Sometimes the steam from the cup was enough, sometimes I had to blow on the window, gently, as one might warm a lover's hands. On each one the words appeared, ghostly against the dark. Clearly Cass had kept herself busy while she waited for my return. I wiped them off impatiently, tired of playing games, but they were stubborn and the marks reappeared, insistent, implacable. *Thou shall not suffer a witch to live.*

Giving up, I left the words to fade and wandered restlessly about the cottage. The silence outside pressed in against the windows with the darkness. It was a stupid prank but I could not shake off the feeling of unease it had engendered. I stepped out, into the moonlight. The courtyard was filled with its shifting uncertain light, the shadows deep as wells. Janet's car was gone, her cottage still dark. Even the owls had fallen silent.

I got the feeling, unshakeable, that I was being watched. I could almost glimpse out of the corner of my eye a figure that gathered all the moonlight, upright, slight, watching. I froze, then slowly turned my head, straining to see. There was nothing there, I thought. Nothing but the shadows of the trees, my own imagination. It was only when it moved that I could make it out, the silent hare, turning and loping away into the dark.

part three

witch hunt

'WE DON'T WANT a witch hunt,' the head had said. I remember her words exactly, one of those phrases that always means its exact opposite: for isn't that exactly what we do want? A rooting-out, an uncovering of the evil that lurks within, a great cleansing sweep through the population. How satisfying it must be to find out at last those who are to blame, for everything, even the things we'd never suspected were all someone else's fault.

How do these things happen? Even after being at the centre of my own small witch hunt, I still couldn't tell you, not with any precision. I had heard that the story of the girls fainting had made the local paper; clearly it had been something of a slow day. Then some of the more excitable tabloids had picked it up, fuelled by an interview one of the parents had given, photographed sitting beside their daughter's hospital bed. They neglected to mention that almost all of the girls had been discharged the very same day, with absolutely nothing wrong with them, instead playing up the number that had been, however briefly, hospitalized. It was not a paper I would ever normally read but there were plenty of people who made sure I heard about it, including a couple of anonymous cuttings pushed through my door.

That was the first inkling I had that any of this was deemed to concern me. I had thought it would be clear to everyone that I had been no more than an innocent bystander when the girls fainted. But in the absence of any concrete explanation for what had happened, people had begun casting around for someone to blame – for what good is a story without a villain? A scapegoat was needed.

Not that I realized any of that when I was called in towards the end of the Easter holidays. The school was filled with workmen, the smell of fresh paint everywhere. Sensible enough, I supposed. They had closed the school early for the Easter break and although the building had quickly been given the all-clear, no noxious substance or leaking drain or blocked flue found, it gave the sense that something had been done. The ancient sash windows of the main block, notoriously difficult to open on hot days, had been chipped free of accumulated paint and flung open. Even in the head's office the breeze had been allowed in. It set the papers piled on her desk in motion, a light ruffle of noise.

When I went in, there were three of them, facing me across the table, ranked as if in judgement. The head, the chair of governors – a woman of great silliness, I had always found – and another woman who I didn't know and who was not introduced to me. She was plainly dressed, no makeup, with an air of some intelligence and she sat with a file in front of her, hands folded over it so I could not see what was written on the front. Even as I sat down, making a joke about confessing everything that fell quite flat, it didn't quite dawn on me that something was amiss. I asked after the girls – no more than making conversation, really, for I had heard that they were all more or less recovered.

The trio glanced at each other. 'We're a little worried about Melissa Harris,' the head said. 'She still hasn't been discharged from hospital.'

'Melissa! What's wrong with her?'

The nameless woman smiled carefully. 'We were wondering if you might have an idea.'

'Me?'

In reply, she left the sort of silence that fools might blunder into, filling it with unwary speech. I said nothing. The chair of governors said something about rumours going around and I thought I caught a small twinge of annoyance from the other two at the interruption.

'Well,' she said defensively, 'I mean, no smoke without fire. That's what people say, anyway. Are saying.'

I might have dismissed that as obvious nonsense but it was dawning on me that this was not just an informal chat about how to approach the pastoral issue of the girls returning to the school, any groundless fears they might have had about returning to the classroom where the incident had happened.

'We do want to get to the bottom of what really happened that day,' the nameless woman added. She handed me her card: Dr Joanna Fairfax. Doctor of what was not specified. 'Perhaps it would be best if you just, in your own words, told me the full story.'

In other circumstances I can imagine we might have been friends, Dr Fairfax and I. There was something about her, a quality of listening I found attractive – seductive, even, in a strictly platonic sense. I'd already told the head what had happened, the ambulance staff, the man with the clipboard from the Environmental Health department, but they had all been simply impatient to get to the answers to their own questions, not to listen to my story. Now, with her, I had the feeling that I might be heard; heard and understood. I closed my eyes briefly, gathered my memories. It was not difficult to take myself back to the stuffy classroom, the starling pitch of the girls' voices raised in a sudden clamour.

'They were caught up in some fuss about something,' I said. 'Some manufactured injustice, invisible to the naked eye.'

The tiniest of smiles of appreciation from Dr Fairfax.

'And this was your year twelve class. With Melissa Harris among them.'

'Yes.' Their faces were before me, clear as day. Seventeen, just blossoming into adulthood, a room full of hormones and half-understood desires. A close-knit gang of them, who had earned a reputation in the school for being something of a handful. They had started to make me feel old, those girls, for the first time in my teaching career. Perhaps because I had grown old – older – waiting for a man who I was realizing would never leave his wife.

'What was the outrage about?'

'They seemed to get worked up about almost anything, that particular set. I think I threatened to keep them in after school because they were late settling down. Five minutes, after the bell, just to make up for lost time. You would have thought I had denied them their human rights.'

'And Melissa among them?'

'Oh yes. I suppose you would call her the ringleader.'

'In this particular instance, or always?'

She wasn't the normal type for a ringleader, Melissa. She was pretty enough, with a doll-like face that you might describe as weak – pale blue eyes set wide apart, fair curls that looked as if they belonged on a much younger child. She had a thin-skinned look, as if she would bruise easily. I had felt sorry for her once, because when she had started at the school – later than the others, once all the friendships had been formed – she had been ostracized at first. I had attempted to be kind and, as so often, kindness had been rewarded with contempt. Now she had become the queen bee and the other girls, who had once had some respect for me, followed her lead.

'It was happening more and more frequently,' I said. 'She had got it into her head that I was singling her out, unfairly. She had some after-school thing she wanted to go to and keeping her in would make her fractionally late. That, it seemed, was enough to openly challenge my authority on the matter.'

'So what actually happened? Talk me through it.'

'As I said, they were all a bit worked up, all talking at once. And standing up. Melissa, the others. I told them to pipe down and that the longer they continued to argue, the longer they would be staying in.'

'And did that work?'

'It seemed to. At first. They started to sit down, some of them anyway, but they were still worked up. Some of them.'

'Including Melissa.'

'Including Melissa. In fact, she was one of the ones who didn't sit down when I told them to. She remained standing with her arms folded, and that encouraged some of the others to stand up again. They were sort of hovering between obeying me and following her lead. They were watching her, all eyes on her, not me, so that when she fainted they were all sort of caught up in it. And it was hot in that room that day, and stuffy.' I glanced at the head, who looked down at her papers. The school was very keen that this not be about the lack of ventilation in the classrooms.

'But there was no unusual smell.'

'Nothing unusual, no.' They all wore perfume, of course, although the school rules forbade it, and highly scented deodorant, and hairspray, all clashing. A warm spring day, with the radiators still on, and the scent of hot humanity, and the close stale feeling of air that has been breathed a thousand times.

'Are you all right?'

I realized I had closed my eyes again. 'Yes. Fine.' I mustered a smile.

Dr Fairfax smiled back, all compassion. 'It's very helpful to get your side of the story. Melissa's memories of just before she fainted are somewhat fragmentary, and the other girls' too. And what they do remember cannot necessarily be relied upon.'

A small silence fell while I took the implications of this in. 'Why, what have they been saying?'

She didn't answer me directly but went back to her notes. 'So, Melissa was standing the whole time in the run-up to the fainting incident?'

'Yes,' I said. 'She was defiant. You understand that I couldn't have that. This is an A-level class, they're supposed to be able to get on with their work independently, not to have to be told what to do all the time. So I was a bit sharp with her, but discipline is important. I was going to tell them that if they didn't want to work they could leave, but they would need to find another A-level subject. But I didn't get to that because at that point she fainted. And then they all started going down, like dominoes. That's all.'

I thought I had nothing to fear, but I had not realized that in some cases it's enough simply to be under suspicion. I had not realized that when people say 'no smoke without fire', they deploy the cliché as if it were some revealed truth, inarguable. And I had not realized, when I sat down in the head's office and faced the three of them ranged against me that my fate had already been decided, the trap set. I didn't stand a chance.

The head asked, 'And you said or did nothing that might have triggered it?'

The chair of governors interjected, 'Well, something must have happened to leave that poor girl in a wheelchair.'

Dr Fairfax said, 'Is there anything else you'd like to tell us?' She regarded me with patient interest. 'Melissa was definitely standing throughout?'

It was then, as I hesitated, that the head stepped in and said, 'We don't want a witch hunt.'

I looked from one to another of them, and then back to her. Three very different women but in each of their faces I saw the same desire: the zeal of the witch-finders, their urge to burn them all.

Chapter 11

C ASS DID NOT go back to school that year. A few days
after the incident with the hares, there was a knock on
my door so diffident I barely heard it, and I found Grant
standing on the doorstep, half turning aside as if to leave before
I'd had a chance to answer. He had brought some eggs from
his new hens and they sat before us on the kitchen table, pale,
smooth and still warm, while he blew on his tea and I waited
for him to come to the point of his visit.

'You never worked out what happened to the old hens?' I
asked.

'No, it's a mystery. They do just die, sometimes,' he said. 'They
were getting on a bit anyway, and they weren't laying as much,
so perhaps it was just as well. The new ones are fine, but they
don't seem to have as much personality. The white ones never do.'

He lapsed into silence again and then he roused himself
and looked around. 'I came to make you something of a prop-
osition,' he said.

'Oh yes?'

'It's Cass, basically. I remembered you said you tutored
people. I was wondering . . .'

'You don't want to send her back to school?'

'I don't see how I can.' He had been staring out of the window as he talked, but now he looked at me with all the full candour of his gaze. 'When our parents died, Gran was always insistent it would be the best thing for her, a bit of stability in her life. Maybe she was right then, but it's getting harder and harder to insist. Cass is seventeen now, I can't actually make her go. And I'm not sure I've got the stomach for the battle, but she does still have her Highers to sit.'

'Have you spoken to Cass about it?'

'I thought I'd better see if you were interested first. In fact, I thought about, you know, just going online and finding you there and signing her up remotely, but that seemed absurd.'

What might he have found if he had done so? I am fortunate in having a common enough name that I don't google well, but even so, I was relieved he hadn't made the attempt. I forced myself to breathe normally.

'If you're not keen . . . It's just she likes you, we both do. And it would be a weight off my mind, knowing she was in good hands. I'll pay you whatever you normally charge, whatever's the going rate.'

I should have said no. I should have sympathized and explained I was far too busy, pointed him towards some reputable agencies, walked away. I should have stayed in my little niche I'd carved myself, my round of walks, the bike rides, my quiet life. I didn't need the work or the money and nor did I need to get caught up in the Hendersons' problems, whatever they were. I had found a place, if not of happiness, at least of peace and calm, where I needed nothing and nobody, and where nobody needed me. Where nothing I said or did could possibly affect anyone else.

But perhaps it was already too late. As I met his eyes I knew I would do none of those things, that our lives were already inextricably entangled in ways that I didn't then fully understand.

'Of course,' I said. 'I'd be happy to help.'

'You would?' The relief in his eyes was tangible, and it was only now as he smiled and reached once more to shake my hand, that I could see the tension that he'd been carrying. His grasp, warm, enclosed my whole hand, seemed to enclose me.

Did that handshake go on a little longer than was necessary? Was there more than relief and gratitude in his eyes as he took his leave? I stood at the cottage door and watched him walk away, and for once it didn't bother me when I turned and saw Janet, her arms full of washing from the line, watching me, watching him, watching us both.

And so began what I still remember as some of the happiest few weeks of my life. It wasn't just that I was teaching again, it was the way I felt welcomed, invited in to share their lives, by Grant and Cass both. From nine to twelve, I taught – although if I could get Cass started on the dot of nine, I was doing well – and then I would inevitably be invited by Grant to join Cass and himself, and Davey if he was around, for lunch; just soup, normally, homemade or out of a tin, but welcome after a morning's work. The talk flowed around the table, banter, family jokes I barely understood. It didn't matter. I liked the fact they no longer treated me as a guest, but just let me join in as best I could. As I remember it, the weather that November was uniformly fine and dry, and as I walked up through the crisp cold to the house each morning, my folder of notes tucked under my arm, it was with a spring in my step, looking forward to my morning, glad to be alive.

I had thought we might work amidst the warmth and clutter of the kitchen but Grant, perhaps sensibly, suggested the study instead. It had an ancient cast-iron radiator that did little more than make the smell of damp books a little stronger and Cass would perch on it, refusing to settle at the table. Sometimes, as the chill deepened, I considered joining her there, sharing what little warmth there was – for after all, where does it say that teachers and pupils must sit in opposition to each other, instead of side by side, heads bent over the same text?

But I didn't. I kept up my professional facade, the teaching persona that had stood me in good stead for so long. I had spent a number of evenings researching Cass's Highers subjects, putting together several weeks' worth of lesson plans, tailored to what I assessed would be her strengths and weaknesses. It was something I was good at; I have never turned up for a lesson unprepared. I like to think that during those few weeks she did learn something, certainly more than her expensive school seemed to have managed to teach her.

She was bright enough, although not academic, and completely undiligent, prone to seizing on anything she sensed would waste time. She had an acute ear for the sound of the back door, darting out to see who might be coming in before I could stop her. Sometimes it would just be Dougie, looking for Grant to discuss some matter to do with the farm, and then she would slink back in quite promptly, often leaving the poor man standing in the kitchen in his socks for ages after she completely forgot to tell Grant that he was waiting for him. But when Cass heard Davey's tentative hello, the click of Jess's claws against the stone flags of the kitchen floor, she would shoot out to greet the dog with fondlings and kisses which Jess for the most part endured until she could fling herself down with a sigh in front of the kitchen fire. Davey might sit himself down with the same sigh, stretching out his stockinged feet to the fire, and it would then take me a while to coax Cass back to the chill of the study and her schoolwork.

If she concentrated on anything, it was on her art. Those mornings when I showed up and she was not waiting for me at the kitchen table – or when she dashed off, ostensibly to the bathroom, and did not return for a good twenty minutes or more – she could invariably be found crouched in the hallway with her sketchpad. She drew the hares in their cases obsessively, giving them human, knowing eyes. And not just their eyes, either. Sometimes I recognized someone in her scrawled drawings, scrappily picked out yet indefinably themselves: a hare with Janet's mirthless smirk, one with Dougie's wide and somewhat gap-toothed grin. Was I in there somewhere? There was a harried-looking, creeping creature, a rabbit really rather than a hare, that cropped up sometimes on the margin of the pages, clutching a sheaf of papers. I did not think it looked in any way like me, but I could not think who else she meant it to be.

But we got on well enough. She knew my weaknesses, too. I would let myself get sidetracked sometimes, especially when she was telling me tales of family life. She knew I could not resist the little snippets she let drop, about her brothers growing up, about Rory – especially about Rory. There was something about that otherworldly portrait of him that looked over us, about the sad silence that everyone else seemed to surround him with, that had fed my curiosity about him. Only Cass spoke of him with any naturalness, and I tended to encourage her, thinking it would be good for her to remember and recount. To bear witness to his life, the anecdotes he had brought back on leave from the army, understated tales of heroism lightly worn. The bright, beloved, older brother, the brave one, the reckless one, the glamorous one. She brought him to brief flickering life with her stories and I thought I had come to know him, if only at second hand. There is little point detailing them here, for they were all lies, of course, those stories, as I found out later. But even so, I have not forgotten the Rory she managed to conjure up. I feel as if I know him still.

I had quickly fallen into a routine. After my morning's teaching and lunch, I was outside for as long as the afternoon daylight lasted. I cycled regularly into town, or just round the empty roads, climbing out of the shadow of the enclosing hills. As the days drew in, the sun on my skin became a precious commodity, the light of those short cold days all the more necessary for being so fleeting. In the evenings I spent a lot of time preparing, researching Cass's subjects late into the night and cutting back on my other work. I turned down, for the first time, a request for an essay and I felt the surprise – albeit unspoken – in the curt response from S. Robinson. He still sent me work, but more slowly after that and there were days when I did not know when the next job would be coming in. It did not matter, for Grant was paying me handsomely, and my needs were anyway pretty few and frugal. I had savings, if I needed them.

My cottage had begun to feel very still and silent after the clatter and life of the main house. The only sound beyond the ones I made myself were those of Janet's faint movements on the other side of the wall. We seemed to have settled into a state of suspended hostility, for she had not said one word to me since our last encounter. We managed never to bump into each other, yet whenever I was in my cottage she was somehow just there, a constant presence audible through our shared wall; a cleared throat, a scraped chair, made all the more oppressive because we didn't speak to each other any more.

Cass had never let up on her pretence that she thought Janet was a witch, even though the joke – never funny in the first place – was wearing very thin. It was mostly nonsense, garbled snippets of folklore about Janet never crossing water, which I simply ignored. Sometimes I was forced to pull her up sharply, though. I wouldn't stand for her implying that Janet was actively wishing anyone ill, or any nonsense about curses.

'She's just an ordinary older woman who lives on her own,' I told her. 'Society has been prejudiced against such people for centuries. You might as well describe me as a witch too.'

'Yes, but you've seen the way she glares at people as if she's hoping they'll burst into flames. And muttering to herself –' and here she gave a pitch-perfect impression of Janet with someone she disapproved of pinioned in her sights, so good that I had to suppress a smile. 'Seriously, you see her doing that, you know for sure something bad will happen to that person. And she's always just *appearing*, out of nowhere, just when you think you've managed to avoid her. It's uncanny.'

I hadn't dignified that with a response, although I couldn't help but notice the way Janet did seem to be often just disappearing into her house as I went out, or emerging, a flicker of movement out of the corner of my eye, as I went in. I could have stopped, caught her, said something – but what was there to say between us now? It was only that it made me unaccustomedly restless in my own home, as if she had indeed cast some ill-wishing spell upon the place. The main house, by contrast, increasingly became the place I felt I belonged, the place I began to think of to myself as 'home'.

One day, after I had been teaching Cass for about three weeks, Grant suggested a walk after lunch, the invitation a general one although he must have known that it was only I who would take him up on the offer. Davey was heading out to work on the wall, and Cass refused, leaning against the Aga and affecting to shudder at the thought of going out into the cold. And so we walked together and, as is often the way when you walk side by side, we fell into talking too. Nothing personal, not at first. Just the turning of the season, and the wildlife all around us, some local history from Grant, a few reminiscences of places we both had known in London. I felt, tentatively, that we were becoming friends, certainly more than just landlord and tenant, employer and employee.

We took the path that led up to the spring and were walking under the trees, silent then on a still afternoon. He told me how his father and his grandfather before him had planted the forests. I was surprised by how recent they were, for they felt as if they had always been there, clothing the hills.

'You'd be surprised,' he said. 'Things change even here, you know.'

'So what had been here before?' I asked.

He gestured at the tumbled remains of the wall that ran alongside the path. 'Much the same as you see everywhere else,' he said. 'Fields, farms. Cattle, sheep.'

'People?'

'The people had long gone,' he said.

When we got to the spring, the great old ash above it had been festooned with little dangling creatures, folded out of paper. Hares and humans and something halfway between, twisted into crude but lively animation. Had there been a breeze, they might have danced, but hanging in the still air they took on a different mien among the tattered, fading scraps of cloth. It could only have been done by Cass, but Grant said nothing, just gathered the macabre creatures up and thrust them in his pocket. I stood by, saying nothing, something in his manner forbidding comment. Had he brought me up to see this? Or had he feared finding something here and brought me for moral support? Either way, he didn't seem to need any response from me.

It was as we turned to walk back that he said, 'And how do you find your new pupil?'

I said something noncommittal.

'She seems happier, anyway.'

'Oh good,' I said.

We walked along for a while, briskly because it was cold.

I had my hands stuffed in my pockets but I could see that he had pulled out one of the little paper creatures and was playing with it absently.

'This time of year is hard for her,' he said at last. 'It was coming up to Christmas when our parents died. Same thing with Rory.'

I could not help but notice the hesitation in his voice before he said Rory's name.

'Hard for you too, I would have thought.'

He flicked his head, as if shaking off any sympathy. 'She's got some nonsense in her head.'

'The family curse.'

I thought he might demand to know where I'd heard that. I said quickly, 'I told her it was nonsense, of course. Girls like to self-dramatize, that's the thing. They have to be the heroine of the story.'

His smile was faint, but I thought relieved. 'Yes, yes, there's that. There's that. Sometimes it's hard not to get drawn into these things. But then again, Cass is all I have left now.'

He had quite smoothed out the folded creature, trans- forming it back into no more than a creased sheet of paper which he then scrunched into a ball. For a brief moment all his usual reserve was stripped away and his face was naked, raw with emotion – sadness, yes, but not just that; something harder. We had stopped walking and were standing where the path turned off the track, back to the main house. The silence of the forest seemed like a held breath. There was nothing to say that would not break the spell, so I kept silent too and after a while we turned and walked down together, and when our ways parted he said goodbye with a brief hand on my shoulder. I watched him make his way back through the trees and I stood there for a long while after he had gone.

I went back to my empty cottage and sat for some time in my coat, staring at the empty grate, thinking I should light the fire, thinking I should get on with some work, yet doing nothing. It was Grant's face I saw in my mind's eye, the swift twist of his hands, the set of his back as he walked away. He had placed his hand upon my shoulder and other than hand-shakes it had been the first contact he had made between us. A gesture of simple friendship, and no more, as casual as Cass's kisses. But I found myself kneeling there, my hand uncon-sciously on the same spot, and it was as if I could still feel the warmth of his touch, burning through the fabric of my coat.

I lost my lover shortly before I lost my job – although in truth, I had been losing him long before then, had I but been able to admit it to myself. I wish that I could say I had been the one to break it off, but I can't afford myself even that dignity. He was not a man for confrontation and I think he hoped that he could let things die a natural death, allowing the lengthening of his silences to do the talking. Increasingly he did not pick up my calls, was slow to ring back, was busy on the nights when we normally had our trysts. I should have just responded in kind myself until we had managed to drift apart – yes, that might have been the dignified course. But instead I had tried to cling – to hope, to straws, to him. It's not attractive, needing to be loved, not once the other person has stopped loving back.

I burn now at the thought of how ridiculous I must have

made myself in his eyes, how pathetic. I knew it even then, if I'd been honest with myself, but I was unable to stop myself. Jealousy undid me; it left me defenceless. He had once said he loved me for my independence, for how self-contained I was. How little he knew me, at the end of the day. How little we know ourselves.

They flirted with him, the girls at the school. They always had, and there was a time when I'd found it amusing. In an all-girls' school there weren't many men for them to practise on. As they reached that age – fifteen, sixteen, seventeen – when they became aware for the first time of the power they held over men, even the most awkward among them, they began exercising it in the way a fledgling bird flaps its wings in the nest, barely conceiving what it's limbering up to do. It hadn't bothered me back in the days when I could walk into the art room and see them all there, clamouring for his attention, and he would look up and his glance was for me alone. We were good at keeping our secret then, the charge it gave us. He was practised at it, of course; I see that now. It never occurred to me that one day he would turn his skill for deception on me. Or that one day I would walk into his room and it would be as if I wasn't there, his eyes sliding off and past my face as if I were the wall.

It must have coloured my teaching, that last year, perhaps even been the root cause of the problems I'd had with Melissa Harris's set. I had never had any problems with discipline in my lessons before, but then I had never been suffering from unhappiness before, raw and unfocused but ever-present. I wondered sometimes if Melissa had divined the relationship, and its slow death. She was one of the crowd that hung around the art room and there was a sharpness sometimes in her glance when I dropped by there with some excuse or other, a twitch of almost imperceptible amusement. I had been used to getting respect from my pupils, warmth even, but never from her. Her contempt – imagined or real – lent an edge to our every encounter. I felt the undertow of chaos lurking when she was in my classroom, ready always to pull me under.

As for him, I couldn't blame him, not really. Having the girls clamouring around him fed his male ego, and who wouldn't want to be the centre of such hero worship? And I could see that they were lovely, so lovely, collectively and individually. Fresh and young, skin like rose petals, gleaming hair. Perhaps it was true that I was jealous, bitter, ready to do them down, as the rumours had it. They were young and I was not and the last of my youth had gone while I was waiting for him. Anybody would have hated them. Anybody would have wished them ill.

Sitting in my cottage with the ghost of Grant's hand still present on my shoulder, I began to let go of all that at last. I felt it almost as a physical thing, the laying down of a burden. The last knot of unhappiness from that time slipped free, and with it came a sudden rush of tears that then passed as quickly as they had arrived. With their tracks drying on my face, I resumed lighting the fire and then sat and watched the dance of the flames, finally freed of the last traces of my past.

Chapter 12

I T WAS SHORTLY after that that the weather changed. People said afterwards that winter came in early that year, earlier than anyone could remember. It rolled in on a wave of fog, day after day of murky mornings that never dawned properly, the sun a sullen disc of glare, sucking all colour from the landscape. If the fog did lift, it was only for the cloud to scrape the hilltops and unleash an unrelenting raw rain. For days it was too cold and wet to walk, too foggy to cycle, impossible to get out. The wall that surrounded the house's grounds became the edge of the known universe, and we its only inhabitants. It became hard to believe that there was a world beyond us any more.

With the weather, Cass's mood seemed to change too. She became more and more difficult, demanding of attention yet refusing to listen, filling the page in front of her with her disturbing drawings instead of concentrating on her piece of art history coursework she was supposed to be completing. She announced she did not see the point of it; would not admit, even, to the importance of her coming exams. I had tried to get through to her how those few exams would shape her entire life, and probably I pushed too far. She ended up throwing my words back at me.

'So what have they done for you, your precious exams? Where exactly have they taken you?' I must have looked shocked because she laughed and apologized but for a moment I saw myself in her eyes: a pitiful failure, eking out no more than half a life. It was just a flash and then it was gone, but it had enough truth in it to hurt and when she bent her head to do a little perfunctory work before the doodling started again, I said nothing more, resolving not to press her too hard again. I didn't want to sever the last tenuous thread of connection that still joined us together.

Yet, for all my resolutions, with every day that passed she seemed to grow further away from me, even as Grant and I had begun to grow closer. She stopped volunteering stories about Rory, or anyone else; grew monosyllabic if I attempted to draw her out. In her restless way, she turned her attentions to others, particularly Davey, and I felt she was all but throwing herself at the poor man. With the weather so bad, he was not spending much time out working and so was a constant distraction to her. Even with her hair hacked off and dressed as she usually was in a mixture of Grant's old cast-offs, she was an attractive young girl and I felt sorry for him having to deal with her. The dog had taken to slinking off at her approach, unnerved, I think, at her extravagant attentions, and I sometimes wondered if Davey wished he could follow suit.

And it wasn't just Davey; she had found a new friend in Kirsty, who sometimes popped in looking for Dougie and seemed to hang around – unnecessarily, to my mind – once she'd discovered he wasn't around. Even though I found Cass's effusive habits annoying – the arm sneaking through yours when she wanted to drag you somewhere, the way she grabbed your hand and clutched or hugged – I missed them when she decided to cold-shoulder me instead. Suddenly it was Kirsty whom Cass was flying out to greet, dragging her into the kitchen for a cup of tea – without so much as checking with me whether that was OK.

Kirsty was, apparently, pregnant, although I could see no outward sign of this. She remained thin, tense, hunched and whispering, as unlike the blooming mother-to-be of popular myth as could be imagined. She had said nothing of her condition, letting Cass do all the talking – a relief to me, as I never knew quite what to say to her. I remembered our encounter at the spring, and even though rationally I knew it could not have been the cause of her pregnancy, it just added to my sense that there was something not quite real about the whole thing. As if some bargain had been struck whose repayment terms were not yet fully clear.

I didn't like to lose face in front of Kirsty by attempting to order Cass back into the study on these occasions, knowing I would most likely fail. So I would leave Cass alone until she left. I would remain restlessly prowling the study, exploring this space that was at once mine and yet not mine; my 'domain', as Grant had jokingly put it when he first suggested I teach Cass there. The books on the shelves were old and forbidding, leather bound into uniformity, long unread and uninviting. Grant preferred to do the estate paperwork in the kitchen, so the desk in the corner had become no more than a dumping ground – an unstable pile of papers, old chequebooks and half-empty packets of envelopes that had partially spread to the chair in front of it and threatened always to topple onto the floor. Grant had originally promised to clear me a space at the desk for my notes, but he had never quite got around to it, so I was still carrying them back and forth from my cottage. It made the place feel temporary and slightly grudging and I sometimes thought it was no wonder Cass seemed to want to be anywhere but there.

On one such morning, abandoned again by my pupil, I decided to put the time to good use by finally clearing out a space for myself in one of the desk drawers. The top drawer was stiff, and opening it threatened to send an avalanche of papers in motion. I had just managed to extract the folder that was jamming the drawer shut and had my arms full when Cass bounced in to tell me Kirsty was reading fortunes from tea leaves.

'No time to be nosing around there,' Cass said. 'Your tea is getting cold.'

'What we've no time for is to be messing around with nonsense like that,' I said, although it had been an unproductive sort of morning and I knew from experience we weren't likely to get anything more done that day anyway. 'I wasn't nosing, either,' I added, but I was talking to the closing door. It was typical of Cass to assume that I was. She herself never entered a room without opening a drawer or peering into a cupboard, or turning over a letter to see if she could work out who had sent it. As it was, I piled the paperwork roughly back on the desk and retrieved the folder from the floor where it had fallen when I yanked it free. It was only as I went to put it away that the name on the front caught my eye: Rory

Henderson. There was no way to get it back into the drawer without starting another landslide of paperwork. I placed it on the table with my own papers, meaning to put it back when I had more time. That must have been how I ended up carrying it home.

When I got to the kitchen, Cass seemed to have forgotten that she had summoned me, and if there was any tea waiting for me, it wasn't obvious where it was. She and Kirsty were hunched over the same cup, head to head. I stood in the doorway, watching the pair of them, but Kirsty especially as she swirled the leaves and muttered something, staring into the cup with the same peering intensity she brought to everything. I didn't catch what she had said, and when I asked, neither of them looked up or gave any indication that they had heard me. Cass was flushed, her short hair even more wild than usual. I spoke again, more sharply.

'What is she saying, Cass?'

At this, they both looked up, both for a second blankly hostile at the interruption, before Cass widened her eyes and said, 'Terrible things,' as if it was all a joke, but there was a hectic edge to her I didn't like. Kirsty said nothing and as I walked back to my cottage after lunch that afternoon I was thinking that, irrespective of my own feelings on the matter, Kirsty was not the best person for Cass to be spending time with.

It was later that I found the folder in among my papers in the cottage. I didn't read its contents then; indeed I never meant to. When I found it, I left it on my own desk along with everything else, ready to be carried back and replaced in the morning. But somehow the next morning, and each morning after that, I managed to leave it behind. Each time my eye fell on it, I made a note to take it back to the house before it was missed, yet somehow I never did, and it lay among my things until I had all but forgotten it was there.

It could not have been long after that that Cass and I properly fell out. It was a stupid thing, my fault perhaps. She had started to grow increasingly fascinated about my past, my previous teaching career, my current tutoring work. The more I attempted to deflect her questioning, the more she pressed me.

At first it had seemed like just the normal egotism of that age – am I the worst pupil you've ever had? Do you have Skype so you can stare disapprovingly at your pupils online? Who's your favourite person to tutor? That sort of thing. But then the questions grew more frequent and more probing. It came to a head that day when she unleashed a relentless barrage of questions, the way a child might. What was the school like where I used to teach, where was it, was it in London, what was its name, why did I leave, was it all girls, was it a private school? It was a long time ago, I said, and it's not important, but then she just wanted to know how long ago, when had I left, why didn't I like it, why was it not important?

'It just isn't, Cass. Now come on, if you don't get this essay even started, you're going to fail, believe me.'

I had mustered all the strength I could in my voice, all the confidence I didn't feel. Cass had a look in her eye that I knew too well, and for once it was I who got up and began pacing, although I knew it would be a mistake to betray my agitation.

'Did you leave or did they kick you out?'

Something in Cass's voice made me alert. 'Of course they didn't kick me out,' I said.

I stilled my pacing and stared out of the window at the greyness beyond, avoiding her eyes. The fog that day was so thick that we'd had to turn the lights on even in the middle of the morning. We could have been anywhere: there was no view, nothing but the gravel drive sweeping into nothingness, even the road gone.

What had Cass found out, if anything? Or was she just guessing, pressing on the tender spots, with something of Janet's genius for knowing which stones to turn over? I started to say something mollifying to her, but even as I turned I realized the silence in the room felt wrong, and that Cass was gone.

I went out into the hall and was unsurprised to find her there, apparently absorbed, crouching over one of the glass cases. But she wasn't drawing this time, she was just staring. There was something artificial about the way she stood with her back to me even as I approached, the way she slowly turned to face me, even the look of fear upon her face.

'What is it, Cass?' I asked.

She didn't answer, so I approached the case. It was the one holding the schoolroom, and I knew, somehow, even as I approached it, what I would find there. The hare that was the teacher stood where it always stood, its pathetic scrap of mortarboard and ragged gown less badges of authority than of ridicule. At its feet, the leverets – dressed in their shorts and pinafores – lay tumbled from their places, still frozen rigid into their sitting positions, curled foetally around their desks.

It ought to have looked ridiculous and yet it didn't. To me it looked horribly real.

I turned to Cass and saw – or thought I saw – mocking amusement on her face. Something inside me snapped. I grabbed her by the shoulders, digging my fingers in hard. I heard my voice saying something, barely coherent, words I would never ordinarily use, spitting them out in her face. I had the satisfaction of seeing her expression change, mockery giving way to real fear. Who knows what I might have gone on to do had I not felt hands on my own shoulders, firm and strong, pulling me gently backwards until I let go, until I faltered to a halt.

'Whoa, whoa,' Davey said. 'What's all this stushie about?'

Too late I recalled myself. A reaction, of course, was what she wanted, what they always wanted. I took a few deep breaths, concentrating on the rush of air in, the release, the gradual slowing of my heart. Cass still looked terrified; hamming it up, perhaps, for the benefit of her new audience.

'I'm sorry,' I said. 'It's just Cass has been messing about, and I overreacted.'

'Overreacted?' Davey rolled the word round in his mouth and raised an amused eyebrow.

'It's been a long week.'

It was a feeble excuse, and he knew it, but he seemed to accept it with his usual wry detachment. He glanced at Cass, but missed the flash of triumph that I had seen in her face. Suddenly she was all injured innocence, still trembling, very young.

'It wasn't me, I never touched them. There's something going on in this house, something very bad. I tell you, we're cursed, cursed, and this is just a warning.'

'Cass . . .' Davey said, but it was too late, she had turned and fled upstairs.

'We'd better get these put back then,' he said. He went to the case but it was locked. 'Grant must have taken the key.'

'Or Cass,' I said.

'Aye, maybe,' he replied after a moment. We both peered through the glass at the scene. The teacher held a book in its paw, leather bound and tiny, a book whose pages I had always assumed to be blank. But looking at it now I could see that they were not, and that someone had inscribed in a minute hand the familiar coded phrase, Exod 22:18.

Once home, I could not stand the confines of the cottage any longer. The fog had not lifted but I went out on the bike all the same, seeking the relief of movement. The air was cold and still, the dampness clinging to every surface, soaking my clothes as surely as if I had been caught in the rain. Riding through the fog, the whole world seemed to have contracted to just what I could see, created afresh in front of me, consumed into the murk behind. There was only the road ahead, the walls unrolling on either side, the shadows of the endless trees, the darkness beneath them. It was only as I climbed up and to the end of the trees that I came out into thin sunlight, just enough to touch my face with warmth in the cold air. The fog still lay in the valleys beneath me, as if it might never disperse. I stood in the brightness and felt a strange reluctance to plunge myself back into the hidden world below.

The fog resumed in patches on the way down, concentrated

in thickening clumps so that things drifted in and out of vision, there and then gone again. At one point – just where I could see down to the crossroads below – it lifted and I caught a glimpse of a figure, bright in a green coat. Something about the way the air cleared, just for a moment, gave me the sense of someone standing abnormally still, as if frozen in time, and then the fog swirled back and the sense was gone.

Two shapes darted out of the fog in front of me, grey and fast and low, and I grabbed the brakes by instinct. Although it had been a cold morning, I had no thought of ice on the road, for it was not yet freezing. But the crossroads was obviously caught in a temperature inversion, the cold air pooled there in pockets, unreached by the sun. The thinnest film of water had spread across the road, halfway frozen into ice. I felt too late the slide of the back wheel, the world slowing down as I fought to stay upright. My back wheel shimmied over the ice for a moment that lasted forever, and then slid out beneath me. I was caught in a tangle of metal and fell with it, the road a hard shock against my hands and then my hip, the tree branches spinning above me, all in silence. Whatever it was that had crossed my path had gone.

I felt the cold first, my cheek resting gently against the crumbled asphalt of the road. Only as I moved did the sting of cuts and grazes kick in; the ache of the bruises would come later. I sat up into the faces of two hairy dogs, the lurchers I had met at the spring before, looking at me for all the world as if they were concerned. Behind them I recognized their owner, and realized that she was the figure I had seen before, bright in her coat. She came hurrying over, asking if I was OK, and skidded too as she reached the patch of ice, arms flying out to balance. She gathered herself and made more cautious progress to where I was.

'I'm fine – be careful,' I said, staggering to my feet. She took my hands, although who was supporting who at that point wasn't entirely clear. Together we reached the safety of the verge and I disentangled my hands from hers and surveyed the damage. My palms were raw and peppered with road grit, my elbow grazed, and I could feel that my leg likely was too.

'I'm so sorry, the dogs must have startled you,' she said.

'That surface is lethal,' I said. 'No wonder there have been crashes here.'

'It's a wicked spot.'

Even knowing how slippery it was, the road looked innocuous, the surface no more than damp. It was hard to believe we'd struggled to keep our footing on it. Further on, the ditch beside the road was blocked, the water overflowing to form a deeper puddle. I could see the feathers of ice forming around its edges. It was this water which had crept and spread and frozen in among the tarmac of the road.

'It's always flooded here,' she said. 'And the ice forms before it forms anywhere else and lingers long after the rest of it has gone.'

We stood beside the single twisted tree. She reached up and touched it as she spoke, a seemingly unconscious gesture. We both looked at where the bike had ended up, caught in the gap in the wall, its front wheel only now finished spinning.

'I wouldn't replace that wall, then, if it was me,' I said.

'No?' she stood there, her head cocked, as if listening for something. The dogs came back and sat beside her, heads cocked too.

'At least they should sort out this flooding,' I went on. 'No wonder people have been killed. And grit it, if it's such an accident blackspot.'

'And who's "they"?'

'Well, whoever. The council.'

She smiled. 'Oh, the council'll not come all the way out here,' she said. 'Their writ barely runs this far.'

'Somebody should do something.'

'Oh, well, yes. Do something.' She smiled again and I got the sense that I was being mocked. 'It's easy enough to do something.' She bent and pushed her coat sleeve back and reached her hand into the clogged ditch, pulling out a handful of leaves. The water, freed, started to run again. 'You can always do something.'

'So why doesn't somebody sort it out?'

She held up the handful of leaves, considering it as if it held the answer to some puzzle. 'It's not a simple matter. You can drain the water or grit the ice, or move the wall. It makes no difference in the end. It's just a bad spot here, and always has been. A crossroads. The place where they buried folk like suicides and murderers. Witches. Bury them at the crossroads so their spirits get confused and can't find their way home.'

She was still smiling, but there was a glint in her eye, a dark sort of amusement. The leaves in her hand were still surprisingly intact – thin, elegant, still retaining a sunny yellow colour, a few withered berries clinging to the twigs. 'Rowan,' she said, showing me. 'A magic tree. Almost as magic as the ash. Planted to ward off evil. That's why it still stands at the crossroads. Even a Henderson wouldn't chop one down. There's a time when there wouldn't have been a house in the area that didn't have a branch in it over the door to fend off the little people. In fact, if you look around, you'll see there still is a bit of it in many houses. Tucked away in some corner.'

I had seen them, I realized. Little sprigs of leaves in odd places, unremarked and unremarkable. The cafe in town, for instance, the bright one on the high street, had a small branch tucked above the door. I had thought it mistletoe at first, left over from Christmas, but the berries were red, not white, I recalled now, the leaves different.

She set her handful down, all but one sprig, which she rolled between her fingers, the leaves trembling in the light, and then tucked it into her pocket.

'All the same,' I said, 'a bit of gritting might not go amiss. Might have saved some lives.'

Her eyes sought mine, seemed to search my face for some reaction I could not give. I kept my expression flat, bland, the blankness I had long perfected and I saw – or thought I saw – a slight disappointment, a diminution of interest.

'And yet, perhaps you don't feel it,' she said. She whistled for the dogs and together we walked over to the bike and looked at it. It seemed undamaged. I picked it up reluctantly, wincing as the movement awoke the grazes.

'I recognize this bike,' she said.

'I think it was Rory Henderson's,' I said. 'His sister lent it to me.' Her face looked a little blank and I thought I'd better elaborate. 'The soldier. He was killed last year in Afghanistan. Cass thought he'd want it used.'

She touched the handlebars lightly. 'Is that what they told you?'

'That he'd want it used?'

'That he died in Afghanistan.'

'Didn't he?' I frowned at her, trying to think where I had heard that from. Perhaps Janet, but she had never said much about him. Or Cass. I could not bring her exact words to mind, but then they came to me.

'He died a hero. That's what his sister said.'

'These things are a matter of public record, you know,' she said. 'Still, there's more than one way to die a hero, I suppose.'

'So where did he die?'

'Right here,' she said. 'Right here at this very spot.'

'Where his parents were killed?'

'I told you it was a wicked spot.'

There was nothing to say in response to that. She pointed me to a shortcut home – taking the road through the forest, which ultimately joined up to the track that turned up to the church. We walked side by side, me wheeling the bike. I could not face getting back on it, I was still too stiff and sore, and a little frightened of the way I had so easily fallen.

When our ways parted, I stopped her before she disappeared up a forest track, remembering something.

'I never caught your name,' I said.

She smiled. 'I don't think I ever told it to you. Ann. You can call me Ann.'

'Ann,' I said. 'Thank you for helping me up, anyway. I would shake hands but –' I held up my bruised and grazed palms and she smiled, and it was only after I walked away that I realized she had never asked for mine.

That evening I went online and checked through the records of British service deaths – in Afghanistan, in Iraq, anywhere. As Ann had said, deaths of serving soldiers are a matter of record, and I quickly discovered that there was no Rory Henderson listed anywhere among the dead, nor any variant upon that name.

I tried elsewhere and finally found the online archive of the local paper. It wasn't particularly complete, but there was a brief article, which was enough to fill me in. Ann had been right. *Local Man Killed in Car Tragedy*, the headline of the first article read. Rory Henderson, 23, killed in a single vehicle crash. His sister escaped from the car unharmed. No further details, no mention that it had been at the same spot where his parents had been killed. Had I misunderstood? It seemed to me that any journalist worth his salt would have picked up that spicy little detail. The description of the crash site matched, though, and the detail of the ice. The article even described it as an accident blackspot.

I paged forward through the weeks, to see if there was any follow-up. The news was all farm stock prices and minor burglaries and council business, or events like the switching on of the Christmas lights, a child winning a national competition, snow chaos on the roads . . . Finally I saw another small item: *Police Call for Witnesses in Death Crash*. An appeal for more information – and reading between the lines, a bit of frustration. 'We believe there were other witnesses at the time,' the police spokeswoman had said. 'We're still appealing for them to come forward.' I wondered if they had got anything useful from Cass. I couldn't imagine they had.

And that was that, at least for the local paper. I tried

searching back further, to the time when the parents would have been killed, but the paper's online records did not go back that far and I gave up. The computer hummed and whirred as it shut itself down. In the silence that it left behind, my thoughts were loud in my head, unignorable. My eye fell on the folder I had left on the desk, waiting to be returned to the main house. It was stuffed thick with paper. It was wrong of me to open it, but I was in the grip of a strong curiosity by then. And after all, what harm would it do just to look?

Not an officer, after all. Not a war hero. Not even a soldier, technically speaking. That was my first surprise, the first lie, and the biggest one. All Cass's stories about him vanished like soap bubbles. Oh, he had joined the army all right – that was always on the cards, right from when he was a boy. He had been in the school CCF, played in the pipe band, applied to Sandhurst as soon as he could. Excelled in his first year – there were letters home from him to his parents, briefly hinting at some of his achievements. And then they died in the car crash, and that's when things began to go wrong. He had come home for the funeral and gone back to Sandhurst when the formalities were over, saddened but not apparently disturbed. It seemed the first time the family knew that something was going wrong came was when the redcaps showed up at the house, looking for him. They found him soon enough in the forest, living rough. It appeared he had been there for almost a week.

What followed then was largely medical. Doctors' reports, appointments, prescriptions. The whole magnificent military bureaucracy required for a medical discharge, once the disciplinary system had ground into action. Precious little human information, except for one short note from Grant and Rory's grandmother, writing to Grant to ask him to return from London. She didn't say much except to say that Rory hadn't made much sense once they had tracked him down. 'It was painful to witness,' she wrote. 'I have never seen your brother frightened of anything before.'

I read the whole file through twice, trying to piece together from the hints and remarks in the sidelines what had actually happened. There was nothing about Rory's death, nothing even about his life after he had left the last of the private institutions where he had been treated. He had lived here, that was all I knew, and as I read through the paperwork a second time, I found myself looking up from time to time at the walls around me. Fed by Cass's stories, I had fallen into the habit of imagining him here; living as I lived, perhaps, self-contained and content, in the intervals between his army postings. His shadow – his imagined shadow – had accompanied me on the bike, his bike. I am not superstitious; I don't believe the dead live on in any way, or that inanimate objects can absorb emotions, however strong. And yet I had received some small sense of comfort from this imagined presence, a comfort I only noticed once it had gone.

The walls remained as bland and blank as always, silent except for the mice whose scurryings I had never minded before. Now they seemed to animate the whole cottage with a hidden and malevolent life. The noise surrounded me. I got up and closed the file and, without thinking, thumped the wall where the scurrying was loudest. 'Shut up!' I cried. 'Just shut up!' and for a moment there was stillness before, tentatively, the scratching started up again.

Chapter 13

The next day was Saturday, a milder, softer day, the fog relenting at last. I had planned to take the bus into town, avoiding the bike until I felt less stiff and sore, and less nervous. I had spent a disturbed night, haunted by the sound of the mice in the walls, and when I did sleep I found myself reliving the memory of the fall off the bike, the slide, the battle for control, all in eerie slow silence. I woke earlier than normal and sat and watched the dawn reclaim the sky, doing battle with myself. By the time it was fully daylight, I had decided. I was prey to too many fears already. If I did not get back on the bike now, I never would.

It took me a second cup of coffee – black, I had run out of milk – to nerve myself up to it. It would be fine, I told myself. I would take it slowly and it would be fine. I eked my coffee out till it was almost cold, trying not to replay the memory of the fall again in my mind. I zipped up my jacket firmly and pulled on a hat and gloves, wound my scarf around my neck, settled my backpack properly on my shoulders. I had done this trip half a dozen times by now and always enjoyed it. It would be fine.

The bike was where I always left it, leaned up against the

wall beside the wood store. As I wheeled it out into the court-yard I thought I saw a flicker of movement behind Janet's window, but I ignored it. Just gripping the handlebars woke the grazes on my palms and brought back the moment of falling with painful clarity. *Enough*, I thought, and tentatively stood astride it. This time I definitely saw a flash of movement at the window.

The drive seemed to slope more steeply than I remembered, and the bike gathered speed too quickly, bouncing me over the potholes. I grabbed the brakes then hurriedly released them as I thought I felt the back wheel skid on the loose grit. It was only for a second, but enough to set my heart pounding. I braked again, more cautiously, and brought the bike to a halt at the bottom of the drive, already breathing hard. The road lay ahead of me, damp with dew, softly gleaming in the slant of the sun. It would be fine, I said to myself again. I had not given it a thought before. There was no need to be fearful now.

And yet, I didn't move. I couldn't. The rush of acceleration had been too much, the conviction that I would fall. It was as if the bike – always so easy, so natural – had become unstable. Even at rest, with one foot squarely on the ground, I felt the sick churn of fear. If I closed my eyes, I saw again the spinning of the trees and the sky and the trees and the earth as I fell. If I opened them, I saw the road, smiling and innocuous, full of unseen treachery.

How long I might have stood there battling with myself, I don't know. I might eventually have won, conquered the ir-rational fears and cycled into town. But then I heard the rattle of an engine and Grant's battered Land Rover appeared and slowed, pulling up beside me.

Grant leaned across the seat and called out to me through the half-open window. 'You all right?' he asked. 'Heading into town?'

I'm all right, I should have said, and smiled, but the wrong words were out of my mouth before I could recall them. 'I'm not sure I can do this.'

'You're not all right, are you? Hop in. Don't worry about the bike, just stick it behind the dyke there, no one will take it. Get in, get in, no need to apologize.'

I hesitated. I could see nothing but warmth and concern on his face. He watched me as I got in, trying not to wince as pulling the door handle set off all my grazes once again. The door didn't shut properly and he leaned forward across me and pulled it closed.

'That's how you tell the difference between a Land Rover and a Jehovah's Witness. You can shut the door on a Jehovah's Witness.'

I laughed and caught the welcome flash of his smile again. 'What happened?' he said.

'I hit a patch of black ice yesterday and came off,' I replied, only just preventing myself from saying where. 'It just rattled me a bit, that's all. I shouldn't let it put me off.'

He smiled a half-smile. 'There's no point beating yourself up.'

I felt myself weaken. 'I should really get back on the horse,' I said.

'Rory always used to say that. Never saw the point, personally. Ride the bike when you're feeling better. You were white as a sheet just there. And you're moving quite stiffly. Nothing broken, I hope.'

'Cuts and bruises,' I said. 'Apart from that, just dented pride.'

'Your hands OK?'

Before I could stop him he had teased my gloves off and turned my hands to look at the raw seep of the grazes on my palms. His fingers were gentle.

'Nasty,' he said. 'At least let those heal before you start riding again. We can't have you coming to harm, you know.'

I pulled my hands free and tried to tug on my gloves again before giving up. 'I'll be a bit stuck if I can't ride the bike.'

'Nonsense. I'll always give you a lift. All you have to do is ask.' He turned the key and the engine restarted with a harsh clatter. 'Only, I forgot, you won't ask, will you? In that case, we'll make it an arrangement. Tuesdays and Saturdays. One lift into town, and in return you can keep me company on the drive. Seeing as how Cass is refusing. Unlike you, she's not a great one for facing up to her fears, that girl.'

'She won't come into town?'

'She won't get in the car full stop. You think not being able to ride a bike is a problem.'

'Is she all right?'

'She'll get over it,' he said, pulling away. 'She's in a strange mood these days. Even for Cass.'

He glanced over at me and I thought there was a question there. I wondered what he had heard about our spat the day before, what Davey or Cass might have told him. I looked down at my hands and then out of the window, anywhere but at him. I should have said something about it, but after the warmth with which he had greeted me, I didn't want to fall in his estimation. He didn't say anything further on the matter and all through the drive, although we chatted away easily enough, I had the feeling that I had failed some test of courage. All the same, as he dropped me off once more at the bottom of the drive, he had not forgotten his earlier promise.

'Now look, I mean it. I'm going in again anyway on Tuesday afternoon, so I'm not going to hang around waiting to see if you'll ask. I'll just pick you up. We can't have you breaking your neck on that machine. We need you in one piece.' And then, after the tiniest of pauses, 'Me and my sister both.'

Janet was waiting as I wheeled the bike up the drive, my shopping bags dangling from its handlebars. She made no pretence of just popping out, but stood on her doorstep with her arms folded, watching me approach. It had been so long since I had properly seen her that it was a shock to realize she was, in fact, quite ordinary. Cass's dark hints, and her invisible omnipresence beyond the wall, had built her up into something stranger in my head, not this commonplace woman in her sensible flat shoes and anorak.

'You never rode that thing all the way back wi' your messages, did you?'

'No,' I said, although I was tempted to let her assume that I had. 'I got a lift.'

'Aye, I thought I heard the Land Rover. What a racket that thing makes.'

'I was grateful for it, though,' I said. 'Noisy or not.'

'Aye well. You watch that family. All over you, nothing's too much trouble, when you're a use to them. Drop you like a hot potato when you're no. You'll see.'

I took a leap in the dark. 'A use to them? You mean with Rory, when he was ill?'

I saw that my guess had shot home. Emotions played across her face – surprise, a certain jealous wariness, and then a brief transforming smile. It softened her whole face, just for a moment, like fleeting sunlight through the clouds.

'Aye well,' she said. 'That boy.'

'You kept an eye on him, when he lived here.'

Caution fought pride in her face. 'More than that. Aye, much more than that. Times were, they could do nothing wi' him, except when I wis there. He wouldnae be helped by anybody else but me.' She stopped abruptly, as if she had said too much. 'But they'll no want you talking about that time. And you'll no hear anything about it from me.'

All softness vanished from her face, and when she smiled again, it was the old Janet smile, more malevolence than pleasure. 'Aye, they may not think much of me up at the big house, but they know where they can place their trust.'

When I returned to the house on Monday morning for my next session with Cass, she made no mention of our argument, but sat meekly, submitting to the lesson, bending her head in a simulation of work, gazing at me when I spoke in a parody of attention. For all that, there was something wound tight about her, wound tight and getting tighter. She complained constantly about the cold. Even leaning against the radiator, she would start to shudder, her hands against her throat, plucking at the neck of her jumper as though it might choke her. When reading, her fingers went unconsciously to where her hair was growing back in, working away at the short tufts until they stood up everywhere. Or she would rake her scalp with both hands before pushing the book aside and standing up, restlessly prowling the room. Always slim, she was growing thinner – the bones standing out at her wrists, her cheekbones sharper than ever. I thought she looked drawn, her eyes shadowed, although she denied doing anything but sleeping like a log each night.

She lived in a constant trail of dropped and forgotten belongings and then grew wild when she couldn't find them, storming round the house raging and accusing people – Grant, Davey, me – of stealing them or going through her things. I noticed Davey took to slipping out of the kitchen whenever Cass came in, the dog close on his heels, in case she started one of her tirades about people rummaging through her drawers or reading her diary. She liked to interrupt our lessons by leaping out of her chair as though stung and claiming someone – something – had grabbed her, poked her, caught her by the hair, tweaked her ear. She was restless, distracted, impossible.

The weather had turned cold, I remember, bone-chillingly cold. Grant and I walked anyway, almost every fine afternoon, his invitation to me grown almost routine. We walked through a landscape bleached with frost, the earth standing hard and frozen. Ice crept everywhere. Even the streams had begun to freeze, ice fingering out from their edges, tombing them over. Yet the cold left me feeling alive, as if we were indeed the only things out there that were still living, the only things moving in the whole landscape. The air was still and the clear skies thinned and paled overhead, the setting sun sending them sugar-almond shades of pink, fading to old gold. Some days we came back after dusk, having walked out the whole of the shortening winter day and barely noticed it.

'Perhaps it's time we took a break,' I said to Grant during one of these outings, as the year was winding down towards the shortest day. 'With Cass, I mean. It's almost Christmas anyway and she's all but unteachable at the moment.'

'It's this time of year,' he said. 'It reminds her of everything that happened. It's better that she's got things to do, to be honest. It's better that she's got someone to talk to, someone who isn't me.'

'I'm not sure how much use I am,' I said.

'You're our rock at the moment,' he said.

I was silent, taken aback.

'I mean it,' he said. 'I told you, we need you.'

'Thank you,' I said at last.

And then, slowly, gradually, as if the freezing of the earth had released something inside him, he began to tell me about Rory.

'You know how he died, of course,' he said. 'Rory, I mean.'

'It was a car accident, wasn't it?' I said after pausing to consider what to say. I thought the memory of reading the file must have burned in my face, but he wasn't looking at me, and the car crash at least was a matter of public record.

'He skidded on the ice,' he said. 'We never really understood why.'

We walked on in silence and when Grant spoke again it was quietly, almost to himself. 'He was ill, had been ill for a long time. Not himself.'

What would I have said if I had not already known? 'Not himself?' I tried, my voice as even and uninquisitive as possible.

This time he was looking at me and I found it hard to meet his eye. 'I suppose Janet told you all about it,' he said flatly.

He looked at me and this time I did meet his eye, and though I said nothing I let my silence be the confirmation that he sought. It was cowardice, I suppose; cowardice and a thread of malice, too, for she had had his confidence and I had not. Not until now.

'We trusted her,' he said. 'We had to, I suppose. The whole village must know then.'

'I don't think so,' I said, for I could grant her that much.

He smiled thinly. 'Well, that's something, I suppose. We don't – well, I never wanted it, him, to be the subject of gossip.'

I did not press him then, resolving to let him talk only if he wanted to, and we walked on together in the cold in silence.

But the subject, once broached, seemed easier for him to return to. Another day, driving into town, he asked me how I was getting on with Janet. I responded cagily, not quite certain how best to respond.

'She was good, offering me lifts in the beginning,' I said at last, 'before I got the bike.' I didn't mention that I still hadn't got back on. I had told myself it was the cold weather, the likelihood of ice, but I knew I was still frightened. And besides, I had come to cherish our drives together into town, brief though they were. Like the walks, they offered another moment of closeness, a chance to talk or not as the mood took us.

'She can be very helpful, when she chooses,' he said, and then, as if he regretted lapsing into waspishness, he corrected himself. 'I mean, there are times when she has been invaluable.'

'With Rory?' I ventured, aware that I was testing the ground.

'With Rory. You know he lived in your cottage?' He looked at me as I nodded, and I was pleased at the way he described it – not 'Hare Cottage', but my cottage, casually conferring something on me, a sense of belonging. 'It was after he came back. And Janet kept an eye on him, she made sure to do that.'

We had arrived in town by then and the brisk rattle the Land Rover made when it was turned off drowned out any further remark he might have made. I wandered round the town doing my usual errands, wondering if he would expand on the subject, but when we got back in the car for the drive home he said no more about it until we reached the cottages. Normally he just pulled over beside the gate to let me out, but this time he turned up the drive and took me right to my door. He didn't say goodbye immediately but sat looking at the two cottages, side by side.

'Are you all right?' I asked.

It took him a while to respond. 'Yes. Just thinking back. You like it here? Not sorry that you came now that you've seen what the winters can be like?'

'Not at all,' I said. I did not move to get out. He was still looking at the cottages, but not at mine, at Janet's.

'She's been a good friend to the family,' he said at last. 'With Rory. I don't want you to get the wrong impression. She can be a bit difficult at times, but we owe her a lot. He wanted to come home, here, be able to roam the hills the way he used to as a boy and she made that possible. It seemed the least that we could do for him.'

'I can see why he'd want to come back,' I said.

'For a while – well, you can fool yourself, can't you, that someone's getting better. I don't know what Janet's told you . . .' I gave a small shrug, as if sparing him the details. He opened his mouth to say more and then shut it again. I acted on impulse.

'Come in,' I said. 'I'll put the kettle on. I owe you that much, for all these lifts.'

I saw him ready himself to refuse, but then he switched off the engine. 'Why not, after all,' he said. 'Yes, why not. Cass tells me you make excellent coffee.'

I sat in my cottage that night, curled under a blanket watching the fire, weaving the little snippets Grant had told me over our coffee into a coherent story. Always a private family, they had told almost no one about Rory's illness – not keeping it a secret exactly, but not doing anything to encourage prurient speculation. All the time he had been away in various hospitals they had let people think he was still at Sandhurst and then, as time passed, away somewhere – Iraq, Afghanistan. And when he came back, well, you might expect a young man who'd been through a war to act a little distant and strange. Perhaps people had guessed, or speculated, but if so, they kept it to themselves. Only those who had needed to know had been admitted into the circle.

Janet was chief among them. How could she not have known, after all, living next door as she did, and being Janet?

But it was more than that, Grant had said. She had been fond of Rory as a boy, putting up with him the way she had never put up with Grant or Cass, and she had stayed fond of him, despite everything that followed. Rory had always been the charmer, the bold and reckless one, able to beguile his way out of every scrape. With his illness, all charm had gone, but the ghost of it must have lingered on for Janet. Of all people, it was she who defended him and gladly put up with him at a time when even his family found him hard going.

'We were just so grateful at the time,' Grant had said. 'Not only for the practical help – although we couldn't have done without her. But just the way that she seemed to be on his side. And more than that; the way she liked him still, as if he was the old Rory. You're so grateful to anyone who remembers that.'

Janet. I could hear her through the walls, the way Rory must have been able to hear her. It seemed in the cold, still winter night that every sound became magnified, every cough, every step. I could all but track her movements, to the kitchen, the sitting room. I had an image of him, sitting where I sat now, hearing the same noises. Had he found them reassuring? Or had he felt the oppression I was starting to feel, knowing she was always there? Knowing, perhaps, that there was no escape.

Grant and I took what was to be our last walk together the next afternoon. Brief and formal though his visit to my cottage had been, it seemed as if we had grown into a new level of intimacy. We stopped, I remember, and leaned against a gate and watched the sky turn every shade of pink and green, the hills around us fading into darkness. The moon had not yet risen and the air was sharp and clear and cold. When Grant spoke, his voice was soft and low, and I did not say anything, not wanting to break the mood.

'We had a real humdinger of a row, Rory and I, just days before he died.'

All this time, he had circled the moment of Rory's death, never quite bringing himself to speak about it. I still said nothing, not looking at him, giving him space to go on.

'He refused to listen to what I was saying. Said I was part of the conspiracy against him. Denied that I was even his brother. I thought he meant it metaphorically, but then he started to shake and he was calling me every name under the sun. And looking past him, over his shoulder, I suddenly realized Janet was there, just sitting there, taking it all in, and the look on her face . . .'

I thought I could imagine it, her grim, satisfied smile.

'We had to repaint the whole place, you know, your cottage. It was . . .'

'What?'

He shook his head, smiled. 'I forget you have to live there. Nothing filthy or anything like that. But he'd been writing on the walls, every clear surface.'

'And you didn't realize?'

'He wouldn't let me into the place – he didn't explicitly refuse me entry, but he was cunning about it, manoeuvring things around so that when I was up here from London he'd always come up to the main house. He was quite good at evading the issue, so it didn't even occur to me until that day that that was what he'd been doing. But that time, I had just arrived – literally just off the train. Cass was coming home for Christmas a few days later. It was weather like this, cold but sunny, such a contrast with London. Only an hour or so of daylight left, and I thought I'd surprise him, thought maybe we could go out for a walk together the way we'd used to do before he got ill.' He shook his head.

'What happened?'

'I don't know if he'd taken a turn for the worse, or if he'd just been managing to conceal from me – from everyone – how bad he was. The state he was in. His hair and his fingernails, patches where he'd missed shaving. And he was so thin. He'd gone through stages when he'd been bloated with the drugs, and that was bad, and then he'd started to look a bit better, and I'd taken it as a hopeful sign. But really, I know now, it was just that he'd stopped taking them. Although . . . I don't know if they were doing him any good, anyway.'

I glanced across at him, saw him swallow.

'He told me I couldn't come in, that I was the Devil in human form, and once I'd crossed the threshold he'd never be able to get me out. At first I thought he was joking but that just set him off and he got angry and then I got angry, which was pointless, but I couldn't help it. And it was Janet who calmed him down. One minute he was raving at me, and then she just came over and put her hands on his shoulders and he fell silent, like turning off a tap. She said she'd put him to bed, call the doctor. I was grateful then, still am. I really am . . .'

'But?'

He shook his head. 'Saying it out loud to someone so

sensible and matter of fact – it seems mad. After all, he was beyond reason by then. But I remember the look in his eyes when she came over and put her hands on him. He gave me this look and I can still see it as she led him away. A kind of pleading, for all the vitriol he'd been spouting a moment before. As if he had somehow been recaptured.'

I could feel from the shift of his weight that Grant had turned to look at me, although I could be no more than a silhouette to him in the dark. The sun was quite gone now, the sky taking on the velvet blue of dusk. The first bright stars pinpointed the air.

'There was nothing you could have done,' I said.

'I think Janet felt a sense of loyalty to Rory, and she never really told us quite how bad he was. She must have borne the brunt of it, living next door. And maybe she got a bit caught up in it in some way. We thought he was getting better, we all did. It was wishful thinking, perhaps.'

'What did the doctor say?'

He burst out, 'You know, I think sometimes future generations will look back on how we treated mental illness with the same horror we reserve for leeches and barber surgeons now. If I learned anything from Rory's illness, it's that the medics know nothing. Nothing. They tried him with all sorts of drugs, one on top of the other. The side effects were barbaric, some of them. And at best they just kept him quiet. Docile. It was heartbreaking.' There was a heavy pause and then he added, 'The doctor wasn't called. There was no point. And Rory turned up the next morning at the house and he appeared so much better. I hadn't mentioned the incident to my grandmother – she was quite frail by then, and I hadn't wanted to burden her. Living up at the house, she hadn't realized the state he'd been in and when Rory showed up, having smartened himself up and pulled himself together, I told myself it had just been a one-off. A bad day or something. It's funny what a shave and a decent set of clothes can do. He looked tired, and a bit pale, but he was carrying on a conversation as normal, as if nothing had happened.

'He came with us, me and Gran, to pick up Cass from school for the holidays. And Cass – well, I can remember them whispering together in the back all the way home about something and thinking that it would do him good to have her around. I never thought about the effect it might have on Cass. And if I'd known, really known, I'd never – I'd certainly never – I'd never have let—'

The catch in his throat became a coughing fit and he couldn't go on.

'Never have let what?'

He gathered himself and when he spoke again, his voice was calmer, more measured. 'I didn't even know he'd taken the keys to the car, that day. We just leave them all hanging up in the hall. Cass just shouted that she was going out with Rory. I assumed they were just going for a walk.'

'You can't blame yourself,' I said. 'You can't have known—' what Rory was going to do, I was about to say, but Grant broke in, speaking quickly and in a voice that would brook no dissent.

'The medications made him unsafe to drive. They altered his reaction times. Rory would never have crashed like that otherwise, ice or no ice. That's what the doctor said. It was an accident, a tragic accident. It broke Gran's heart. She didn't last a month after that.'

A silence fell. And then, above us, calling through the dark, a skein of geese filled the evening with their cries. We both looked up, searching for them, but it was Grant who saw them first, barely visible, just catching the last light from the sun. We watched them until they were gone, their calls fading. As if it had been a signal, we both pushed ourselves upright from the gate and began the walk back towards the house.

'Thanks for putting up with me bending your ear,' he said. I told him it was no problem, that he could bend my ear any time he liked.

'It's made such a difference having you here,' he said. 'Just living in the cottage, filling it with life again. And looking after Cass. We both appreciate it, even if she's got an odd way of showing it.'

'The pleasure's all mine,' I said. We picked our way along the path and under the trees where the last light had faded into deep shadow. Unable for a moment to make out the way ahead, I stopped, and he – his eyes better adapted perhaps, knowing this route from boyhood – laughed and turned to look back at me.

'You're all right, just follow me,' he said. 'Here –' and he reached out his hand – a gesture, I now realize, quite meaningless beyond the simple courtesy of showing me the route.

I had forgotten, in the quiet intimacy of our walks, the gulf that realistically lay between us. We all feel seventeen inside, deep down, forgetting the picture we present to the outside world. He always came across as so mature, responsible beyond his years. It did not occur to me that he would recoil from the touch of my hand as if I had burned him.

He said nothing, and I said nothing. He stuffed his hands back into his pockets and stiffened his back. We started walking again, quickly now, and though I stumbled a few times in the darkness I managed to keep my balance and bite my lip to stop from calling out. At the back door, he recovered his voice and almost naturally asked if I was coming in.

'No, better go,' I said. 'Work to do.'

'OK,' he said. 'Tomorrow at the usual time, then?'

'Tomorrow at the usual time.'

He did not linger at the door. It shut behind him and I envisaged him pulling off his boots, shrugging off his jacket, padding down towards the brightly lit kitchen. Davey might still be there, Cass, the kettle beginning to whistle on the stove, my own cup even waiting for me by the others. Would he say anything, pass some flip remark? I hurried off, not wanting to hear the laughter.

There's a memory burned indelibly into my brain. I imagine I will die with it there, unfaded, and that if science could learn the secret of deciphering how our neurons encode these things, it would be visible still after my death, scarred into the tissue, as real as any wound. It's of laughter, the comfortable deep rumble of my lover's laugh, the high light silver of a teenage girl. The laughter that bursts forth after the silent agony of having to keep a straight face while the subject of the laugher is there. I can hear it still, ringing down the corridor of the silent school. I can still summon the burning of my face through the unaccustomed makeup, inexpertly applied – as I saw when I went to scrub it off, clownish in the bathroom mirror – in an attempt to mask the traces of the years. I had prepared myself so carefully, even worn the outfit I had worn when he'd first painted me, as if that might have done something to rekindle the relationship between us. Pathetic. I knew it the minute he opened the door and I saw the stab of pity in his eyes.

He had tried to hide her presence, keeping the door half closed behind him, but she was brazen, hopping off the stool where he liked to seat his models to see who it was. I had managed to say, 'Hello, Melissa,' and she had managed a barely insolent 'Afternoon, Miss.' I gave him a look and his face told me everything. A furtive shame, a bit of defiance, and under it all, the foolish male pride at having proved his virility again.

'So much for making a go of your marriage,' I had said.

'It's not what you think.'

I looked between them, the pair of them and I had no words, not any more. Him, I suddenly felt sorry for, risking his career like that. But her, as she smirked beside him, childish triumph in her eyes – her, I knew I hated.

The rising moon was sending a silver halo over the hills as I passed into the courtyard of the cottages, pursued by the memory of laughter, of every humiliation I had ever felt. I did not stop at my door but kept on, down the driveway, out into the road. I wanted to walk and keep on walking, past the bus stop and the village, past the town, not stopping until I reached the anonymity of London. The moon cast everything in a shadowy light, grey, elusive, shifting. The cold air pinched my fingers, found every gap in my clothes. The road surface was slick with frost and I kept to the verge, my feet crunching on the frozen grass, loud in the stillness of the night.

The hare came silently, though, silently and easily, sure-footed on the slick road, on its long legs, gathering the moonlight. It passed me so close it almost brushed my legs, unafraid, stopping to turn and look at me with glittering eyes. I was filled with the urge to grab hold of it, ridiculous as that might seem, to confirm that it was indeed made out of flesh and blood and not a phantom of the moonlight. But I did not move. I watched it and it watched me and then it turned and ran onwards, easy and silent, until it was out of sight.

CHAPTER 14

I AWOKE THE next morning to the memory of the afternoon before with Grant, the deep and spreading sense of shame and humiliation jolting me awake. It was Saturday. Ostensibly a day off, although I had some work to do, a fresh deadline looming. This was a big job, a master's dissertation I had taken on at the special request of S. Robinson, and it would be a lucrative one if I could only get it finished. For the past week or so I had been neglecting it, caught up in my daily walks with Grant, my evenings spent far too often daydreaming beside the fire like a silly teenager. For the first time since I'd started this work I was in danger of missing a deadline, or turning in a substandard piece of work. The thought only added to my displeasure with myself. I flung myself out of bed, resolving to get on with it. I had no idea if I would get my regular lift into town or not, but fretting about it wouldn't change anything, whereas working would. At least I could salvage one part of my life from what felt like a total wreckage.

For all my resolve, as the time approached when Grant would normally pick me up, I started to spend as much time standing at the window as I did sitting at my desk. There was a sick churn in my stomach. When I did hear the Land Rover approach I wasn't sure whether to be relieved, or more nervous. As I scrambled to get my jacket on and gather my bag, I found my hands were shaking. I was too worked up even to notice that Davey had come along for the ride until I got to the passenger-side door and saw him there, with Jess at his feet in front of him. I had to quickly change tack and scramble in the back. It was perfectly natural, I suppose, for Davey also to need a lift into town, but I could not help but feel that Grant had engineered it so that he would not have to face me on my own.

We drove out mainly in silence, broken only by the occasional scrabble of claws as Jess sought to keep her footing in the corners. It had rained in the night and then frozen again and the road looked slick and treacherous, but Grant did not slow down. Davey muttered something about black ice, but he just laughed.

'It's fine as long as you stay off the brakes.'

'Oh right, well that's reassuring.'

'Better stock up, though,' Grant said, as we pulled into the supermarket car park. 'There's snow on the way and they don't clear or grit the roads much out here. Last year we were snowed in for a week.'

I did my shopping in a hurry, not wanting to hold him up. The drive back was a repeat of the drive out and though his handling of the car was sure and confident, I was relieved to be dropped off at the bottom of the drive to walk back home alone. The sky was heavy with clouds and I guessed that Grant's forecast would prove accurate. I wasn't thinking of anything much but getting back, lighting the fire, drawing the curtains. The fading light as the clouds gathered felt colder than the dark.

When I saw Janet at her door my heart sank, and I dropped my head, hunching my shoulders as if I might escape being seen. She was glaring, but not at me; she barely flicked a glance in my direction. She was muttering something under her breath until she caught me looking at her. Then she stopped abruptly, chucked her head upwards once in greeting and withdrew with a slammed door. Puzzled, I set my shopping down to search for my keys. I jumped when Cass emerged abruptly from behind the woodshed.

'God, that woman's such a bitch.'

'Cass, please.'

'Well, she is. Just because we're not going to jump and fix some stupid slate slipping off her stupid roof. She thinks we're made of money and we're completely not. You should see how many slates have slipped off at the house for a start. We've got like a million buckets for when it rains.'

'Even so, that's not the sort of word we use about people.'

'That's not the sort of word we use,' she parroted back at me. 'Stop being so middle class. And besides, she is a bitch. Are you going to let me in? I'm absolutely freezing my tits off here.'

I unlocked the door and Cass pushed inside, making no move to help me with my bags.

'It's freezing here too. Christ, don't you heat the place?'

'Not when I'm not in it, no.'

'Haven't you got a timing thing that makes it come on before you get in?' She went to fiddle with the central heating controls. 'It's like the grave in here.'

'Cass, please, just leave it.'

'All right, fine, I was just trying to help.' She flung herself into a chair and watched me as I put my shopping away. 'Got a lift with my brother?'

'Yes, and Davey,' I said, not sure why I felt the need to underline to her that we had not been alone.

'Lord, so they'll be there now, wondering where I am.' She threw herself backwards, head lolling, arms limp. 'God, I'm so bored. Another night of boring farm talk. Do you know, he's only got dial-up internet there, can you imagine? It's like the Stone Age.'

'You could always go back to school.'

'Oh please. I swear they're trying to bore me into returning. Do you know what they talked about last night? Stones. Rocks. Different kinds of rocks. I swear to God. And then cows. Different kinds of cows. Like, name that cow. Cows they have known. I thought I was literally going to die of boredom.' She slumped onto the table, letting her tongue loll out. 'It was that bad.'

'Well, you could get some work done if you're that bored. Finish off your coursework.'

She made a mock choking sound and lay still. I eased past her to put the milk and butter in the fridge.

'Cass, if you're set on going to art college, then you'll need at least a decent mark in your art history if nothing else. You can't just waltz in with your portfolio and assume they'll take you.'

It was tired old ground and I knew it. She said nothing but raised one hand and made a motion, opening and closing her fingers: yackety-yack.

I sighed. 'If internet access is the problem, you can use my computer. You can even use it to check Facebook if you'd like to keep up with your friends.'

She did not lift her head. 'Facebook? Do I look middle-aged? And besides, I have no friends. I have nothing in common with the girls at school because they're all bitches.' She gave the last word unnecessary emphasis and then sat up to look at me, checking to see if I had noticed the challenge. 'Bitches bitches bitches.'

'That's enough, Cass.'

'That's enough, Cass.'

I took a breath, counted to ten. 'Do you want to use my computer or not?'

'I've got a better idea.'

A moment ago she had been a spoiled child, but she had changed again with the swiftness I could never quite get used to. She stood up as one might to meet a challenge. I met her eyes and they were cool and level, with the careful blankness of the poker player. Something made me catch my breath and be still, the way an animal will when it's threatened.

'I know what your big secret is,' she said.

'What do you mean?'

'Isn't this the point where you're supposed to say, "What big secret?"'

'I don't have time to play games, Cass.'

'I was thinking you might actually like to complete my coursework for me if you don't mind. I'm sure you'd do a better job than me.'

'And why would I do that?' I kept my voice even, but I could see from the way she was watching me that she wasn't bluffing.

'Oh, I don't know,' she said airily. 'You like my brother, don't you? I've seen the way you look at him. Ridiculous, of course.

But at the moment he only pities you. I bet you'd hate it if he despised you too.'

She had practised it, I guessed. Perhaps even in the mirror, getting that final cock of the head just right, the little smile. Nerves made her bring out her lines just a little bit too quickly, but it didn't matter that her hand was trembling on the table almost as much as mine were behind my back.

'I don't know what you're talking about,' I said.

'Don't you? People with secrets should be a bit more careful about locking their doors, you know.'

Her face now was half fearful, half triumphant, as if she knew she might have pushed too far. I could see her breathing, the effort she was making to keep it under control. In the silence of the kitchen I could hear my own breath, mirroring hers. I could hear my heart. For a moment she became not Cass but Melissa, standing in the classroom – my classroom – defying me. Her eyes, too, had been full of knowing, as if she had seen right into my mind and knew everything that was there.

But I said nothing. I let her make the next move.

'I know what you do for a living,' she said finally. 'So you could just write my essay for me.'

I almost laughed with the relief of it. 'Oh please.'

'What, you don't think I'd tell my brother?'

'And then what? He'd sack me and send you back to school? Is that what you want?'

I could see she hadn't considered the possibility of defiance. Her eyes flicked sideways as I went on. 'Or I tell your brother you've been issuing threats, snooping around other people's houses. I'm sure he'd get a kick out of hearing that. Realizing that you're mad enough to think blackmail is a way out of your problems.' I saw her flinch as the word 'mad' hit home. 'I'm not the only one with secrets, Cass, am I?'

She opened her mouth, but said nothing.

'Sit down,' I said, and I saw with some satisfaction Cass subside slowly into her chair, deflating with abrupt suddenness.

I pressed home my advantage. 'Let's talk about secrets, shall we? You and your family? Your brother the hero? Are you sure you want to cast the first stone?'

'I'm sorry,' she said. 'I was only joking.' Her face had gone chalk white.

It was harsh, but she needed to be taught a lesson. 'Joking? Or were you trying to threaten me, Cass?'

She was fiddling with her hair – catching the short strands between her nails, wincing briefly as she tugged, as if testing how securely it was rooted. I wasn't sure if she was even conscious of what she was doing, although as she caught me watching she stopped, clasping her hands together in her lap.

'Were you?' I had forgotten the power of pure anger, coldly deployed. She had not expected it from me. All her cockiness was gone.

'No, I swear, I was only kidding. It was just a stupid joke.'

She would not meet my eyes, but her gaze darted back and forth, looking for an escape. I watched her breathing accelerate, grow shallower.

'If you know what's good for you, Cass, you'll just keep quiet from now on.'

I have to admit I enjoyed the way she opened her mouth but found nothing to say. Her fingers flew back to her hair. I could see the skin of her scalp distorting as she pulled at a short strand, the yank and release as it came free. Without thinking, I reached out and took her hand by the wrist, stilling it.

'You'll lose it all,' I said.

She tolerated me for a moment then pulled her hand free, standing so suddenly that the chair flew backwards with a clatter. 'Get your hands off me!'

'OK,' I said. 'OK.'

But I was talking to myself, for she had gone.

The threatened snow started that evening. Fat, soft flakes at first, mesmerizing at the window in the fading light. They settled almost instantly on the frozen ground, piling everywhere, muffling everything. I watched the snow fall until it was too dark to see and in the morning I woke to more of it. The world, bleached pale before by the frost, was now monochrome and silent and the sky heavy as lead. Even as I watched, it began to snow again, lightly but persistently.

I had not slept well. I had woken from the dream, the old dream, and then spent too long running over things in my mind. I had felt certain the day before that I had shut Cass up, but in the darkness of the night, things did not seem quite so clear. Who knew what Cass would take it in her head to do? Probably not even Cass herself. When I finally fell back to sleep I dreamt the scene with her again, over and over, playing out the variations in my mind. Then I dreamt that Grant had come round, angry and bitter, and I'd woken from that one with my heart hammering and lay for a long while, staring into the darkness. Even though I knew it was a dream, there had been enough truth in what had been said for the emotion to linger. I lay there until my watch said 7 a.m. and though there was no more light than there had been at midnight, I got up, wearier than when I had gone to bed.

It was Sunday. I had no reason to go up to the house. If Cass had said anything, I would find out soon enough. All I could do was get on with my day and wait for the blow to fall, but although I tried to work, again and again, I found my eyes drawn to the falling snow. The silence was absolute. Even Janet was inaudible through the thin wall.

By eleven I could stand it no longer. I was achieving nothing, my mind treading over the same few stale thoughts. The snow was still drifting endlessly downwards. I might as well be out in it, I decided. A walk might jolt me out of my mood. I pulled on the heaviest jacket I owned, and an extra pair of socks. My boots were not really suitable for snow, being a cheap pair that had long since lost whatever waterproofing quality they'd had, but I reasoned I would not be going far.

The cobbled yard was slippery underfoot. I had meant to walk out down the driveway and along the road – away from the house – but I realized it would be too icy for comfort, and chose the path through the grounds instead. This looked fresh, untrodden, the snow lying softly and lightly over everything. There were animal tracks, but even these were softening and fading in the falling snow, my own prints blurring behind me.

I had had no intention of going anywhere near the house, but the path skirted the edge of its lawns and I found myself pausing there, looking through the trees and bushes at its dark bulk, wondering what was going on inside. It was then that I saw Janet, moving ahead of me. The day was a gloomy one and the snow had grown heavier, but it was unmistakeably her, in her purple anorak, moving with her flat-footed stumping gait. I thought she must be making for the back door, but she did not head into the courtyard at the back but kept on going around the house. Without thinking, I started to follow her, keeping well back, sticking to the cover of the trees.

I had thought she must be going to the front door, but she did not stop there. She just trudged on, head down, the snow gathering on her hair and her shoulders. She did not look round, although she glanced from time to time at the house to her left. My feet had grown sodden, a dull chill ache settling across my toes. I had reached the edges of the tree cover and to go further I would have to walk right across the open lawn in full view of Janet, and those inside. The shutters were open, I noticed, and anybody could be lurking behind any of the windows, watching this strange promenade. I stopped where I was and watched Janet disappear around the far corner. Let her do whatever it was she was doing. I would return and dry my feet out, thaw my fingers by the fire. I turned to retrace my steps, half blinded by the snow now blowing in my face, driven by the wind.

So mesmerized was I by the dance of the snow in the air, that when the scream came it was hard to work out where it was coming from, or what it was. I stood stupidly looking around me through the trees before I fixed on the house. I ran towards the back door and in, not stopping to take off my boots. The screaming had stopped before I got inside, leaving not even an echo behind. The house was silent as the snow.

I looked in the kitchen first, but it was empty except for

Jess, turning to look at me with a dog's anxiety. The hall was empty too except for its tableaux of hares, the glass eyes staring at me in blank accusation. Then came voices sounding from above, Davey and Grant and an incoherent sound that could only be Cass.

It occurred to me then, I don't know why, just to turn around and slip away before they knew I was there. But it was too late, the voices were coming down the stairs, and the moment to escape was lost. Being caught leaving would be worse.

'Is everything all right?' I called up. 'I thought I heard someone cry out.'

Upstairs it went quiet.

'We're fine, thanks.' Grant's voice was clipped, tense.

Davey spoke over him. 'Oh well, see, that might explain it.'

The three of them appeared one by one, coming down the corner of the staircase, looking down at me. Davey, Grant, and finally Cass, frail as a snapped twig. She was wearing a man's jumper pulled on over what looked like pyjamas, her feet bare. The jumper was huge on her, stretched and frayed at the cuffs, and she looked about twelve. I met her eyes uneasily but the look she gave me was blank.

'What happened?' I asked after the silence had stretched out just that little too long.

I thought I saw Grant shake his head fractionally at Davey, but Davey ignored him. 'The wee lass thought she saw faces, peering in the windows. Gave her a fright.'

'Faces?'

'Faces, a face. The upstairs window, mind. That would give anyone a funny turn.'

'She was dreaming,' Grant said shortly.

Cass did not say anything, did not react, just kept on staring blankly down at me. Something about that blankness seemed false, willed, as if to remind me what she knew, the threat still held over my head.

'I'm sorry you've been troubled,' Grant added, but for once I didn't take the hint of dismissal in his voice.

'Whose face?' I asked Cass. She kept on looking at me, unspeaking. I saw Davey glance over at her and then back at me.

'Did you maybe see someone out there near the house?' he asked. 'While you were out on your wanders.'

'Not peering in through any windows,' I said.

Grant stirred. 'But there was someone?'

Why did I feel such a reluctance to speak? 'Only Janet,' I said at last.

'What was she doing?'

'Just walking,' I said. 'Walking round the house.'

Something passed between the two of them, Davey and Grant, something over Cass's head. They started downstairs, leaving Cass on the landing, and headed for the back door. I followed in their wake, Jess's claws clicking on the stone floor behind me as she sensed the chance to get outside. My footprints were still there, leading straight towards the door. The snow was still falling.

'Where?' Grant said. 'Where was she?'

I waved my hand across the expanse of whiteness that was the lawn. 'Somewhere there. But she was just walking, and nowhere near the windows.'

'And where were you?'

'By the trees.'

My prints were clear enough, skirting through the cover of the trees where the snow was thinner. But though we crossed the lawn, there was no sign of any other footprints going round the house.

'I saw her,' I said. 'Clear as I see you now.'

I caught another glance between Davey and Grant. What they might have said in response, I don't know. But we heard a faint noise, barely a cry, and turned to see Cass out in the snow with Jess. The girl was hanging on to the dog's collar, the dog was straining forward. They were both right in the middle of the lawn, the place where I'd first seen Janet, as far as I could tell in the disorienting blankness of the snow. As we came over I could see that the dog's hackles were raised and it was growling the same low menacing growl as when I had first encountered Davey.

'Look,' Cass said faintly. 'Look, look, look, and they're going round widdershins.' She was breathing in accelerating gasps, succumbing to a fit of hysterics. I didn't see immediately what she was pointing at in the snow for I was concentrating on trying to get her to calm down, to breathe slowly, all in vain. She was shuddering all over, trembling or shivering or both. Her fingers lost their grip on the dog's collar and Jess raced away, flattened against the ground, a streak of black and white. It was only then that I saw what Cass had been talking about, what Grant and Davey were looking at in such silence. Nothing but the track of a hare's footprints, clear against the snow.

The strangest thing was the way that nobody would talk about it. At first, we were too caught up in the immediate concern of getting Cass indoors, calmed down, warmed up. Davey simply picked her up – her feet were still bare – and set her down in front of the kitchen fire. Her shuddering subsided gradually, but she would say nothing further, shaking her head and closing her eyes, whatever I asked her. Eventually Grant led her upstairs with a hot-water bottle and came back down alone.

'She gets like this,' was all he said. 'She'll be better in the morning.' I saw Davey glance up at him, a shadow of doubt on his face.

'It was Janet I saw,' I said.

'I'm sure it was,' Grant said.

'If we looked properly, we'd find her footprints.'

I thought I saw another look pass between him and Davey. 'It doesn't matter,' Grant said.

'Well, but what was she doing?' I pressed, and this time got no response. 'Don't you think it's a little odd?' I appealed to Davey but he just shrugged, looked around him – anywhere, it seemed, but at me.

'I wonder where that dog's got to,' he said. 'Normally she'd be back by now, wanting in.'

'She'll be fine,' Grant said, but Davey was standing already.

'I'll just away out and give her a wee shout,' he said. 'I'll no be long.'

'Wait, don't, you'll never find her –' Grant was halfway to the door after him, stopping to turn and look at me with something like panic in his eyes.

'It's all right, I'm leaving,' I said. 'I just wanted to know if you still want me to come round as usual tomorrow. If Cass is likely to be up to it.'

'Oh Lord. I'd forgotten about that.' If anything, his discomfort had redoubled. 'Look, don't worry about it for now. I'll let you know, OK?'

'I don't mind popping round, just to keep her company,' I said.

'I'll let you know, OK? I mean, obviously we'll pay you anyway, don't worry about that.'

He could not have been more dismissive if he'd slapped me. 'That's hardly necessary,' I said. I put my cup down in the sink, keeping my back turned until I was master of my own expression. When I looked back his face was flushed, his eyes anywhere but on me. I could see myself saying something I might later regret, so I left, saying nothing at all, grateful for the sting of cold air against the heat of my face.

Janet's light was on when I got back to the cottages. A little square of yellow, almost cheerful in the stark landscape of the snow. I paused, hovering outside my own door. All I had to do was knock and she would come to the door, ordinary in her slippers and her buttoned cardigan, just another older woman with nothing on her mind but what to have for her tea. I could simply ask her what she had been doing, circling the house like that, where she had gone to. Why didn't I? I didn't know then, and I don't know now. I know only that the thought of it filled my stomach with a clench of something: anxiety, fear even. The closed door, the lighted window, repelled me. I told myself I didn't want her to think I made a habit of spying on her and withdrew, switching on my own lights to beat out their fitful defiance against the gloominess of the day.

What daylight there was had almost gone before I ventured out again. I was stiff from sitting at the computer, cold even with the heating on, turned up full blast. The evening would be endless if I didn't get out, get some exercise. I would stay away from the house, away from any possibility of bumping into anyone. I would walk myself weary, and that way maybe sleep would come.

The cottage door opened oddly, a soft heaviness that made me wonder if snow had piled up against it. But it was not snow that was weighting the door, but a hare, dead, its back legs mangled. I stood staring stupidly at it and could not shake the idea that it was the one that I had failed to dispatch, somehow come back to accuse me. I did not stop to think further, but slammed the door shut and locked it, drawing the bolts too. Then I leaned back against the wall, fighting nausea. I could not get the image from my mind. The dead hare was still out there, waiting for me to open the door. I would have to deal with it, but I couldn't just then. Not in the fading afternoon, the gathering shadows waiting around me. I would do it in the morning, in the light of day.

Chapter 15

I WOKE THE next morning to a chill that pervaded every-where, sending its fingers under the covers, pulled in with every breath of air. It was dark outside, dark inside. My watch said seven, the luminous hands standing out sharp against the blackness. I huddled further under the covers and waited for the whumpf of the heating starting up before attempting anything more. Nothing came. I lay in the half-daze between sleep and wakefulness and watched the edges of the curtains lighten gradually to grey. It was still silent and cold.

The room was full of dawn shadows by the time I could put it off no longer and got out of bed. I reached for the light but the click of the switch did nothing. I hurried myself into some clothes and went to have a look. None of the lights worked, although the fuse box was fine. Power cut then. The boiler sat mute, needing electricity to work its pump. I could see my breath in the kitchen air, and when I pulled open the curtains ice was flowering inside the panes, the usual pools of condensation frozen solid along the bottom. The snow outside was a pale shadow through the filigree of ice. The day was dawning lurid pink above it.

I was kneeling, attempting to light the fire, when the knock at the door came. I went to answer it, confused when the door didn't open as I turned the latch. It was only after a further knock that I remembered my fears the night before and hurriedly fumbled with the lock and the bolts, unaccustomed to such defences. Davey stood on the doorstep in his shirt-sleeves, apparently oblivious to the cold.

'Are you all right?' he said. 'Grant sent me down to fetch you.'

'I'm fine,' I said. 'I'm lighting the fire. I'll be fine.' Even as I said it, I knew that I was lying, that the fire would do little to warm the room, that I would not even be able to comfort myself with a cup of tea. The thought of the big kitchen, the Aga, other people – even Grant, humiliating though it might be – was tempting.

'You won't be. It's minus five, and it's getting colder. Half the valley has lost its power, and it's all the way into town. They say it might be days.'

'Days . . .' Pride fought with practicality, but it didn't matter because Davey wasn't really asking, he was telling.

'Grab your stuff, some clothes, and come up. I'll drain your pipes before they freeze and burst.' He stepped in, and I couldn't help but glance at the doorstep where the hare had been, but there was nothing to be seen, not even a trace of any blood. He must have cleared it up before he knocked, and I was grateful to him beyond measure.

I gave up any pretence of reluctance and hurried to get my clothes. He whistled while he worked on the plumbing, a cheery background noise that filled the chill of the cottage with a sort of warmth.

'Where's Jess?' I asked from the bedroom as I gathered

together my warmest clothes. The whistling stopped abruptly and I emerged and looked at him.

'She's no come back. I couldnae find her.'

'That's a bit worrying, isn't it?'

He gave me a flat look and said nothing further. The chill of the air outside hit our faces and made me fumble my keys as I locked up. I looked across at the other cottage, up at its chimney. There was no smoke, no sign of life.

'What about Janet? She can't stay there either.'

'Good point,' Davey said. We looked at each other for a while, neither of us sure what to do. 'No, you're right,' he said at last.

Still, we hesitated before I knocked on the door and we stood there waiting. I was starting to hope that she was out, had found herself some other haven – even though her car still stood outside the door – when we heard the slide of bolts and the door cracked open. She was wearing her anorak and a woollen hat. She said nothing, just waited for us to speak.

'We were wondering if you wanted to come up to the main house, where it's a bit warmer. Just till the power's back on,' I said.

'Oh aye,' she said, looking at Davey and then back at me. 'Awfy big of you, handing out the invites to the big house. This come from the laird and master himself, did it?'

'You can't stay here,' I said. 'What if it's off all day, and overnight? You'll freeze.'

'Will I now?' she stared me out, then shifted her glance to Davey. 'Got that daft bitch of yours under control yet?'

'Jess is fine.'

'Oh aye, the dog too. It was out running wild the other day.

If they catch it at the sheep, they'll have it shot, you know. They'll no wait till they lose one. Blam. Shoot first, ask questions later.' She smiled at him, almost sweetly, and turned back to me. 'You can tell those Hendersons that I'm grateful for their concern – if they ever actually were concerned, though I have my doubts. But I'll no freeze and I'll no starve, and I've no need for their charity, thank you very much.'

The door slammed shut. 'Well, that's us tellt,' Davey said.

I hadn't realized how chilled I had become until we opened the door into the kitchen in the main house and were hit by the wave of warm air. I was relieved to see that Cass was up, albeit still in her dressing gown, standing at the Aga boiling a kettle and making toast on the hotplate. She glanced up when I came in, and smiled, but said nothing. Grant, seated by the fire, smiled in greeting so naturally that for a moment I forgot everything except my pleasure at being in comfort once more, and able to sink down in my normal place with a hot cup of tea between my hands.

There was no sign of Jess, though. I saw the drop of Davey's shoulders as he took in the room, as if he had been hoping that she would be there waiting for him. He took his tea standing up, peering up and out at the window, going to the back door again and again to see if she might have returned.

'You're letting the draught in,' Grant complained, as he returned for the third or fourth time. 'That dog will be fine. She's holed up somewhere, or found someone to take her in, or else she's having the time of her life hunting rabbits.'

'Aye, you're likely right,' Davey said, but he didn't sit down and he didn't stop his glances up at the window.

Cass made the last round of toast and brought it to the table, stacking it up on a plate and then offering it to us with a gesture, hands open, palms out. I was struck by the self-conscious eloquence of it, and thinking back, I realized she had said nothing since I had come in. There had been such a clatter of plates and cups and greetings that her silence hadn't really stood out, except that Cass could usually be guaranteed to talk over everything and everyone. She sat down now at the table, straight-backed and self-contained, hands folded in her lap. Another role she was playing, I guessed.

With some reluctance, Grant and I dragged ourselves away from the fire and settled at the table to join her.

'You've not seen Jess, have you, Cass?' I asked.

She shrugged and shook her head and caught my eye with something that might have been a challenge. I glanced across at Grant. He shook his head slightly.

Davey, too distracted to notice, went again to the back door. We could hear him calling, and then the slam of the door as he went out.

'He loves that dog,' Grant said. Cass just smiled.

'In this cold, I'm surprised she stayed out,' I said.

'Well, that's dogs for you. Totally irrational,' Grant said easily. He finished his toast and Cass stood up again, her hand out for his plate, and then mine. I watched him watch her walk to the sink. 'You're making me feel cold, Cass,' he said. 'Go and put some clothes on. The bedrooms are pretty arctic,' he added to me. 'Hot-water bottles all round and extra blankets, I'm afraid.'

'I'm very grateful that you've offered at all.'

'Well, of course. Bit of an adventure really. No power, snowed in. It's fine if you've got a source of heat and can huddle round. We'll have to get the candles out and play Monopoly or something in the evening.' He was still watching Cass, his mind clearly barely on what he was saying as she rinsed off the plates and dabbed around the counters ineffectually with a cloth. Eventually she drifted out of the room. 'Best if we don't make a fuss about it,' he said. 'The not speaking thing. It's happened before.'

'Is that what the doctor says?'

'Oh well, doctors.'

'You haven't spoken to her GP?'

'Bit soon for that. And in this weather. Besides, the chap's a bit of an idiot, frankly. He wasn't much use last time.'

He stood up, the gesture signalling that was the end of the matter. I could do nothing else but stand up too, fetching my bag from where I had left it in the doorway, going to find my room. I moved through the shadowy darkness of the house, familiar now, my eyes adapted to the gloom. Someone – Cass? – had made the bed up already and piled it with woollen blankets, slightly moth-eaten. I folded back the shutters and the daylight crept in. The snow was still clinging to the branches of the trees, too cold to melt. There was no sign of life outside.

Cass had slipped quietly into the room beside me, her hand creeping out to take me by the crook of my elbow. I wanted to say something – my mouth was open to say it – but I didn't. Perhaps Grant was right, and making a big deal about her silence would be counterproductive. I was surprised to see that she had her schoolwork folder in her other hand and she led me downstairs to settle at the kitchen table, getting out her papers and pen, meekly bending her head over the previously despised coursework.

Grant had been right about one thing – the missing dog aside, at first it all felt like a bit of an adventure. Dougie joined us halfway through the morning, his face bright red from the cold, banging his hands together to warm them. 'Came on the quad bike, over the fields,' he said. 'It's the only way you can move. There must be three cars in the ditches down at the village. Old John Sturgeon slipped and broke his hip trying to post a letter and they had to take him out on a tractor. The main road's like an ice rink, it's pure bumper cars down there. Even the snow plough came off on a bend, apparently, and totalled a gritting lorry.' He rubbed his hands together and beamed.

'Are you and Kirsty all right in the farmhouse?' Grant asked.

'Oh aye. Right as rain. Got the genny if we need it. Got the wood burner going, had bacon and eggs this morning, stuck the pan right in it. Best breakfast I ever had. We'll no freeze and we'll no starve.'

I was struck by the echo of Janet's words and wondered anew how she was. But we had done our best by her, and she had made her own decision.

'Where's Davey?' Dougie asked.

'Out looking for that dog,' Grant said. 'She's been missing

since yesterday morning, went after a rabbit and not been seen since.'

'The wee border cross? That's no good in this weather.' Dougie had stopped beaming now. 'I'll maybe go out and help him look.'

Something in his concern affected us all, and we ended up all going out, piling into our coats and boots and hats, even Cass. Without discussion, we split up and spread out, and I ended up walking past my cottage, which already looked as if it had been abandoned forever. The sky was blank and sullen, promising another snowfall. Every so often a branch would shed a load of snow with a soft detonation, but otherwise everything was still.

In a monochrome world, something caught my eye, the merest dot of scarlet. I remembered the mangled hare, and wondered whether after all a dog might not have found it, have carried it off to consume in privacy. Another dot caught my eye, and then another, hard to make out against a jumble of blown and trodden snow. I could see no clear prints, but I followed the faint trail, past Janet's cottage, around behind the barn where I had once hid.

The dog lay in the snow bank the way she used to like to lie stretched out before the fire. One ear was even half cocked, as if she had heard Davey's voice in conversation and was waiting for his command. I thought at first she might even be asleep, for there was no obvious sign of violence. Black and white, she merged into the black and white of the landscape and I was close up before I saw the blood in the fur around her muzzle, rusty brown and brighter red, and the way her head lay, twisted as if by great force. Her eyes were half open and dulled, all life gone. The snow had restarted and was settling on her body, flake by flake. My first irrational thought was that she must be cold.

I turned to go and find the others, but Davey was already there behind me. In one movement he was kneeling down, his hands bare in the snow.

'I'm sorry,' I said. He said nothing, only cradled the dog and buried his face in her fur.

'What could have happened to her?' I asked, but I might as well not have spoken for all the impression it made. I had to help him as he staggered to his feet, his arms still tight around the dog's body. Her head lolled horribly, even though the rest of her body had stiffened with cold and death. I could not shake the impression that someone or something had pulled it half off.

Davey started towards the house, and I hurried in his wake. Kirsty was trudging up the ice-bound track of the drive, carrying a bright red blanket as if she were bringing supplies to the wounded. She gave it to him without hesitation to wrap the body in.

'What happened?' she asked.

Davey jerked his head towards the two cottages, Janet's and mine, side by side like partners in crime.

'She said something would happen to Jess,' he said.

'She can't have known, though,' I said.

The look he gave me was blank, almost hostile. For a long moment I thought he might hammer on Janet's door demanding answers, but he set off again and Kirsty and I followed. As we headed along the path back to the house the others found us, falling in with our little impromptu funeral cortege. First Cass, and then Grant and Dougie coming down from the woods around the back. Davey laid the dog down gently by the woodpile, still wrapped in the blanket. The rest of us hesitated for a moment then went inside, leaving him out there with his hand still resting on her head, saying a final goodbye.

We were still thawing out when Grant, clearing the table for lunch, noticed the container of chicken feed and the empty egg basket.

'Cass, did you do the hens?' he asked sharply. She looked evasive. 'Oh, come on, I give you one responsibility and you don't even do that. They desperately need food in this weather, you know that. And the chances are their water will be frozen too. What were you thinking?'

Cass threw her arms out in an exaggerated teenage gesture of exasperation.

'I'll go,' I said quickly, seizing the chance to make myself useful, and to get away from the house. For all its size, the kitchen was beginning to feel crowded. Kirsty and Dougie had stayed and she was bustling around helping with the lunch preparations, and somehow I always managed to be standing where she needed to be next. What little conversation there was kept drying up; even Dougie lapsed into an abstracted silence.

'It's Cass's job, really,' Grant said.

'I don't mind.'

'Have a look for some eggs, although you'll be lucky. They've pretty much stopped laying for the winter.'

I hurried out with the scoop of feed in one hand and the

egg basket crooked in my elbow. At the back door, I hesitated. My boots were damp with melted snow and I did not fancy putting them on again having only just warmed up my feet. Easier just to slip into Cass's wellingtons, left higgledy-piggledy beside the door. They looked too big for me, but they would do for the short walk up to the hens. The path up to the enclosure was already trodden with a muddle of tracks, and was slippery underfoot in my borrowed boots. The temperature had dropped further in the short time we had been indoors and the cold was relentless, pressing against my face. Once more I was struck by how the snow made the silence absolute, even the sound of running water frozen now to a standstill. Not a bird sang and not a creature moved.

Shoving my free hand into my pocket for warmth, I found something there and pulled it out to have a look, turning it in my numb fingers. No more than a twig, a few pale leaves, a shrivelled berry. A rowan sprig, just like the one Ann had retrieved from the ditch – perhaps the same one. I had no memory of where I had got it from, whether she had given it to me. I was not the sort of person who would have put it in my pocket for luck. I looked at it, thinking I should just discard it, and yet I didn't. I was still turning it absently in my fingers as I pushed open the gate to the walled garden.

Immediately I was struck by a sense of déjà vu – the silence, unbroken by the crooning of the hens, each bird just a heap of feathers lying where it had fallen. Only this time they were white hens in the white snow, their combs like spatters of blood. And this time there was no Cass, and no footprints, for the snow had erased everything, smoothing it over like the tide smooths a beach, leaving only shadows of what was there.

I set down the basket and the grain and rushed back through the gate, thinking for a moment that I should get help, as if there might still be something to be done. But there was nothing and nobody and I did something then which I can't explain, even now. I went back into the enclosure and picked up my basket and the scoop of grain, and scattered the feed around in the snow just as I might have done had the birds been alive. I even went over to the hen house and checked the nest boxes for eggs and smashed the ice on the frozen drinking container so that I left them fed and watered as if I were expecting them to spring back into life the minute my back was turned. And when I returned to the house and the kitchen with my empty egg basket and my empty scoop I said nothing, not even when I glanced across the room and met Cass's eyes, the ghost of a question forming in her gaze.

That night I crept up to my bed by candlelight, past the jumping shadows of the hares in their cases. The evening had been sombre, Kirsty and Dougie gone, the rest of us left with our own thoughts beside the fire. There was no sign of the power being restored. By common consent we turned in early. My room smelled of long-closed air and damp and the sheets on the bed were cold as the grave. I lay curled around the small space of warmth that the hot-water bottle afforded, grateful for the weight of the piled blankets, tucking them close around my shoulders. The air in my nostrils was sharp with cold. The house settled around me with its own symphony of noises – sighs and creaks, the scuffling of mice in the walls.

I did not think I slept but I woke in the night to a soft noise and a shift in the quality of the darkness. I had not closed the shutters and the window was a grey shape, the door another, an area of less-dark than the surrounding walls. It took me a moment to orient myself, remembering where I was. It took me a moment longer to realize someone else was breathing in the room.

'Who's there?' I asked, half raising my head. The only answer was the door closing and a soft weight landing on the side of the bed, no heavier than a cat. No words. I heard the drop of a dressing gown sliding to the floor and then the covers lifted and Cass got in beside me with feet like ice. 'Are you all right? I don't think . . .'

Her only response was to shuffle herself in more firmly to the middle of the bed, turning her back to me and curling up so that I was forced to turn and curl myself around her, one arm over her ribcage. She caught up my hand in her own and held it there, shivering like a dog. Then gradually she warmed, relaxed, and fell asleep, leaving me awake in the darkness.

I must have dozed off for when I awoke again I was still lying on my side on the edge of the bed, my hand on something satiny smooth. I shifted and felt softness, the yielding brush of fur. I snatched it back and sat up, blinking in the dim light of morning. It was the hare in the green dress, its back turned, its head on the pillow beside mine, and Cass was gone.

CHAPTER 16

I HAD SLEPT late. It was daylight, but fog was pressing hard at the windows, the outside world vanished. The ice had spread its flowers right across the inside of the panes and showed no sign of melting. I hurried to wash and dress, grateful for the gushing hot water from the tap in the little sink by the window. I pushed the stuffed hare under my bed, resolving to deal with it later. Whatever games Cass was playing, I didn't want to exacerbate the situation. Down in the kitchen she greeted me with the faintest of smiles, still silent. She passed me a cup of tea and went back to making toast on the Aga. She and Grant were both wearing fleeces, and after a minute or two I went and got mine as well. Even in the kitchen it was too cold to be sitting around for long.

'Apparently some important piece of kit blew somewhere and it's all gone belly up across the county,' Grant said, coming off the phone. 'No power back for at least a day.'

'Is that the official word from the electricity company?' I asked.

'No, but almost as authoritative. I've just been speaking to Helen. She's been raising it at the highest level, as only Helen can. I can only imagine they're holding a special board meeting now to address the crisis.'

Davey came in, dressed for work, and silently began lacing his boots.

'You're not going out in this?' I asked.

'Dykes'll no build themselves,' he said shortly, and went out with a bang of the door.

'Let him go,' Grant said. 'Work's a great therapy.'

Cass and I settled down to another fruitless morning until I tired of the sound of my own voice and freed her to crouch in the hallway in fingerless gloves, sketching the hares. She paid no attention to the missing one, but settled beside the school tableau, and I left her to it.

'How long can she keep this up?' I asked Grant. 'The not speaking.'

'Who knows? She went a month, last time, but that was our fault, making her the centre of attention. Doctors, shrinks. She'll get bored of it.'

'But she must have been traumatized? Do you think the trauma is coming out again? You can't just leave her to fester.'

'I've hardly any choice at the moment. And besides, the shrinks know nothing, absolutely nothing.'

He had his back to me, chopping carrots, preparing a pot of soup for lunch. I was leaning against the Aga, holding what seemed like my tenth cup of tea that morning. The light was filtered, grey, the kitchen a place of shadows.

'Something must have triggered it,' I pressed.

'You tell me,' he said, and it might have been a throwaway remark, except that the knife had stopped and he was clearly waiting for an answer.

'I have no idea,' I replied. 'Maybe it was that business with the face at the window. That was about when it started, wasn't it?'

'No. It was before then. She came back from somewhere on Saturday wound like a spring. Wouldn't say anything but silly nonsense. I thought she must have been over with you.'

'She was, but she was full of nonsense with me too,' I said, as lightly as I could manage. Grant turned and looked at me with level eyes. I felt myself prick with sweat, my mouth grow dry. Nonsense could mean anything or everything. It could be Grant's polite way of letting me know that she had carried out her threat to tell him what she knew. I did not rise to it, and in the end it was he who looked away first, turning back to the task at hand.

'I just thought something might have set her off. Something trivial.'

'Like what?'

'Being asked to keep a secret. Or told to keep her mouth shut.'

'It's not as if Cass ever does anything she's told, though.'

'No, true.' He turned to face me, smiling, but he was still waiting for an answer. 'It's just . . .' he trailed off, then put the knife down. 'Look, I don't think it would be anyone's fault if they'd said something that might – as you put it – have triggered this. It could have been done completely innocently. But I think it would help if Cass knew that it hadn't really meant anything. You know, that it was just a throwaway remark.'

Could it really be that simple? That all I had to do was shrug and mention that yes, I had told Cass to keep her mouth shut in a moment of frustration but that I hadn't meant it literally and we could all laugh and return to normal – or what passed for normal for Cass, anyway. But that would only mean more explanations, complications. And Grant would not laugh, not if he learned everything I had been concealing. The last shreds of the esteem he held for me would be stripped away. Cass had been right about one thing: I could stand being pitied by Grant, but not despised by him.

'Even if it seems ridiculous to you, it might not to Cass,' he said. His eyes were on mine, waiting, open, all encouragement.

Just then a memory came into my head, clear and vivid, conjured up before my eyes. Not the Saturday, but before that, weeks before. Not Cass, but Janet, waiting for me in her doorway, the dusk, her smirking face. It was ridiculous, and yet I felt my scalp tightening at the memory of her words. One could not harm someone simply by wishing them ill, and yet perhaps that concentrated malice had to go somewhere, could leak out through word and gesture, tipping an already unstable girl over the edge.

I almost didn't say anything. I opened my mouth, then shut it again.

'What?' he asked.

'Just something Janet said,' I finally replied. 'A while back. It can't be that, though. Cass wasn't even there.'

'What happened?'

'Just Janet threatening her. Saying something would shut her up one of these days. Once and for all.'

My words sounded stark, too stark. I had not meant it to come out with quite such a ring of melodrama. Certainly I would have held my tongue if I had noticed, if either of us had noticed, Cass's presence in the doorway. She did not make a sound as she fainted, nothing except a soft thump as she hit the floor.

You can tell the genuine fainters, in my experience, because they are invariably inelegant. There's nothing glamorous about losing consciousness, nor about regaining it. Cass came to shaking and moaning, a moaning that stopped the moment she opened her eyes and registered our presence. Then she clamped her lips together and squeezed her eyes shut and went limp again, faking it this time. She was rag-doll floppy when I tried to sit her upright.

'Come on Cass, you only fainted,' I said. Her shoulders felt birdlike beneath the thick wool of her jumper. I was visited by the memory, almost physical, of her in my bed, each rib distinct. Was she even eating? I had seen her around food, making it for others, holding it in her hands. But when I cast my mind back I could not recall when I had last seen her taking a single bite herself.

I left her propped awkwardly between the door and the arm of the sofa, her head still flopped sideways. I took the tea I had been drinking, still warm, and stirred in sugar, then wrapped her two hands around the mug. She had not moved.

'You can drop this if you like, but it will just end up in your lap if you do,' I said, and caught the flash of life in her face, the acknowledgement behind closed eyes. I pulled my hands away and waited. She held on to the mug. 'And I'm expecting you to drink it.'

Was that a smile? She did not open her eyes, but she lifted the tea to her lips. She wrinkled her nose at the first taste of sugar, but swallowed the first mouthful, and once she had started she gulped it down. Only when the mug was empty did she open her eyes.

'The magic of tea,' Grant said weakly. He looked suddenly young, and out of his depth. I felt the gratitude in his eyes and it was something, a small step towards repairing the friendship between us.

'When did you last eat, Cass?' I asked her. She looked away and shrugged. 'Of course you're going to faint if you don't eat,' I said.

'Ah no, not that,' Grant said. 'She's always had a healthy appetite, haven't you, Cass? Never had much time for the eating disorder crowd.'

It's true, she didn't seem the type, lacking the rigid discipline it takes to maintain anorexia. But perhaps she had closed her mouth to more than just speech.

Or had it closed for her.

I pushed the thought aside as absurd, but it lingered. Although I was taking pains to conceal it from Grant, I too felt out of my depth, that there was more going on than just a disturbed and slightly histrionic teenage girl. The kitchen no longer felt like a cosy sanctuary, and it seemed as if there was more than just cold out there beyond its walls.

I left the pair of them and went upstairs, thinking it might be an opportunity to replace the hare in the green dress before Grant noticed its absence. I didn't want to add to the feeling of inexplicable things going on that was beginning to prey on all our minds. Although it was the middle of the day, it felt darker upstairs than in the kitchen, the corridors barely lit by the daylight filtering through the snow on the skylight above the stairs. Once in my bedroom, I could not find the hare; it had gone from under my bed and was nowhere in the room that I could see. After spending far longer searching for it than made sense, I gave up and went back out into the dim corridor. I had grown chilled again, hunched and tense against the cold, looking forward to thawing out beside the kitchen fire.

I barely caught the movement the first time, right at the far end of the opposite corridor. I registered only a sense of someone being there, someone who froze as I froze, and who was watching me now even as I peered into the shadows concealing them. I could see nobody and I shook my head, thinking I must have imagined it, and started down the corridor again. This time the movement was unmistakeable. Janet. It had been Janet, still in her coat, stumping towards me, not even trying to hide her presence.

I opened my mouth but my challenge died in my throat. My heart pounded, loud as footsteps in my ears. What was she doing here, sneaking around? What designs did she have on us? Still though she was, I could feel her watching me. Before I could think better of it, I darted forward with no real plan in mind other than confrontation. But she wasn't there. The corridor beyond the stairs was empty, and so were each of the rooms off it. She had been there, right in front of me, and then she was gone and I could not explain it, except that I was somehow going mad.

Below I could hear the sounds of the household, carrying on as usual – the rising alarm of the kettle coming to the boil, the thunk of a piece of wood being thrown on the fire. They ought to have felt comforting, these little reminders of normality, but in my shaken mood they only left me feeling more unsettled. I stood with my hand at my throat, waiting for my breathing to return to normal. It took an effort of will to turn my back on that empty, menacing corridor and return downstairs as if nothing had happened.

Cass ate the soup, under Grant's watchful eye. I took some down to Davey, a thermos of it, and some bread, needing the excuse to get out of the house and stretch my legs. I took the shortcut through the forest, where the snow was lighter, just a powdery dusting filtered by the overhanging branches. The fog had lingered and had frozen onto everything it touched, coating each twig and branch, each needle on every tree. The forest was spectral with it. The trees appeared and disappeared like ghosts as the mist shifted around me. It was a relief to emerge out into the relative normality of the crossroads and see Davey standing there.

He had almost finished the wall. The gap now was no wider than a few stones and I thought at first that he was standing back and admiring his work, but as I approached he put a hand up and then a finger to his lips and returned his eyes to where he had been looking, deeper into the frozen forest. I moved towards him as stealthily as I could and followed his gaze, but I could see nothing.

'Only roe deer,' he breathed. 'But they're so close.'

Even knowing what I was looking for, it took me an age before I saw the first one, its eye fixed on mine, still as a held breath. It was no more than a few yards away. The second one was even closer, betrayed by a flick of its ears and the whisper of a branch beneath a shifting hoof. Two more stood head on, further out among the trees. They seemed to vanish as you took your eyes off them, only to be found again by the angle of a leg, the dark liquid glance of an eye.

'It's the wall. They sense it's between us now, and they'll come closer,' Davey said. 'And they're hungry too.'

We watched until something broke their nerve and with a sudden crashing they were gone, no more than bounding white tails between the shadows of the trees. I smiled in pure delight and Davey smiled back, the first time I'd seen him smiling since Jess had gone.

'They'd no come near with Jess about,' he said, as if he'd read my mind.

'You'll miss her.'

'Aye well. She was just a dog,' he said unconvincingly. 'That's what folk say, anyway.'

I gave him the soup and was ready to return, but he detained me. 'Hang about a minute if you'd like. I'm almost done here.'

He worked swiftly, slotting in the last remaining stones, but I was still frozen from standing watching by the time the wall was completed. It looked stark and hard against the softness of the snow, solid where everything else seemed lost in the swirling fog.

'Bravo,' I said, because it seemed something needed to be said.

He pulled from his pocket a small flat bottle, whisky, its colour warm against the world of whites and greys. 'Mark the occasion,' he said, twisting off the cap and handing it to me.

It was harsh in my mouth, flooding my senses. He laughed at my expression and took a swig of his own, then trickled some over the wall.

'Got to be done,' he said, and handed me the bottle once more. The second mouthful seemed easier, mellower, sweeter almost. I forgot the deadening cold spreading up from my feet. He took a bigger swallow, grinned, poured another helping over the stones. My third swig was almost welcome though the tears sprang to my eyes as it hit the back of my throat and it was all I could do not to splutter. He tipped his head back to take his last drink, then tucked the bottle – still with a finger of liquid in the bottom of it – into a chink in the wall and patted it.

'That whisky'll be gone by morning, I can guarantee it,' he said. 'Taken and the lid screwed tight. Always the same.'

I was seized by the urge to laugh, but Davey looked deadly serious.

'Come on,' I said. 'Who'd take it here?'

'Nobody. That's exactly it. There's nobody to take it, and yet it's always gone. But that's what you do, give them a wee dram to keep them sweet.'

'Who though?'

He shrugged and I sensed that he didn't care if I believed him or not. He unscrewed the thermos and looked inside. 'Have you had any yourself? There's loads here.'

I had hurried off without eating and he could see it in my face. 'Away and sit in the van out the cold. I've a couple of pieces with me an all, we can have ourselves a feast.'

The van still smelled of dog. We sat and stared at the wall through the windscreen and the soup was warm and welcome and it was a companionable sort of a meal, in its own way. In the end, my tongue loosened by the alcohol, I said, 'So it's a kind of blessing then, the whisky? A sacrifice?'

He was chewing on his sandwich and for a long time he didn't answer. Eventually he said, 'I'd no call it that. Insurance maybe.'

'Against what? Another accident?'

A second long pause. 'Accident. Aye, well, I suppose you could call it that.'

'Well, what then?'

He gave me a look and even through the whisky buzz I knew I'd get no proper answer. I had finished my half of the soup and was thinking about starting the walk back before he spoke again.

'I've got her in the back.'

'Who?' I asked, stupidly.

'Jess. The ground's rock hard and I cannae bury her. I couldnae stand to see her just put out for the bin men to take away. I thought I'd build her a wee cairn out here. Keep her from the scavengers.'

All I could see of him was his weather-beaten profile, and the dip at his neck where his shirt opened and the paler skin appeared in the hollow of his throat.

'Oh, Davey,' I said.

He shrugged. 'You'd think it would be safer loving a dog. At least you know they'll love you back. But that's gone too now. The dog and all.'

I left him to his melancholy task and walked back through the fading afternoon, still feeling slightly drunk. The day felt dislocated, out of kilter. The thought of going back to the house filled me with a mild oppression. By the time I got to the grounds the light was already going, the short afternoon all but over. The mist still hung through the trees like a ghost.

I didn't notice Grant until I was almost upon him. He stood with his back to me, shadowy between the trees, still as the deer, peering down the barrel of a gun. He was aiming somewhere beyond the woods, into the open ground beyond. Startled, I took a step backwards and he heard me and looked up, his face unreadable. All the vulnerability I had seen in him earlier in the kitchen was burned away, and there was a hardness there, even as he granted me a mocking smile.

'It's all right,' he said. 'It's just an air rifle. I'm hunting wabbits.'

He handed the rifle to me and I took it without thinking. The weight of it in my hands was surprising.

'Be careful with it, it's loaded,' he said. 'I suppose I should have warned you I would be out. You'd be hard pressed to kill someone with one of these, but all the same, best to be safe.'

I found myself squinting down the sight.

'You look like you know what you're doing,' he said.

'Haven't a clue, I'm afraid.'

'I imagine you'd be quite a good shot.'

'What makes you say that?' I asked.

'Well, unlike Cass, I expect you wouldn't close your eyes before pulling the trigger,' he said. 'Could you hit that rabbit?'

It took me a moment before I could see it, crouched in the snow-covered grass beyond the trees, quite still.

'The gun's pretty accurate. I've just zeroed the sight,' he said in an undertone.

It was cold against my hands, cold against my cheek. I would have thought the creature would take fright at our voices but it remained where it was. I had it framed in the sight, caught right in the crosshairs.

'They're a terrible pest, rabbits,' Grant said. 'Especially in a hard winter like this one. They go for the young trees; the poor things don't stand a chance.'

It wasn't a rabbit, though. Even I could see that. A rabbit would have scampered off already. It was a hare, pressed low against the ground, its great long ears flattened against its back. Its eyes seemed to meet mine through the scope.

My finger was on the trigger. I could feel the cold of the metal sinking in through my skin. I felt no nervousness at holding a weapon, my heartbeat steady as a rock. I had never shot a living thing in my life, and yet I felt the urge to do so now, to see if I could do it. Grant was beside me, only an inch between us. I could feel his eyes on me, as if he were urging me on, but I did not turn to look. I narrowed the world until it was just me and the waiting hare. I had only to choose my moment and then fire.

What stopped me? I still don't know. Only that a memory came to me out of the blue, of Ann, her face grave and yet kind, her hand restraining mine from some over-hasty act. A memory almost vision-like in its vividness, that brought with it – not disapproval, but disappointment that I had almost given in to the atavistic urge to destroy this creature simply because it was in my power. I let the barrel drop, shaking my head, handing back the gun.

'It was a hare,' I said. 'It wasn't a rabbit.'

Grant seemed unsurprised. 'Oh well,' he said. We watched

the animal lope away, unhurried against the snow. 'I really came out just to clear my head, I suppose.'

'How's Cass?' I asked.

'Oh, you know. The same.'

'What are you going to do about it?' Even as the words came out of my mouth I wondered if I'd overstepped the mark, too emboldened by the whisky to read the boundaries any more. He lifted his chin, but then sighed, rubbing his forehead. He looked startlingly young again, all the hardness falling away in a way that made my heart ache.

'I don't know. I just don't know.'

'You really should talk to your GP if it continues. Get her referred.'

'No.' His reply was so firm, it was almost a shout. I must have looked startled because he went on. 'You don't know – you can't know – what things were like before. The doctors are no use. They're just no bloody use. We're on our own. Me, Cass – and you.'

In a gesture that seemed entirely unrehearsed, entirely natural, he turned to me, hands open, bringing me into his circle. Then we walked back to the dark house together through the dusk.

That night I woke again and thought for a moment that the power had come on, for the room seemed flooded with light. The door to the hallway was partly ajar and the light poured in, cool and ethereal. I got up and realized it was just the moon, risen high overhead, shining through the glass roof above the landing, filling the house with moonlight. All was still and quiet, but I was seized by an urge to share this moment with somebody, anybody. Without thinking, I stopped by Cass's door, pushing it gently open. Her room, unshuttered, was bathed in the same light. Her bed was empty, the covers flung back, the sheets like snow in the moonlight. In the silence of the sleeping house, in that unearthly light, I could not shake off the feeling that she had been spirited away.

part four

witch trial

THEY WEREN'T LOOKING for a witch hunt, the head said. A witch hunt, after all, presupposes that there's nobody actually guilty at all, at least in these enlightened days. Nor, presumably, were they looking for a witch trial, a byword for travesties of justice, of duckings and drownings, superstition gone wild. Although, in fact, historically, witch trials were nothing like that, even at the height of the witchcraft hysteria. Witch hunts, witch panics, may have ripped through whole communities, sparing nobody from suspicion, the merest twitch or mole or wrong word spoken enough to condemn someone in the popular mind. But the trials were conducted with all due appearance of legality and justice. Witnesses and affidavits, depositions, magistrates. Acquittals, even. Witches were not condemned on supernatural grounds – sink or swim, the witches' mark – or at least not on that alone. It was the women's own words that burned them, mostly. They confessed. Perhaps coerced, tortured into it – or perhaps even believing their own words. For who wouldn't want, in some small sneaking corner of their heart, to hold the power of life or death over a hated neighbour? Or at least have others think you did?

They didn't want a witch hunt, but they got a witch trial. I didn't realize it until it was too late. That this chat – cosy in the head's office, all informal – was in reality a softening-up so that I might condemn myself in my own words. Dr Fairfax – I never did discover what she was a doctor of – didn't exactly spell it out but it was clear that there were just two ways to go. I could allow myself to be eased out quietly, with a good set of references, into another job, another school, no harm done. Or I could go hard: disciplinary proceedings, tribunal, my reputation besmirched and tainted by any mud they had to throw.

All I had to do – and Dr Fairfax hinted this with such sympathy, as if she, and they, were all doing me a favour – was say that I had been struggling in the classroom, that I had lost control of discipline, that I had just let things get out of hand that day. No mystery, no fault of the school – except that they had perhaps been too lenient on me when I was obviously struggling. That perhaps my obvious stress should have been picked up on, and I could have been offered more support. Other than that, there was nothing to see here, folks. Just one of those things. No mysterious toxic gas, no failure of health and safety, definitely no reason to pull your girls out of this exclusive private establishment and let them sink or swim in the local comp. And as for me: a refresher course to brush up my skills, an appointment with a sympathetic GP for 'stress', and then in the fullness of time when I had 'recovered', a good word put in with some other schools and I would be on my way, the whole imbroglio forgotten.

And if I didn't play ball? Well, it was amazing what they had built up on me, in this file in front of her right now. An improper relationship with a fellow member of staff – a married member of staff, no less – that hadn't even been all that discreet. Had I not read the code of conduct I had signed when I joined? Were there other boundaries that I had overstepped, perhaps in my relationships with the pupils?

I was too angry at the double standards to think straight. 'I assume you'll be sacking him as well, then,' I blurted out. 'And besides, if you want to look for overstepped boundaries with pupils, then it's him you should be looking at, not me.'

If I had thought that would be my trump card, I was mistaken. I felt the temperature drop in the room. The head got a frozen look on her face; no doubt working through the unwelcome implications of what I had just said. The chair of governors was less guarded, her dismay obvious.

Only Dr Fairfax seemed unruffled. She drew her eyebrows together with a look of professional concern. 'And the pupil in question being?' she asked.

'Melissa Harris.'

The head picked up her pen to make a note, but Dr Fairfax stayed her with an upraised hand.

'Are you saying then that you wish to make a formal accusation? It is a very serious allegation.' Her eyes were gentle, soft, understanding. 'It implies you might have borne a grudge against Melissa. Although, of course, she would have been the victim in this case. That might make things look even worse for you, if this should all go to a formal hearing.'

'But this is insane,' I said, for some part of me still didn't quite believe that this was happening. 'The girls got caught up in an episode of mass hysteria, that's all. It happens with girls of that age, occasionally. It had absolutely nothing to do with me or what I thought of Melissa or anyone else. I was just there when it happened.'

'And you know about mass hysteria?'

I didn't see the trap, even as I heard it spring in her voice. 'I looked it up, googled it. Anyone would.'

A rustling of papers in the files. A printout brandished like a weapon, there in black and white. A list of URLs visited, search terms used.

'After the event, they certainly might. Yet these are dated three days before.'

There were to be two ways to go, the easy way and the hard. I went down hard.

CHAPTER 17

T HE NEXT MORNING, the thought came to me as I awoke
that I had completely missed my work deadline, for the
first time ever. I had no way of getting online, and no other
way of contacting S. Robinson to explain. It ought to have
come as more of a shock; something that would have filled me
with anxiety only days before, but instead it barely registered.
The problem seemed a distant one, as if it was someone else's.
Time had slipped out of joint, the outside world already fading
into insignificance.

Down in the kitchen that morning, seated by the fire, the
four of us were each as quiet as the other, as if whatever had
silenced Cass had spread out its reach and gradually taken
hold of us all. We sat and drank our tea, and we might have
sat there all day, wrapped in a strange passivity, had the sound
of an engine not drawn Grant, Davey and me out into the
courtyard behind the house, leaving Cass still staring at the
fire. It was Helen, on the back of the quad bike, bolt upright
and imperious despite being wrapped in an old blanket. Kirsty
was at the controls, bundled in a vast coat that must have
belonged to Dougie.

'You need to get onto the council about that road, Grant,'

Helen said without preamble, waiting for Kirsty to hand her down from her perch, and pass her her stick. 'Even the blasted Range Rover can't get up it.'

'Where's Robert? You didn't leave him in the car, did you?' Grant said.

'Hmph. Might as well have done. No, he's in London, claims he's stuck because of the snow. The whole country has come to a standstill, apparently.'

'Dougie's going to try and get the tractor to move the car,' Kirsty said. 'The road down to the village is just a sheet of ice.'

'Right, well, standing around out here isn't going to achieve anything,' Helen said. 'Let's get indoors.'

It was deadeningly cold again, but she was dressed with no apparent concession to the weather in a tweed skirt and stout shoes, a padded sleeveless jacket over the top. She handed Kirsty back her blanket, already neatly folded, and put out the crook of her arm to Grant. Together, they moved slowly towards the door, the rest of us following behind in the cautious waddle needed to keep upright. The snow in the yard had not been cleared and now it had compacted hard over the cobbles, trampled in places to sheer ice. It was a clear day, weakly sunny, and yesterday's fog had left a glitter of frost over everything, beautiful but deadly.

She did her best not to show it, but Helen was shocked when she first set eyes on Cass. I saw it in the slight recoil of her head, and then the brightening of her smile. Cass had seated herself at the kitchen table, her knees drawn up tight against her chest, with her jumper pulled down over them. She had changed so gradually over the past few weeks that I had not registered the full impact, but seeing her now through

Helen's eyes, she looked dreadful. She had become gaunt, her hair still patchily growing in. Her once-luminous skin was merely pale now, grey in places, shadows gathering round her eyes. Even as we watched, her hand drifted up to her temple, her hidden fingers working away at the scalp. She smiled weakly at Helen and then sat up straighter, pulling her legs out from under the jumper at least.

'I hear you're being a bit silly,' Helen said, her brisk tone sounding forced. 'Not eating properly. Fainting. And this silence nonsense. Clearly there's something going on, Cass, but you have to talk.'

Cass's shrug was beautifully eloquent, calculatedly infuriating.

'Come on, Cassandra, you have to tell us what is wrong, or nobody can help you.'

Silence. Of course. And then Kirsty, half forgotten in the kitchen doorway, spoke up in her small voice.

'Can she write things down?'

Cass cocked her head and smiled. I scrabbled in the pile of estate documents and found a pad of paper and a pen that, after a few scrawled passes, produced some ink. I handed them to Cass and she bent her head, writing the way a child might. She pushed the pad out into the middle of the table and we all tilted our heads to read the words from whatever angle we could.

'I have been bewitched.'

I thought someone would laugh, must laugh. Even now, playing it back in my mind, it seems that someone ought to have responded with a snort of disbelief – or that Cass herself, delighted at the effect she had created, should surely have burst into delighted giggles. I looked around at the others, waiting for someone – Helen, perhaps – to dismiss her words. But on every face I saw the same uneasiness. Even I felt a pricking at the back of my neck. Cass wrote nothing further. She placed the pen down, gently and finally, and folded her hands.

'Who by?'

It was Grant who spoke, after a silence that seemed to have gone on too long. Cass said nothing and made no move to pick up the pen again. Her eyes passed from one to the other of us, coming to rest finally on my face with a look that might have been an appeal.

'Tell them what you told me,' Grant said, turning to me.

They were all looking at me now, with various degrees of curiosity in their eyes.

'This is ridiculous,' I said, finding my voice at last. Their faces didn't change. Helen was watching me with narrowed eyes, Kirsty with her head poked forward like a creature emerging from a hole. It was Davey I ended up looking at, standing behind Cass. I thought I might see some scepticism there, if nowhere else, some faint flickering of sense. But his hands, which had been resting on the back of Cass's chair, had moved to rest instead upon her shoulders. She tipped her head up slightly to acknowledge him, leaning back against him. She was keeping up her part well, just the right mix of exhaustion and fear in her eyes. Her breathing had quickened and shallowed as if she were under some threat.

'Tell them what you told me,' Grant repeated.

It was Helen I spoke to. 'She's just being a silly girl,' I said. 'We can't seriously believe she's been bewitched.'

'And yet, something is making the girl ill,' she said. 'Something or someone.'

'She's making herself ill,' I said. 'Surely we can all see that.'

'Ask her again,' Kirsty said. 'Give her the pen. Get her to give us a name.'

'But nobody did it,' I said, infuriated. 'Can't you see that?'

Even as Helen leaned forward and handed her the pen, Cass started to shake, a tremor that spread from her hands right through her whole body. It sent the pen skittering across the table, the notepad slithering to the floor. Suddenly she went rigid, arching herself backwards with such force that she drove her head into Davey's stomach, sending him staggering a half-step backwards. It seemed to take all his strength for him to maintain his grip on her frail shoulders. Her eyes were half closed, only the whites showing, her bottom lip caught in her sharp little teeth. She had her arms locked straight, pressing against the table edge, her feet scrabbling for purchase on the floor. We all stared in horror at her; all except Grant, who had kept his gaze on me.

'Tell them,' he said.

I looked at my own hands and they were trembling too.

'Tell them.' His voice had softened, become gentle, as if coaxing something out of a child. The only emotion on his face was sadness.

'You have to say the name,' Kirsty said. 'It breaks the spell.' Her voice was as matter of fact as someone explaining a recipe. Everyone ignored her.

A small trickle of blood appeared at the corner of Cass's mouth, a tiny flowering of colour. I could see the pulse fluttering in her arched throat, the rapid flickering of her eyes beneath her lids. Her left hand came up to her face. She began to make a horrible choking noise, animal like.

Kirsty was repeating her words, over and over until Davey, still holding Cass, turned to me in alarm.

'Just say it,' he said. 'What's the harm?'

What was the harm? Cass was twisting wildly now, threatening to shake free of Davey's grip. I spoke to the table, as undramatically as I could. 'Janet,' I said. 'Cass overheard me telling Grant that Janet had said something to me about shutting Cass up. And that's it. That's all it was.'

The effect was immediate and striking. Cass's body relaxed, the front legs of her chair hitting the floor with a retort. She closed her eyes fully and seemed to sigh, letting her head drop against Davey's hand. And then out of her mouth came a cascade of tiny feathers, white as snow, drifting in the sunlit bars of the air.

Kirsty and I stood side by side, staring at the bodies of the hens. They were almost as I had left them, except that they were shrouded with a further layer of snow. She had said nothing, and nor had I, not sure if I would manage to strike the right note of alarm and surprise. Checking them had been Kirsty's idea, leaving Helen dealing with Cass, although what there was to deal with exactly, I wasn't sure. She was still not speaking, just sitting there, white and exhausted, staring into her tea as if she might find some answers there.

'They've been there a while,' Kirsty said at last. 'It's no snowed since last night. Was she not up feeding them this morning?'

I could not say. If she had been, she had come and gone so quietly I had not noticed.

'Could those be Cass's footprints?' Kirsty pointed to the footprints in the snow, the narrow shape of Cass's elegant green wellingtons.

'Well, that explains the feathers, I suppose,' I said.

Kirsty looked at me with a small smile. 'Oh aye, there's always ways of explaining things,' she said.

'What do you mean?'

'Well, I'm no daft. I can see how it can be done. But it doesnae explain why she'd do such a thing, though, does it?'

'So why would she?' I asked, but there was no answer beyond a look of blank impatience, as though I were a slow pupil.

We walked back via the cottages. We were running out of food at the house, milk especially, and I had restocked the day before the snow came.

'Helen will have to stay the night and all,' Kirsty said, enumerating the supplies we'd need. 'They'll no get her home today.' We had left Davey trying to start the Land Rover, producing nothing but the repeated whine of the starter motor, no answering cough from the engine. 'Minus fifteen it was last night. The diesel froze in the tanks up at the farm.'

The courtyard outside the cottages was trampled hard and icy in places and we stuck to the fresh snow where we could, but even then we sometimes felt the treacherous slide of ice underneath. I opened the door and we were hit by the damp chill smell of shut-up air, a taint of mould and decay. The curtains were still half closed, admitting little of the dim winter daylight.

'Young Rory's place,' Kirsty said. 'I mind he was happy here, for a while anyway.'

'That's the first time anyone's told me that,' I said. 'I thought he moved here because he was depressed and didn't like the main house.'

'Aye well. Folk were quick to brand him mad, just because he saw things differently. Some would say he saw things the right way.'

'Everyone's out of step but our Johnny.'

My words sounded flip and I regretted them instantly for they made her clam up again. Everyone seemed to have a different response to Rory, as if he were not so much a real person but some sort of a Rorschach test, a canvas everyone projected their own emotions onto. Kirsty stood in the dim kitchen, looking around her. Now that we had stopped moving, I was beginning to feel cold, and suddenly anxious to be out of the place and back in the big kitchen of the house, with people around me.

'You might as well just empty the fridge,' I said. 'Take whatever we need. It should all still be fresh; I can't imagine it's any warmer in here than outside.'

What happened next, I cannot explain, except as some figment of my imagination. And yet, that was not how it felt at the time, and nor is it how I remember it, even now. It was as real as everything else that happened in those days and in the weeks and months beforehand. I left Kirsty staring into the dark fridge, apparently lost in thought, and went to pick up some fresh clothes from my bedroom. Here it was fully dark, the curtains still closed tight. Surely I had opened them before, to have some light to pack by? Without thinking, my hand went to the light switch and flipped it on, the same automatic motion we all make as we enter a room. The bulb in the bedroom was one of the low-energy ones that takes a moment to respond, and the light came on but not immediately. It seemed to seep into the room, creeping outwards towards the walls. I stood stupidly registering first that the power must have returned, and only then what I was seeing. It was my bedroom, and yet not my bedroom, an utterly different room. The bed had only a twisted heap of blankets on it, an uncovered pillow, the room otherwise unfurnished. The light bulb was stark and bare and its light was dimmed by the darkness of the walls.

Writing. When Grant had told me about Rory writing on the walls, I had imagined something larger, a graffiti-style scrawl. What I had not pictured was what I saw then: closely spaced lines of handwriting, as if someone had lacked paper and simply used the wall instead. From the highest point a tall man could reach, right down to the skirting boards, all around the room. Neatly enough done, too, although there were crossings-out in places, things added between the lines, all in the same black ink, the same square hand.

All this I took in as the light slowly strengthened and then abruptly gave up again, plunging me back into darkness. I had not moved, my hand still resting on the light switch. My breathing was shallow and I felt the urge to swallow, yawn, like a nervous dog trapped in a corner. I flipped the light switch again, uselessly, off and on again. There was no sound in the rest of the cottage. I stood frozen, knowing that I should go in and pull open the curtains to let in some light, but I was unable to move. I did not want to see that room again, the close-packed words, the stained and sorry bed. Even in the darkness, the image haunted me.

I stood there until I heard Kirsty call my name from the kitchen and went back to find her standing there in the doorway.

'Did you see the lights come on?' I asked her. 'I thought we had power there for a moment.'

She flipped the light switch up and down to no avail and shrugged. 'The fridge light never came on.'

'It was only for a moment,' I said, but I was doubting even now what I had seen.

'Did you get what you wanted? Your clothes?'

'Not quite.' The words formed to ask her to come with me, for I did not want to go back there on my own, but I did not say them. I stalled a little, toying with things left on the kitchen table, then took a breath and went back towards the bedroom, opening the living-room curtains on the way to give me the courage of the daylight, or what little there was of it. My eyes were more used to the half-darkness by now and the light coming in through the doorway was enough to see by. The walls were as blank and innocent as a sheet of paper, the bed made as I had left it, my clothes still folded where I had left them on the chair. I stood there in silence, telling myself that I had been imagining things, breathing my way back into calm. Everything was as I had left it – and yet not quite. There was a taint still in the air, the stink of sweat and fear.

I don't know what made me examine the fireplace on my way out. Perhaps the prickle we get when we think we are being watched. The grate had been swept, the way I usually swept it, the fire laid ready for a match, the same sort of neat pyramid of scrunched paper and sticks I would have laid myself. I had, after all, been preparing to light the fire when Davey called. But it did not look, somehow, like my fire. And it would not have been me who placed atop it, like a body on a pyre, the little clay figurine that was staring back at me now. Gingerly I picked it up, wary of the fragility of the dried clay. There was hair pressed into the surface as before, but it was not Cass's, not this time. It was a soft mat of greying brown, a mouse's nest of it, familiar as my own hand. It was the same mat of hair I cleared out monthly from my own hairbrush, smelling faintly of my shampoo.

Kirsty was still clattering round in the kitchen, sounding as if she was rummaging in the cupboards. I hurriedly put the figure in my coat pocket in case she took it into her head to come and see what I was doing. I didn't have any idea what to do with it, but I knew I couldn't leave it where it was.

As we left, Kirsty detoured to peer through one of Janet's windows, glancing back at me as I came up to her.

'There's no smoke from the chimney,' I said.

'She can't be in there, not without a fire.'

The interior was shadowy but empty. We trekked around, looking in each of the windows in turn. The curtains were open, the place neat, unremarkable.

'She must have found somewhere else to go,' I said. We both glanced at the car under its blanket of snow. There were no tyre tracks in the yard.

'She's no gone far,' Kirsty said. 'She's no gone far.' The look she gave me was full of complicity. 'I preferred it when I knew where she was.'

I said nothing. Ridiculous though it was, I could only agree.

Grant and Davey were in the mud room when we got back, dressed to go out, their heads bowed over what I saw was the air rifle, laid out on the bench. Davey had another gun beside him, a shotgun, and a string of cartridges looped around his shoulder. Helen sat, as if presiding over them, her stick planted in front of her. There was a grim purpose about the scene that I didn't like, and I stopped dead, meeting their eyes and then looking away. Kirsty scuttled on into the kitchen with her bag of supplies.

'What are you doing?'

They looked at me flatly for a moment.

'Pest control,' Grant said, after too long a silence.

'What do you mean?'

'Only rabbits,' Grant said. 'You don't have to look so worried.'

'What else would it be?' I asked, but there was no answering smile and they went back to their work. I watched them, still uneasy.

'You know,' Grant said after a while, looking up at me as if imparting some meaning, 'you have to be very careful with guns, even air rifles. You have to be scrupulous about keeping them clean.'

'Right,' I said.

'You handled this one last, didn't you?' He pointed at the rifle in his hand.

'You were there,' I said. 'I gave it back to you.'

'You mustn't let the barrel touch the ground, for instance,' Grant went on as if I hadn't spoken. 'If it jams, if it clogs up, it could be nasty. Something like this in it, for instance. That could kill someone.'

He held out his hand and something uncurled a little as if under its own steam. Two thin blades of leaves, oiled and dirty, clinging to a twig. The rowan sprig. My hand went to my coat pocket but it was not there; my fingers found only the gritty surface of the clay figurine.

Three pairs of eyes were on me, accusatory. I felt myself blushing for no reason.

'It's an easy mistake to make if you're not used to guns,' Grant said. 'I'm just letting you know.' His voice was all forgiveness, and then he smiled, the flash of a smile that caught me unawares, there and gone before I could react.

'Oh, and now the phone lines are down, by the way.' He shouldered the gun. 'Right, let's go and see what we can find, then.'

The kitchen was empty, full only of the grey daylight, quiet, the fire banked down. At a loose end, suddenly, I stood and looked around me. My eye fell on the phone in its place hung up on the wall. I don't know what I thought – that Grant had been mistaken somehow, perhaps – but I picked it up anyway and held it to my ear. There was nothing. I jiggled the cradle, and still nothing. I looked at my mobile, but its battery signal was flashing and there was no way of charging it. I switched it off to preserve what charge it had left. It wasn't as if I had anyone I wanted to call anyway.

Some indefinable shift in the air told me that I was not alone. I waited, but nobody spoke.

'What's going on, Cass?' I said, suddenly weary of it, of

everything. I did not turn to look at her, not wishing to give her the opportunity to mime a response. 'What are you doing? What is your brother doing? What's going on? I just don't understand anything any more.'

She did not answer. Instead, I felt the air shift again and the door slip open, and when I turned around again, I was once more on my own.

The Land Rover still wasn't starting. I could hear it out in the yard, the repeated whirring of the starter motor, the dry rattle as it half caught and then died. Cold diesel, perhaps, or just something frozen, I didn't know. I didn't know why they needed it, either. Surely if they were shooting rabbits, they would stick to the grounds. The sight of the guns had unsettled me beyond reason. I stood at the kitchen sink, aimlessly washing up and feeling increasingly sick. I didn't know what I dreaded more: the sound of the vehicle finally starting up and them going off with their guns to do whatever it was they were planning to do, or them finally giving up and coming back inside. Ever since that little scene around the kitchen table, I had felt that they were in the grip of some collective madness. The presence of the guns just made it worse. And ever since I had said Janet's name I felt I had made myself complicit in some way. Anything I did would just get me deeper enmeshed. There had to be some way of breaking the delusion that seemed to have us in our grip, but I couldn't think of one.

When I could stand it no longer, I threw down the washing-up gloves and went out, heading up towards the hens' enclosure.

With Kirsty there, I had not had the chance to look at them properly to see what had killed them. It had struck me that the dog might have been the culprit, and all at once it had made a kind of sense, reassuring in its logic. The dog, hungry, might have got into the enclosure somehow and gone after one of the birds. An animal like that might easily go into a killing frenzy, her wild instincts taking over. And Janet – or someone else, anyone, Grant even, enraged at the attack on his hens – might have seen that and, horrified, intervened. An unlucky blow of a boot or a stick – Janet was a strong woman – could easily fell a dog. And then perhaps she had carried the dog away – or perhaps the dog, injured, had staggered off, only to die later where we had found it. It would explain, too, the blood on the dog's muzzle; not hers after all, but the hens'.

Even as I told myself the story I knew it was unlikely, for I had seen no sign that the birds had been attacked when I first found them, but I told myself it was not impossible. And it seemed more probable than the alternative: Kirsty's insinuation that both birds and dog had died due to some – my mind shied away from the word, as if even thinking it would make it true – supernatural cause. The atmosphere in the house, shadowed and fraught with unspoken words, made it too easy to slip into superstition. I felt better in the open air, my lungs opening to the cold; better to be moving, too. As I turned the corner into the enclosure I could almost see the blood on the scattered feathers, the torn throats a dog might leave.

But there was nothing, not a sign. Stiff and cold in death, the birds were otherwise unmarked under their thin shrouds of snow, not even smelling yet of decay. I took my gloves off and overcame my revulsion at touching them, probing beneath the feathers with my fingers, but found nothing. Nor were there any prints, animal or human; nothing other than the footmarks Kirsty had noticed before. Cass's, she had thought, but I remembered now they were my own. It began to snow again, fine light flakes sifting down, feathers on my skin. I put my gloves back on and flexed my fingers, deadened by the cold. I should go back and warm up but I dreaded the thought of returning to the house. I turned instead and continued up and into the trees.

The forest was still ghostly with fog. The grey light seeped everywhere, illuminating nothing. The shooting had started, a few intermittent shots among the trees, echoed by the hills, impossible to work out where they were coming from. Each one sent up a cawing of birds, and then silence before another shot rang out. With no sense of surprise, I saw Ann ahead of me, shadowed by her dogs, as if we had arranged to meet here. She fell in beside me and together we walked in silence. The snow blew and swirled like sand around our feet, frosting the dogs' coats. She did not speak and neither did I. There were words whirling in my head, but I could not voice them. To say the words out loud would be to make them real.

I had expected the spring to be frozen over but it was still running. There was vapour rising from it, thicker than the surrounding fog, mirroring the clouds of our own breath. Where the running water cut through, the grass beneath the snow could be glimpsed, bright and living green in the frozen world.

I felt Ann's hand on my wrist, ungloved, cool but not cold against my skin.

'What do you come up here for?' she asked. 'You seem to be seeking something.'

I had forgotten the searching blue of her gaze. The words whirled faster in my head, my breathing accelerating. It wasn't fear, I recognized, this emotion that had weighed on me all day. It was dread. I could feel the cold weight of the air on my lungs. The sound of shooting had lulled, the world had fallen silent around us. I could not frame my fears into words, even in my own head. It would all have just sounded insane.

I am not a weak person, as a rule. I do not like to ask for help; I never have, especially not of strangers. Perhaps, this time, I could have done so, and things might have turned out differently. She seemed to be waiting for me to say something, to ask, but she didn't prompt me. She just waited and then, when time enough had passed, she called her dogs to her, gave me one last smile, and walked off into the fog, leaving me alone.

I turned, seriously rattled, suppressing the urge to call her back. The shots resumed, growing louder. There seemed to be too many of them for it just to be Davey and Grant, as if the whole forest was now filled with armed men, hunting through the trees. I found myself hurrying, head down, all but breaking into a run. Amid the swirling snow, it was too easy to imagine a figure passing swiftly from tree to tree, and another, and another – all of them sure and silent, vanishing when I looked again. Several times I stopped and whirled about, sure I had seen someone out of the corner of my eye, but each time there was nobody there, or nobody I could see. When I got to the path that led down to the house and the cottages I was out of breath, my heart racing. The trees pressed too close around for comfort. Even as I stood there, I heard another shot, close by. This time the birds it sent up did not settle but went on circling and calling for ages, filling the skies with their unease.

Even though it was only the middle of the afternoon, the day was already closing in. Somewhere out there, I thought, lights were being switched on, houses lit up like pictures in an advent calendar. I longed suddenly to be in one of those bright boxes, warm, among people.

It was then that it occurred to me that I could just leave, just walk away. Even if the buses weren't running, there might be cars and who would not stop and offer a lift to someone on foot in weather like this? Or if the worst came to the worst, I could walk the whole way. It wasn't far, not really. In a few hours I would be in the town, and there, surely, there would be power, light, warmth. I started down the path, turning off to the cottages instead of the house. I could make it down the driveway there completely unobserved. It seemed important that I get away before anybody noticed.

I did not think of the bike until I saw it leaning against the wall, a little hat of snow on its saddle. My fear of falling off completely forgotten, it seemed like the answer to a prayer. So much quicker than walking. I had a vision of the coffee shop, its cheerful staff, their pleased cries of greeting as I stumbled in out of the snow to be revived. I did not hesitate, acting now like one possessed. I cleared the saddle and pushed off, the fresh snow providing a surprisingly good surface. The tyres bit and took hold and I was away, feeling the relief of doing something, being in control. Ahead of me the road lay clean and white and innocent of any tracks. I put my head down and pressed on, as fast as I could manage.

The first mile went easily enough. The snow resumed shortly after I set off but not too heavily, feathering against me, settling where it could, almost warm where it brushed the skin of my face. But as I climbed out of the shelter of the trees, the wind took over, sending the flakes into a wild dance against the darkening sky. The cold began to find me again, seeping into my hands and feet until they ached as though they had been struck by a hammer. I had sweated a little with the effort of the climb, and the sweat was cooling now against my skin. My gloves were soaked through, my boots darkening, snow crusting on the cuffs of my trousers, my socks, the bike. The road surface was harder to ride on, too. In sheltered places where the snow was deep the bike became uncertain, the chain skipping against the cogs, too clogged with snow to drive the back wheel. There were icy patches where the bike skittered and I had to let it slow, coasting along with one foot on the pedal, one hovering ready to stop if I had to. It was only where the wind had lifted up the lighter snow and sent it dancing across the road that I could speed up, the fading daylight at my back.

Regardless, I pressed on. I had no other option. All thoughts of buses, of other people, seemed madness now. The landscape was empty of anything but snow. I reached the crest of the road and looked backwards. There was nothing: the dark blanket of the forest, the bulk of the house, all gone in the whirl of mesmerizing flakes. I did not stop to take it in but rode on, battling the bike and the wind, fighting to keep upright. I kept my eyes on the road ahead, focused on any stray patch of ice or deeper drift. I had forgotten everything else: where I was heading, what I was escaping from, if I ever knew. I was alone in a wide world of snow.

Where was I? All the familiar landmarks had vanished. I knew I had not yet reached the road end where the bus stopped which meant I was miles still from town. I had no idea how long I had been going but it was now after four o'clock. At best I would have another hour of daylight, and then it would be fully dark, sooner maybe in this heavy snow. I was thoroughly cold, wet, and beginning to be frightened. It occurred to me for the first time that I could just die out here, stupidly and foolishly, and that nobody knew where I was to come and rescue me. Unable to think of any alternative, I just kept going, barely pedalling now, scooting the bike with my feet where I had to, walking it up the smallest rise where the snow prevented the tyres from gripping on the climb.

I did not hear the engine at first. Or rather, I heard it but did not register it, sunk as I was in my thoughts, blindly plodding on. Only as it was almost on me did I turn and see the headlights and realize how dark it had become. Relief flooded me, even as I saw that it was the Land Rover, with Grant at the wheel.

I stopped and he stopped and for a moment he did not get out. I stood beside the dark bulk of the vehicle, beginning to shudder in the cold. All I could see was the snow falling through the beam of the headlights. I found myself thinking that it was lightening up, stopping, and that if I persevered, it might get easier. I started the struggle to remount the bike but before I could do so, Grant was out of the car and round to the side of the road, taking me by the shoulders.

'There you are. You had us worried.'

No questions about where I was going, what I thought I was doing. I felt my shudders increase, as if they might tear me apart.

'Let's get you in, before you freeze to death.'

'What about the bike?'

'Don't worry about the bike.' Before I could stop him, he had grabbed it and picked it up and dropped it over the other side of the dyke.

'We'll come back for it later,' he said. 'But first we have to get you warmed up.'

I was made stupid by the cold, too dazed to move. His arm was around me, his body a bulwark against the wind. The interior light came on like a blessing as he opened the passenger door and then I was being helped up, my foot fumbling on the step, too numb to feel. His hands settled me in the seat, reaching over to fasten the seatbelt. He was close, close enough that I could see the glisten of whiskers where he had missed a patch shaving on his neck. I could smell the rough wool of his jumper and I could feel the warmth emanating off him as though it would burn my skin.

I pulled off my sodden gloves. My fingers had turned a dead yellow white. Grant, climbing back into the driver's seat, took hold of my wrists. He said nothing, but enfolded my hands in his. I expected to feel the flow of warmth but instead I felt only the iciness of my own hands. My toes were coming alive, aching with the pain of it. Slowly the shudders started to ease.

'You did have us worried, you know,' he said at last. 'We thought you'd been spirited away.'

He smiled, with all the warmth and sincerity that I might ask for in a smile. I started to pull my hands away but he tightened his grasp.

'Not yet, they're still two blocks of ice. In fact, this would be quicker.' Letting go with one hand, he loosened his jacket and then pulled me closer, placing my hands between his jumper and his shirt. A strong arm gathered me in until my head almost rested on his shoulder. 'Relax. You're OK now. We've found you. We'll get you home.'

Despite myself, I began to relax. I was safe in the car, safe out of the storm. The snow whirled and danced, mesmerizing in the headlights. When he spoke, his voice was as much a rumble in his chest as a sound, resounding through me.

'Can't have you running off like that, without a word. People would wonder. People would talk.'

Chapter 18

WE PULLED UP outside the house and I thought the power must have returned, for the front windows blazed with a warm and welcome light. I expected Grant to continue round to the back as usual, but he turned off the engine and came round and opened the car door for me, ushering me out with his hand on my elbow. I stumbled, almost falling, my legs suddenly weak as spaghetti. His firm grip both held me up and propelled me forward. The front door swung open at his touch and the light danced and I saw that it was not the power returned, but candles, a mass of them, the flames bobbing and flickering in the gust of air from the door.

Two armchairs had been brought into the centre of the hall, placed before a low table. Helen sat in one of them, Cass in the other. Despite the chill in the room, Cass was dressed in her emerald green dress and the fox fur stole, whose glass eyes flickered in the candlelight. Otherwise, the light did little to reach the edges of the vast space. The hares in their cases threw fantastic shadows, moving with the candle flames. I glimpsed Kirsty, lurking in among them, so that her shadow blended with theirs. Davey was there too, arms folded, just casually blocking the doorway to the corridor. In front of Cass and Helen was another chair, armless and upright, empty and waiting.

All eyes were on me. I entered the house, aware of Grant behind me, his hand heavy on my shoulder.

'The wanderer returns,' he said, and though his words were light, all warmth had vanished from his voice. There were cooking smells coming from the kitchen and they wakened a hollow hunger in me that battled with an animal impulse to run away. I stood still and said nothing until the gentle pressure on my back became irresistible and I walked forward and sat down in the waiting chair.

'What's going on?' I asked. 'Is this some sort of a game?' There was in truth nothing playful about the set-up but I hoped at least for some sort of answering smile, something other than the grave stillness with which they all greeted my remark.

It was Helen who moved first. She didn't say anything but placed something down gently on the table in front of her. Cass seemed to flinch as she did so.

'We found this,' she said. 'Is it yours?'

'What is it?' I started to ask, peering in the tricky light, but even without seeing it I knew what it was. The clay figure had gone from my pocket and lay where Helen had put it, crude and grinning.

'It was in your bedroom upstairs,' Helen said, and I did not think to ask what had made them go through my things, nor how it had got there.

'I found it in my cottage. In my fireplace. It's nothing to do with me.'

'When?' Helen asked.

'When I went back with Kirsty. This morning.' I had to think back – was that right? But yes, it had only been a few hours ago.

'You never said anything to me,' Kirsty said.

'You found it in the fireplace?'

Who had spoken? I looked round the shadowy spaces beyond the candlelight. Grant, it must have been, although I had thought he was still behind me, barring the way out of the door.

'I found it in the fireplace. Right in the grate. On top of the kindling. Ready for a match.'

There was a shift in the shadows as Cass gave a little theatrical shudder. She leaned forwards, the movement making the candle flames dance. The light caught the russet tones of her hair, the fox's pelt, both the same. Hard to tell where the animal ended and the girl began.

'The fire was laid?' Helen asked.

'Yes.'

'Who laid it?' Definitely Grant this time.

'I don't know. Me, I suppose. I must have done.'

'You laid the fire?' He almost pounced.

'I must have. I mean, I remember laying it when I first got up and the power was out. I was trying to get warm.'

'And you put this on top of it.'

'No! As I just said, I found it. Just lying there.'

'Just lying there.'

'Yes.'

In the silence that followed, I wondered if I should be protesting my innocence – but of what? And besides, there was still some small part of me then that thought the whole thing was patently ridiculous, a game, a prank taken just that little bit too far.

'So you just picked it up and put it in your pocket?'

It was Davey who had spoken, for the first time. He was still leaning in the doorway to the corridor, a little detached from the rest of them. I felt a wave of exhaustion hit me. All I wanted was to sit down by the fire, warm up, eat something. Drink a cup of tea. Be normal.

'Yes,' I said. 'Yes, I picked it up.'

'Why?'

Why indeed? I thought back, trying to remember. It had looked vulnerable there atop the little pyre of sticks and paper, helpless, but it was, in the end, just a piece of clay.

'I wanted to protect it,' I said.

At some point through that long evening, through that long night, I became aware – more strongly than I was aware of anything else – of the damp of my socks, the cold seeping through them like a slow deadening, up through my feet and into the rest of me until I felt I would never get warm. It eclipsed my hunger, the weariness of my legs, the tiredness that had gathered behind my eyes. And with it spread the dawning realization that I had no idea what these people's intentions were, or what they might do to me.

'What is this?' I asked at last. 'Some sort of a trial?'

Any faint hope I might have had that they would laugh, or deny it, faded. Their expressions didn't change. I watched their faces in the shadowy light and they were suddenly all strangers to me, every one.

I should have walked out then. It's clear enough in hindsight now. Never mind attempting to get to town, I had my own home to return to, not 200 yards away. There was even a fire laid, enough food still in the kitchen that I could scratch myself together a meal. Bar the door and wait till daylight came, and with it, sanity. Why didn't I? I think it was because I was not sure just what would happen if I tried. I was not sure if they would let me leave. For now I was not a prisoner, not yet. But if I stood and walked towards that front door, what then? Would the last pretences of civility disappear? Would they, could they, hold me captive? It was as if as long as I willingly remained in place, we could all pretend that this was something normal, ordinary. I could hold down the fear.

Kirsty had made one of her darting exits and then reappeared, and the smell she brought with her from the kitchen hit me with another wave of hunger.

'The soup's ready,' she said to Helen, and if she meant it to be discreet, she had pitched it wrong, for I was suddenly all attention.

'I'd like to eat something,' I said. 'I think that's allowed, no? Assuming I'm not actually accused of anything. Whatever this little charade is about.'

'It's about Janet,' Helen said tartly. 'And it's about Cass.'

'But you can't seriously think that Janet has had anything

to do with whatever is wrong with Cass. I mean, really, Helen? Kirsty, yes, I can imagine, but you? And you too, Davey?'

Davey had the grace to look uncomfortable. 'You saw what she did to Jess.'

'I saw what happened to Jess. There was no sign it was anything to do with Janet.'

'She threatened her.'

'And the hens,' Kirsty said.

'Well, she didn't even threaten the hens,' I said. 'Why would she have anything against the hens?'

Silence. But if I thought I had scored a point, I was mistaken. Cass was paying attention again, her breathing shallow. Kirsty crept forward too, into the circle of light.

Grant spoke from the doorway, his voice coming out of the darkness, almost gentle. 'It was you who found the hens, of course.'

'Both times,' Helen added.

'That's not true,' I said.

'Did you not?' Grant again, his voice still soft. 'Were they all right the day you went up to feed them on your own?'

I swallowed. To lie now, to brazen it out, seemed absurd.

'You didn't say anything, did you? But they weren't all right. At least, not when you left them.'

Beyond the candlelight his shadow shifted, head to one side.

'It just seemed easier,' I said.

'But why?'

I didn't know. I couldn't think.

'You didn't want to get the blame,' Helen said. 'Finding them twice was unfortunate.'

'The first time it was Cass who found them, not me,' I said. 'For some reason she didn't want to tell Grant that.'

'So you're accusing her,' Helen said.

'I'm not accusing anyone.'

'It seems to me that you're the one accusing Janet,' Helen said sharply. 'And yet it was only when you came on the scene that things started happening.'

'This is insane.'

'So why didn't you mention the hens?'

'And this isn't the first figure you've found, is it? Or made?'

'What brought you up here?'

'Who's helping you?'

'What are you doing here?'

One by one the candles guttered and died until we were left with a single one on the table before me. Cass had seemed to lose interest in the proceedings and was playing with the soft wax that had pooled around the candles, rolling it in her fingers, fashioning it in some way. As she grew more absorbed in her work, she sat straighter, holding the wax occasionally to the remaining candle flame to keep it workable, and I felt as she did so a sympathetic twinge at the burn of the molten wax coating her fingertips.

All the while they kept circling around the same questions: what had Janet said about Cass, how had she said it, where was she now, what might I know about it? I had begun to forget what I had said and what I hadn't said, what had happened and when. This is how people make mistakes, incriminate themselves, even the innocent. I stopped answering and it didn't seem to matter. I stopped listening to the sense and heard just their voices, the raw harsh music that they made. I watched Cass, her hands in the pool of light, the shape of a hare emerging. It was crouching, watching even as it was brought into being. Alive.

They say that there are certain kinds of close harmony where the voices blend in such a way that in the gaps and resonances between them another voice emerges. Three singers become four, four become five, half heard and half imagined, just beyond the grasp of understanding. Perhaps it was just such a phenomenon that was at work that evening, or perhaps the tiredness, cold and hunger had simply addled my brain, for as I watched Cass create the hare I heard a fifth voice joining in, a voice that seemed to come from now here and now there, then from everywhere.

I could not make out any words, could not make out even whether it was a man's voice or a woman's, but in among the leaping shadows that the candle made, it was easy to imagine another figure prowling the edges of the hall, upright, slender, lithe, glimpsed only from the corners of my eyes. I turned my head, trying to get a better look. Always it vanished, revealing itself only as a collection of shadows, ungraspable.

Who was speaking? I no longer knew. I buried my head in my hands, beyond weary, beyond hungry. I entertained the fantasy that when I looked up again, all this would have gone away and I would be in my own bed in the cottage, or my own flat in London with the symphony of the sirens playing out against the orange dark.

'Where is Janet?' Grant asked again, insistent.

'I don't know.'

I opened my eyes to the room, which was unchanged. Cass put down the hare she had been forming and picked up the little clay figure, already frail and crumbling at the edges. Its feet were almost worn away. She cradled it in the palm of her hand, watching me all the while. Her fingers closed loosely around it. Her eyes were dark pools in the candlelight.

'Where is Janet?' Helen asked.

I wanted to say that I had seen her, right here in the house. Or had I? It didn't matter, I couldn't speak anyway. My breathing was shallow, constricted. We seemed to have used up all the air there was in the room.

'It wasn't ever anything to do with Janet, was it?' The voice again, the unknown voice, perhaps just in my head. It was all you. It's happened before. It's why you had to leave teaching. Why you left London. It's not just Cass. There were other girls, a whole roomful of them. A classroom full. They fell, didn't they, because you felled them. You picked them off. Like petals from a rose.

Cass's eyes were still on me, her fingers closing tighter. I started to stand up, reaching out towards her. All the air I could breathe no longer seemed enough. I saw the dance of darkness start up before my eyes. Some disconnected part of me thought, *ah, so this is what it feels like.* Down through the tunnel of my remaining vision I watched Cass's fingers form a fist. I felt the squeeze of her grip around my chest, choking, closing off the air. The world had gone silent. The last thing I remember is the final convulsive squeeze of her hand, the trickle of powdered clay dust through her fingers, and then nothing.

I suppose I must have come to again pretty quickly, although I don't remember. I don't remember either what happened next or how I got from the hall to the kitchen. The next thing I do remember is waking in the kitchen alone in the dark, beside the light of the dying fire. Or not alone. There was someone else there, seated, quiet, no more than a stir of breath in the darkness. As soon as I sat up, struggling to free myself from a tangle of blanket, I felt the shift in the air, as of someone coming to attention. I looked round and could make out nothing in the dark but I felt no fear, just this awareness of a presence.

Despite the fire and the blanket, my feet still felt frozen. That was what had woken me, the deadening chill. I leaned forward and found I still had my damp socks on. Beneath them, the skin felt waxy and dead, too numb to register the touch of my hands. As I tried to rub them back into life, I felt rather than heard the kitchen door open and then after a moment close again, as if someone had gone out and then returned, someone who moved surely and silently even in the dark. Still no words were spoken, but something soft landed at my feet. A pair of socks, rough wool, but warm, so warm and dry.

'Thanks,' I said, and even in that one word I felt the half-crack of my voice as the gratitude threatened to overwhelm me. 'Thank you,' I said again, clearing my throat and mastering myself. No answer came, just a settling, perhaps the creak of a chair. Was I under guard? Or somehow being protected?

Warmth was returning, blessed warmth. The urge came to lie back down, to pull the blanket over my shoulders and head, to sink downwards into oblivion. Only the presence of this unknown person kept me tied to wakefulness. I sensed them waiting, listening, alert yet calm. A benevolence. The socks rough and warm against my feet.

'Who are you?' Even as I spoke, the strangeness of the wording struck me: the question you might ask a stranger. 'Who is it?' would have made more sense. And yet the words seemed right. I didn't recognize this presence, strange as that might seem. Grant, Helen, Davey, Kirsty – all of them would have spoken by now, surely. And it was not Cass. The room was full of calm acceptance. No room with Cass in it ever felt that way.

I leaned back, my head against the arm of the sofa, feet tucked beneath the blanket. I listened. More silence. Not even the sound of breathing. A well of silence to drop words into, to see the ripples they might make. An act of kindness. This is how confessions happen.

Now in the waiting dark, I hesitated. A word or two would be enough. Rory – I knew then with absolute conviction that it was Rory – would understand. More than that, it was as if he already knew, and was just waiting for me to say the words. It might be a sort of absolution. It might even – and this made sense to me then, in the quiet darkness – be what was needed to restore Cass back to herself.

Words pressed against my teeth. It would be a relief. When I lost my job, my friends had mostly rallied round, angered on my behalf. They listened to my bitterness and added bitter assurances of their own. They told me that was the way the world was, unjust and cruel. The rumours had been so monstrous that no one who knew me had thought to give them credence. There was no space there for doubt. The whole thing was absurd. There was no space to tell them anything that suggested any culpability of my own. And if I had, who would have believed me? After a while I didn't even believe myself.

What might I have said, had I succumbed to that impulse? Before I could part my lips to speak there was a shift once more in the quality of the dark, and I knew that the presence I had felt so strongly was gone and I was once more alone.

How do you make someone faint? It's easier than you might think. A moment of heightened emotion, something as prosaic as an empty stomach, hyperventilation. I knew this. I had always known this. I hadn't needed to search for it on the internet. At my own school – another all-girls' school, another hothouse of volatile emotions – we had played what we called the fainting game, teetering on the edges of unconsciousness, sometimes tipping over and into it. Or rather, the others had played. I had always stayed on the sidelines, not taking an active part. It was a game for other girls, the popular ones, comfortable at being the centre of attention, happy to give up control. I had found some small amusement in the way they were so quick to succumb, their bodies easily overwhelming their minds' defences. There was a chant they used, some nonsense rhyme that was supposed to be a spell, but the words themselves really didn't matter. What mattered was the way you breathed afterwards, an accelerating rhythm, flaring the ribs and then forcing the air out hard, faster and faster until the body cannot catch the oxygen it needs and the mind checks out. Simple as that. I had practised sometimes, on my own, but I lacked the nerve to take it the whole way. It was a fad for a while, and then forgotten, as the in-crowd moved on to other thrills. But I had always remembered.

They had been caught up in outrage, those girls, just as I had told Dr Fairfax. A manufactured injustice, just as I had described it, although I hadn't mentioned that it was I who had manufactured it. Threatening to keep them in simply because they had dawdled into my classroom, that was something you did with the younger classes, not the A-level set. But I had known they were only late because Melissa had held them up, detaining her gang in the corridor to stage whisper some salacious detail, and then when she had finally wandered in, she couldn't resist glancing at me, her eyes full of all the mocking knowing of the young.

Dr Fairfax was a perceptive woman. She had detected my only actual lie, a tiny one, an excusable enough mistake that anyone might have made. Melissa had not been standing up the whole time. They had all been standing in the uproar at my announcement they would be kept behind, but then she had sat down abruptly in her usual seat, right at the front, her admiring clique around her, watching to see what she and I would do.

I looked at her and she at me. I remember the dew of sweat across her upper lip, the smell of her, or at least the deodorant she used, and underneath that the smell of hot humanity confined in an airless room. The classroom windows didn't open, but even if they had, they would only have admitted the grimy London air with its acrid stink that seemed to pool in your mouth. The radiators were on too, for it was only just April and the policy was that the heat stayed on until the Easter holidays, whatever the weather.

I let the silence lengthen. She was still glaring at me. I folded my arms, and she, her attention fixed on me, folded hers too in unconscious imitation. I wondered if she was aware of the way it pushed her breasts up so that they threatened the buttons on her school blouse. The lace of her bra was quite visible through the gaps. She would not meet my eyes and I sensed in that a form of weakness. I still had some power over her.

'You can't do that, Miss,' she said. Miss. As if I didn't have a surname, let alone a first name. Only a marital status, spinster, left on the shelf. I hated that Miss, and they – she – knew I hated it too.

'I can and I will.'

The rest of the class were watching now, their minds not yet made up which way to jump. They would do what she did, I knew; mutiny if she mutinied, back down if she backed down. She bit a nail. Her hands were still child's hands, nails bitten down to the quick, a smear of paint on the knuckle flaunted like a trophy.

'There's no way . . .'

I leaned forward, hands on her desk. She faltered. Sometimes silence is the most powerful response. The rest of the class were completely quiet now; I could have wished for this level of attention when I was teaching them. The truth is, I knew I was overreacting, but she was only sharpening my anger. I wasn't going to be faced down, not in this manner.

She was watching me now, sensing something. Her arms were still folded but her defiance was giving way to uncertainty. I let my eyes bore into hers. I was just that fraction too close, invading her space, but she was not going to be the one to back away. Her arms rose and fell with each breath and I noticed that her breathing had fallen into the same rhythm as mine. All around us, the class watched.

I breathed faster, shallower, easy enough to do as I fed my own anger. A small part of me watched with satisfaction as she followed suit, a fresh line of sweat springing up on her upper lip. I caught the scent of something, beyond her sweet and sickly perfume, an animal smell. I let my face draw closer to hers and I don't know what she saw there but this time she did lean back, her breathing accelerating now of its own accord. Still I said nothing. Still there was silence in the room. I kept my focus absolutely on her.

'Stand up,' I said, making it an order, but keeping my voice soft so that they all had to strain to hear. 'In fact, stand up all of you.'

She didn't want to. She was breathing hard now, flaring her nostrils to pull in more oxygen, her body telling her that there was none, for she was breathing too shallowly to take it in. The faster she breathed, the less good it did her. Her hand came up absently to touch her face and I knew the pins and needles had started to set in around her lips. I straightened, giving her space and raised my hand slightly, and repeated my command. A minute – seconds – before, she had been all defiance. But now she rose as if she had no volition but my own, and stood, struggling for breath. She swayed slightly and I knew the room would already be darkening around her.

'Stand up properly,' I barked, and that only panicked her more. Even as she tried to straighten she began to crumple, one hand flung out wildly, reaching for the chair to steady herself but only knocking it backwards out of her grasp. She was properly frightened now, and that made her breathe even harder, panicking as she started to fade. She swayed again and this time couldn't stay standing. She half fell, half stumbled, then slid gracelessly and silently to the floor. Only now could I afford to break my gaze and glance at the others, as they looked wild-eyed back at me, panic in their faces.

I had not thought that it would work on all of them, not really. In truth, I hadn't even been sure if it would work on Melissa. But in the end it was simple enough. You overbreathed and then you stood up, and you fainted, as simple as that. And once one goes, the panic spreads and there was nothing, then, I could have done to stop it. She fell, and then they all fell, one after the other.

Like petals from a rose.

CHAPTER 19

I WOKE, STIFF and cold, to a grey sort of daylight, the late winter dawn. I was on the little battered couch in the kitchen, a blanket thrown over me, the smell of old dog hairs in my nose. I moved and was jolted fully awake by the slither of something soft, furred, slipping over my face. I had flung it off before I recognized Cass's fox fur stole, which had been tucked in around my neck. I sat up and bent to retrieve it. I was still dressed in yesterday's clothes, rough wool socks on my feet. Whatever else I might have dreamt or imagined in the night, that part had been real.

I glanced over and saw Davey sitting at the kitchen table. He started when he saw me up, as if he had nodded off and just woken.

'Are you on guard?' I asked.

He had the grace to look embarrassed.

'Just what was all that about last night anyway?' I asked. 'Am I . . .' A prisoner, I wanted to ask, although I hesitated to say the words.

Before he could answer, we heard Helen's voice in the corridor outside. She was still talking as she entered the kitchen, directing her words over her shoulder to whoever was trailing in her wake.

She nodded to Davey and then glanced over at me, her face neutral.

'Oh. You're up,' she said. Her eyes narrowed as she saw the fox stole. 'Where did you get that?'

'It was just here,' I said. 'Cass must have left it here.' I didn't mention the way it had been tucked in around me.

'Well. She's gone.'

'Gone?'

'Gone. Disappeared. Not in her bed this morning. Not in anyone's bed. Gone.'

Helen and Grant were all for heading out to search for her straight away. Cass's boots were missing, though not her coat – she had taken Grant's, it seemed, and with it the Land Rover keys although the vehicle itself was still in the yard. There might be a trail of her footprints in the snow, although in the mess of freezing and unfreezing it was hard to tell which prints were old and which were new. Kirsty had gone back to the farm to fetch Dougie and the quad bike. After Helen's first announcement, none of them spoke to me, or included me in any plans, or even behaved as if I was there at all except to step around me. Only Davey glanced my way from time to time with something that might have been embarrassment or might have been wariness, like a dog that knows it has been doing something wrong.

I let them rush around and went to the Aga to put the

kettle on and started making toast. I felt Cass had probably had enough of a head start that taking a few minutes more to eat something wouldn't hurt.

'What are you doing?' Helen asked, suddenly deigning to notice me.

'Making breakfast,' I said.

'There's no time for that.'

'Well, you can do what you like, but I didn't eat last night.'

Helen jerked her chin upwards, surprised at being opposed. The daylight had brought me a new defiance. And it was my food, after all, the supplies Kirsty and I had foraged from the cottage.

'Hmm. Well, perhaps it's not a bad idea for the boys to eat something first,' she conceded.

She seemed to assume that I would make toast for them too, so I did – not that they ate much. Grant and Davey stood leaning against the kitchen counter, tearing at the toast, slurping too-hot tea. At one point Davey picked up a crust and looked around, for he had been used to feeding such titbits to Jess. Grant fidgeted, throwing out instructions to Helen and Davey, still ignoring me. I took my time, taking my plate to sit in a civilized fashion at the table. It seemed I was not to be included in the search party.

'We need to cover the forest, the graveyard. Up by the spring.'

'Davey, you might walk down and see if Dougie still has the spare keys for the Land Rover.'

'We'll need to take some blankets, hot tea – the thermos. And there are walkie-talkies somewhere, if the batteries work.'

He was still eating as he bustled out, and I heard the click of the gun cabinet lock, and then more swearing. The shotgun was gone. He came straight back in and looked at me for the first time that morning.

'Did you take it?'

'I wish I'd had the foresight,' I said. 'It didn't even occur to me.'

'Christ,' he said. 'Right, well, that complicates things.'

There was more bustling in the mud room, muttering with Davey.

'Call the police,' I said, raising my voice so I could be heard from the kitchen. 'Call out a search party. You can't handle this alone.'

No answer. Helen shrugged on her padded jacket.

'I mean it,' I said. 'There must be some way of getting through to the authorities.'

It was as if I hadn't spoken. Outside, I heard the sputter of the quad bike. Helen walked out without a word. I heard voices, then the turn of the key in the back door, locking me in. I went to hammer on the door but stayed my hand. That would be playing their game. Instead I listened, marking their departures. Grant took the quad bike and Helen insisted on joining him. Davey was walking back to the farm to pick up the Land Rover keys. I tried to turn on my mobile but it was completely dead now, and the landline was still silent.

As their footsteps died away, I heard another sound, steady as a clock. In fact, I had been hearing it all along but had not registered it until now. The drip, drip, drip of melting snow, the thaw at last.

Roaming round the kitchen, I saw that Kirsty had picked up one of my packets of coffee from the cottage. I had drunk too much tea in recent days; I felt awash with the stuff. I found an old-fashioned espresso pot at the back of a cupboard and set about making coffee, properly, a small act of civilization. I felt as if I was reclaiming myself.

The house was never silent – like all old structures it seemed to constantly creak and settle – but as the hiss of the pot died down, I heard a new noise. I listened, sharply, thinking there had been something human about it, but nothing more came so I dismissed it, poured my cupful, and savoured the first mouthful. I felt sharpened, alive. I had allowed myself to get sucked into the madness for a moment, but it was over now. The minute the roads cleared and the phone line was restored, I would ring for a taxi and be gone. Even Grant could not seriously believe that he could keep me prisoner here indefinitely.

I leaned against the Aga and closed my eyes, enjoying the warmth, the smell of the coffee, the moment. The events of the night before seemed entirely fantastical. It wasn't the world that had gone insane, but the inhabitants of this house, myself included. I thought back to my impulse to confess to some imagined apparition, and felt a sting of embarrassment, like remembering a drunken evening. Oh well, I thought, glad that in the end I had had the sense to keep my mouth shut, even to a figment of my imagination. It didn't really matter in the long run. In a few hours, a day, the outside world would return and we could go back to playing by the rules of civilization. All I had to do was wait.

I heard the noise again, closer now. Unmistakeably the sound of someone moving. I thought of Janet appearing in the corridor upstairs and froze again, straining to hear. It was silent again, but it felt like the silence of someone waiting, holding still as I was holding still, planning their next move. I put my coffee down, focused on the door. Still nothing, still silence, except for the door pushing slowly open.

It took me a moment to register that it was Cass. She had dressed herself in military fatigues, her hair buzzed short like an army recruit. For a mad moment I thought it must be Rory standing there in the doorway, shotgun in hand. I let my hands rise slowly upwards, palms out.

'Cass . . .' I said, but she shook her head, motioning me sideways with a flick of the gun. Never taking her eyes off me, she walked over and picked up the blanket from the sofa, wound the fox stole round her neck. Then she grinned a cracked grin and ushered me out down the corridor.

'The back door's locked, and your brother has taken the key,' I said. I didn't know much about Cass's state of mind, but I had a feeling that she wasn't going to take any surprises well. She didn't seem to register my words, but when we got to the door, she simply took aim at it and fired, splintering the wood enough that she could kick it open. I struggled into my damp boots and coat under her silent gaze. Then she marched me to the Land Rover.

The blast of the shotgun had re-awoken my sense of danger. Grant had been wrong about one thing: she didn't close her eyes when she pulled the trigger. She had seemed perfectly composed, and the damage the gun had done at close quarters was impressive. I dropped any plans I may have had to make a break for it as she was occupied with unlocking the vehicle, and meekly got in the passenger's side. Instinctively I put on my seatbelt and she laughed at that, a rusty cackle like an unused gate. She was struggling to find a way to point the gun at me within the confines of the Land Rover and ended up with it across her lap, the muzzle of it almost resting on my thigh. I could feel the faint warmth of the fired barrel through the fabric of my trousers. She threw the blanket into the back seat. She seemed to have brought no other supplies.

The Land Rover started up first time, shimmying a little as she spun it round on the ice and then gunned it onto the road. The fresh snow had fallen onto the rutted ice of the old. In places, it had blown away and the older snow was visible beneath, milky white ice now, gnarled. The wheels seemed barely to have traction, fishtailing around a bend, Cass fighting for control. The gun had become the least of my worries now, although I was acutely conscious of its presence. Cass kept taking her hand off the wheel to touch it, as if reassuring herself that it was still there.

'Cass, I'm not going anywhere,' I said. 'You can put the gun in the back.'

She ignored me and drove on, but more carefully now. So her intention was not simply to break both our necks in a ditch; she was heading somewhere. She took a familiar turn and my heart sank, for I knew that way led to the crossroads. A suicide bid then? But why the gun? And why me? The blanket in the back seat took on a more sinister light. I remembered Jess's cairn that Davey had built. Was I to end up in an unmarked grave, under a pile of rocks? I could see how, in Cass's twisted world, it might all make sense.

I started to talk, keeping my voice as soothing and as matter of fact as I could manage. I didn't take my eyes off her face, gauging her every reaction.

'Cass, listen,' I started. 'I know about Rory. People thought he was mad, didn't they? Because he left the army and came back here. But he wasn't mad, was he? It was just that he saw through things, the things other people miss. He understood.'

She kept her eyes on the road, concentrating on the driving, but I could see she was listening. I softened my voice further, so that she would have to strain to hear. An old teacher's trick. There's nothing like the pin-drop silence of a class when you have their full attention.

'It was Janet that made him really ill, wasn't it? Grant never understood that, even when it was too late. How she did it, I don't know. There are ancient powers that have never been forgotten. They still work. They haven't gone away.'

Was she listening to this nonsense? We were climbing now, up and over the moorland. The snow had drifted between the dykes in places and I thought we might get stuck, but Cass battled through, backing up a couple of times and taking a run at it, the Land Rover seeming to clamber over the thicker pockets of snow like a creature possessed. I kept talking, because I could think of nothing else to do.

'She poisoned his mind, didn't she? And though he knew what she was doing, he knew too that nobody would believe him. Even you, perhaps. Even you might have doubted him, at times. It would have been easy enough to do.'

It was a pure guess, but I sensed I had struck home. Even as she focused on the road ahead I could see the jump of the muscles in her jaw, the tightening of her hands on the wheel.

We had reached the top of the climb, and were out into the sunshine. Below us, a river of fog seemed to flow over the shoulder of the hill, filling the valley below. I shuddered at the thought of the descent, imagining a crazed, careering tumble, the vehicle coming off the road at the first bend and sending us head over heels down the hillside, but Cass wrestled with something by the gearstick and when we started off again it was at a steady crawl, the engine growling away with a new and laboured note. I had to raise my voice to be heard.

'But you were young, then, Cass. It's understandable. You didn't know what you know now. You hadn't experienced it. It's not your fault, what happened to Rory. You can't undo it, either. You can't undo the past.'

I glanced over at her, alarmed to see that she was picking up the gun again, both hands, steering with her knees.

'Christ, Cass, don't shoot me,' I said and my voice came out as a squeak of pure fear. I swallowed and tried again, but she was laughing, a silent laugh, the vehicle swinging alarmingly close to the edge of the road as she grabbed for the wheel and corrected our course before grabbing the shotgun again.

I thought then that my hour had come. Whether she shot me or just killed us both in a smash was largely immaterial. The unfairness of it pressed at me, larger than anything else. I had not done anything wrong, and yet here I was, about to die. All I had wanted – all I had ever wanted, I realized, with the force of a revelation – was to belong. To be loved. Not by Grant, or at least not solely by Grant. By all of them. Cass, Grant, Davey, even Rory, dead though he was. All I had wanted was my seat by the fire, my own mug, my own place in the family. To be needed. That was all. That had been my crime.

But it was not me Cass was aiming at now. In fact, she seemed to have forgotten my presence. She had wrestled the gun round to aim it out of the window and she was peering forward as we crept back into the fog, her whole attention on what she saw before us.

Fog is never absolute. It thickens and thins, reveals and conceals. One moment something will stand out clearly, the next it will vanish or fade until you doubt your own eyes. Without context, things shift their size, their shape. A branch becomes a reaching hand, a stone a crouching beast, coiled to spring. And a hare, a hare can shift from animal to human, human to animal, as fluidly and easily as it can run.

It can only have been a hare, out there on the high open moor, in that weather. It can only have been a hare, moving at such insolent speed. It vanished and reappeared, seeming in no hurry to get away, yet always just in front of us, for all Cass's efforts to chase it down. When she slowed, it slowed, and once, I swear – I would still swear it, in a court of law – it stood its ground and looked at us, and it was Janet there, clear as day, looking at us both with an expression of amused contempt.

Cass fired the gun. Before I could say anything to stop her. I saw her aim, head half out of the window, the jerk of her finger before I reflexively closed my eyes. The report sounded louder this time, wrong, the smell of powder harsh and acrid. I dared to look. The hare was running now and the gun seemed to have cracked apart in Cass's hands, one barrel peeled and smoking. She flung it into my lap and wrestled the car into a different gear.

The Land Rover roared forward, all Cass's fury concentrated in its noise. She gunned it straight at the creature, a howling coming from its engine, from her. We had all of the weight of the downhill behind us, the ice beneath its tyres. The hare was fast, running hard, but we were faster. Faster until there was a flash of solid shapes through the fog, a splinter of branches, the looming shadow of the wall, the snap back of my seatbelt hugging me to my seat, the shattering of glass. Then silence and the tick of a cooling engine. And voices, calling, people running, the whole cast and crew of them pouring out of the forest as if they had been waiting for us to arrive.

part five

aftermath

I ONLY EVER saw Melissa Harris one last time. It was unfortunate that she had chosen to visit the school the day I too had returned to complete the paperwork around my departure. I saw the hubbub by the gates, her friends clustered around her as I was hurried in by the side entrance. If she or her schoolfellows noticed me then, they gave no sign. I passed like a ghost through the gates, up the steps, pushing open the familiar door one last time to sign my career away, and seal my fate.

When I came upon her again she was alone, slumped in her wheelchair as if abandoned in the corridor. It was during the calm that descends when lessons are in session, pupils and teachers alike confined to the classrooms, the hallways briefly silent and empty. My footsteps sounded unnaturally loud as I made the endless journey down the corridor towards her. Her eyes were cast down, her hands clasped in her lap, only the occasional tremor of her leg, apparently involuntary, betraying any sign of life. She must have heard my approach but she did not look up and the closer I got, the more her stillness seemed willed.

There was nothing wrong with her, I was pretty sure of that. These mass hysteria episodes can leave certain more fragile individuals – mentally fragile, that is – damaged for a while. It's not unknown for them to become wheelchair bound, despite doctors acknowledging that they can find nothing physically wrong. It would not be entirely fair to describe it as malingering; the mind can be a powerful thing, and family, friends, even medical professionals, can collaborate unconsciously to perpetuate the situation.

I debated passing her in silence, if she was so determined to ignore my presence. Or give her just the briefest greeting, the way I would acknowledge any pupil. But something about her stillness got under my skin. Her bowed head looked meek, put upon, framing me as the aggressor. I could not help but loom over her as I reached her chair. Still she did not look up, but instead produced a theatrical flinch, irritating me all the more.

There was a fleeting, mad second when I thought that I could command her to get up. That I could take her and pull her upright and end this whole charade. I didn't, of course I didn't, although I sometimes wonder what might have happened if I had. All I did was say her name, just that. I thought she might ignore that too, but one's name has a powerful magic and this time she did raise her head and meet my gaze. Such a guileless doll-like face. It seemed that only I could see past the limpid innocence in those china blue eyes.

All I did was say her name, whatever might have been alleged afterwards. I looked at her and she looked back at me and it was only when the door to the head's office opened and the hurried footsteps sounded towards us that she started to shrink away and rub her arm, widening her eyes in a pantomime of fear. There was a bustle of panic as her parents reached her, and she was whisked around with angry words that I didn't bother to take in. I could sense the head watching me from her office door, but my eyes were on the girl, her neck craning to get a last glimpse of me as she was wheeled away, triumph in her eyes.

CHAPTER 20

T HE TAP ON the door when it comes is so soft that if I
hadn't been expecting it, I might not have heard it. Cass
is on the doorstep, her head turned away, and for a moment
I catch my breath. She is wearing the same hooded coat she
wore the first time we walked together and for a moment it is
as if the old Cass is back. But then she turns her head and
pulls down the hood and smiles her new uncertain smile. The
scars from her crash soon healed and faded, and her hair grew
back quickly enough, but these days it is duller, coarser, kept
practically short. You would barely describe it as red any more,
and without its reflection to bring out the illusion, her eyes
too have taken on a more ordinary shade. But perhaps it's not
so much that she's changed physically but that her spark has
gone, that quicksilver liveliness that had us all bewitched.

She puts out her arm and together we set off for our walk,
as we do every day. Head injuries are tricky things and she
still needs me, even for the simplest outing. Her fingers tighten
on my arm as I support her weight through a brief stumble;
they say her balance will be permanently affected. We move
along our well-trodden path through the grounds. Our route
is the same as it always is – the same one we took on our first

304

walk together, except that we do not go as far. Although she hasn't said it, I know she has a goal: the churchyard, the family grave. So far we have not made it, for she tires easily, although sometimes we get as far as the spring and the great ash tree that guards it.

It stands alone now, that tree. The forest has gone. It was not long after Cass's crash that the men came to fell it, filling the air with the noise of their machines. A coincidence, Grant said – they were always due to be harvested – but I couldn't help but feel that it was a reaction, a clearing away of some-thing, although of what I am not sure. Cass was just out of the hospital then, and we were drawn to the edge of the forest by the sound of it. Grant stood there too, watching impassively as the winter stillness was ripped apart. Faster than I could have imagined, the ranks of trees were being torn down, leaving a churned world of broken stumps and branches and the air full of the incongruously Christmassy smell of pine needles.

The machines crawled over the hillside above us as we watched. I saw one seize a tree in its grip like a child with a toy, slicing through its trunk and stripping it of its branches before tossing the remains aside. I could have stayed there watching all afternoon, torn between horror and fascination, but Cass shuddered and turned away and we did not linger, not that time. I thought she might want to avoid the sight of the forest after that, but we returned, day after day, until the whole forest was gone and the stacked logs had been carted away. It left a raw and broken landscape of splintered match-wood and churned earth. The whole span of what has become our world was laid bare, shrunken in the light. Even the church, which had seemed so far away, stood visible, fringed with the remaining spindly trees. Only the crossroads, down in a valley, remains hidden from view.

The trees are starting to return now. The planted conifers shouldered their way through the birches which sprang up first, and are now overtaking them. Today is a good day, and after that first stumble, Cass walks a little more freely, although she doesn't say much; these days it is I who chatters away as we walk, filling the silence. Together we make the slow ascent to the start of the forest track and, with a little encouragement, she perseveres along it until we reach the shelter of the waiting ash.

At first, after the felling, the spring was clogged, but after a while the water began to flow again, clear and cold. Fresh ribbons and cloths have appeared tied to the tree's branches, although I never see any other people up here. The place reminds me always of Ann, and makes me wonder what might have become of her, for I have never seen her again since that first winter. Once or twice I asked around, casually, but nobody seemed to recognize my description of her, or her dogs. And yet her face comes to me vividly at times, a memory both unsettling and yet bringing its own sense of calm.

As Cass releases my arm to bend and touch the shimmering surface of the water, I reach reflexively into my coat pocket. For a long time I carried with me a sprig of rowan, withered and brittle, still marked with oil and blackened with soot where I took it from the barrel of a broken gun. For all Grant's warnings, I never thought that something so small and fragile could do such damage. It gave it a talismanic power to my mind and when it finally disintegrated, I felt momentarily bereft, as though I had lost a powerful protective charm.

It was Grant who took the gun, before the air ambulance arrived, and flung it into the forest. It was he who wrenched open the buckled door of the Land Rover and checked cursorily that I was all right. The others had flown to Cass, flung through the shattered windscreen, her face a mask of blood. I blessed the power of the three-point seatbelt and climbed out unscathed except for a few bruises and a stiffness in my neck that would last for days.

'What happened?' he asked, and then: 'No, on second thoughts, perhaps it's better if I don't know. The police will be here soon, and the medics. We'd better make sure we're ready for them when they arrive. And, if you're all right, it would be a lot less complicated if Cass was alone when she crashed.'

At his words, they all turned to look at me: Grant, Davey, Kirsty, Helen. I saw nothing but blank hostility in three of their faces, but not in Grant's. There was a plea there, an uncertainty. All that had passed in the last few days was mine to divulge, or to keep quiet. None of the others would talk. It was my silence he needed now.

I left it long enough to see the fear spark in his eyes, then relented. 'It's fine,' I said. 'You can depend on me.'

I had thought then that I would leave, return to London and pick up the pieces of my old life, but I soon realized I would be needed here. Cass was coming out of the rehabilitation unit and could not manage the stairs in the house and Janet's cottage was the obvious place for her to go. With me to keep an eye on her, make sure she was eating properly, encourage her to go out, there was a chance she could rebuild something of her life. And so I have stayed, and I could not leave now if I wanted to.

Janet herself I saw only one last time. She had been staying with her sister but came back to pack up her things and clear out the cottage. I had not heard that she was coming, and was startled by the unmistakeable sound of her moving about next door. I found myself frozen, listening.

I had not expected her to stop by to say goodbye, but she knocked on my door and I answered, opening the door cautiously. She could not have looked more ordinary as she stood there on the doorstep, in the same old anorak she always wore. The neighbourly thing would have been to invite her in, but I didn't and she didn't seem to expect it.

'Here,' she said, holding up the keys to her cottage. 'You'll be wanting these.' They weighed unexpectedly heavy in my palm, the same set I carry now in case I need to let myself in to help out Cass.

I ought perhaps to have wished her well, but the words didn't come. She waited a beat longer, then nodded, smiled her mirthless smile, unchanging to the last.

'And you can tell those Hendersons I'll no be troubling them again.'

Today, as Cass stands up from the spring, I take her arm again, wary of another fit of dizziness, but she is steady beside me.

'Shall we continue along a bit further?' I ask, for the church looks so close now, almost within touching distance. Cass shakes her head and we continue with our set routine, on to the main house, knocking on the back door unnecessarily as we come in. It's good for her to see her brother, and she makes an effort when she's with him, forcing the words past the stammer that does not seem to lessen, for all the speech therapist's breezy assurances. I used to slip away to leave them in peace together, but increasingly these days I stay on, have a cup of tea with them, settle into the corner that has become my own. We don't talk of much, not of consequence. Grant knows I won't bring up the past. It's our pact, as unspoken as everything else.

This time, as I stand to visit the bathroom, Grant glances up. 'Use the one upstairs,' he says. 'The cloakroom loo is acting up again.' I slip out and pass through the shadowed hall, the shrouded display cases. The hares are in storage, waiting a decision on their fate, for Cass would not enter the place until she was assured that they were gone. I know the house well now, and though the landing is dim I do not reach for the light switch. Returning, I am startled to see somebody else moving towards me on the opposite landing, and for a crazed moment I know that it is Janet, returned, malevolent, threatening to tear apart the fragile rebuilding we have done. My heart hammers and I freeze and in that moment I see what it is: there is an old display case at the end of the hallway and it is my own reflection I have glimpsed. It comes to me that I have made this mistake before. Nothing to be frightened of. I smile.

It is time to take Cass back, take her through her exercises, then leave her for her lunchtime rest while I get some work done. She knows I can hear her through the wall; she has only to call out and I will be there. I push open the door to the kitchen and they are both there where I left them, sitting at the table, apparently in silence, abstracted. Grant looks tired, drawn; Cass too. In that moment, watching them, watching over them, I am flooded with love for them both, all-encompassing, protective. And then they see me and it flashes across both their faces: something akin to fear. There and gone again as it passes, and I smile, and they smile back, and I gather Cass up and take her home.

Acknowledgements

This book has taken far longer to write than it should have, for which I have only myself to blame. My thanks go to my editor, Maria Rejt, and to Charlotte Wright and the rest of the editorial team at Macmillan and Mantle for getting it out into the world at last. Thanks also to my agent, Euan Thorneycroft at AM Heath, for seeing its potential, and to both him and Jessica Sinyor for their insight and advice.

I would like to thank Jake Smith-Bosanquet for his comments on earlier drafts and for kick-starting my career as a published novelist in the first place. I might not have persisted with the early drafts without the support of the Scottish Book Trust mentoring scheme and the advice of Jonathan Falla. I'd like to thank too the staff of the Ewart Library in Dumfries, and the Dumfries and Galloway Archives service for their assistance in my early researches into the history of witchcraft in the region (and in particular for giving me permission to borrow a book from the reference section, a privilege I could not have dreamt of as a library-obsessed child).

Every writer needs a community of fellow writers, and even when I thought this book would never see the light of day, Dumfries Writers' Group has kept me in touch with the world of writing. Special thanks to Mary Smith for being my first reader, and to JoAnne McKay and Hugh Bryden for support, cheerleading and above all a good dose of literary gossip when it was needed most.

Finally, my thanks to Paul for his support that goes far wider than mere writing.

The events, people and individual places depicted in this work are all, of course, fiction, but this book owes everything to the landscape and history of Dumfries and Galloway, both of which deserve to be much better known.